Sunrise
BLUES

A GOOD ENOUGH NOVEL

To my friend & inspiration Martha

Sunrise
BLUES

A GOOD ENOUGH NOVEL

VONNA IVORY JOSEPH

All the best ! Vonna Joseph

To my daddy, who urged me to "Keep living."

How'd I End Up Back Here?

"I'm so sorry about all of this. I really am. It was truly not my intention to be back here encroaching on your space," Sunrise said. She looked up at the popcorn ceiling, and at the yellow balloon valances that sat above the Georgian windowpanes in her childhood bedroom. A small Queen Anne desk and an antique dress form stood unchanged, as a memorial to her long-gone youth. She stroked the soft fur of her only siblings as they sat beside her on the twin sized four-poster bed.

"Surely you can understand my humiliation--being a woman and all," she said to her mother's prize-winning Pomeranian. Amber snuggled closer to the rambling woman and rolled onto her back. "I'm sorry, Stevie Nix," Sunrise whispered to the other dog as he descended the bed and plopped down on the floor as if he'd grown tired of Sunrise's lament.

"Taliesan and Caspian were by earlier; they're itching to see you," her mother said as she rounded the corner.

"Hmmm," Sunrise said as she extended her arm and helped her mother onto the bed.

Ursula sat against the tall, upholstered headboard and took her daughter's hand in hers.

"I know they are, Mom. But I'm not ready; I need more time.

Ursula's eyes dropped. She looked at her daughter and patted her knee. "Do you remember the time you fell out of that big ol' oak tree out back?

"I do," Sunrise said.

"You remember how Taliesan came tearing through the door, screaming bloody murder?"

"Those scrawny little legs flying through the kitchen door? Yes. I remember that," she said, laughing.

"And do you remember what the doctor said about her?"

"He said her name was befitting because she was my talisman that day."

"And you looked up at him and asked, 'what in the world is a talisman?' and he said..."

"A lucky charm," she said, smiling.

"That's right, Sunny. Taliesan is your lucky charm. And she's worried something awful about her best friend. Your daddy had to talk her down. She was ready to jump on a plane to New York to put a beating on Xander and his whore!"

"Mother! Come now," Sunrise chided.

"You can't shut her out, Sunny."

"I know, but I'm ashamed," Sunrise said, turning her head away from her mother.

"Ashamed!" Ursula screamed. "What do you have to be ashamed of, Sunrise Nicole Anderson?"

"Mom, look at me! I paraded her around my fancy New York City apartment, and to my white husband's fancy office. I even had her sit down to a meal with that woman! And now I'm back here sharing my room with dogs! Come on, Mom!"

"I can move the dogs out of here, Sunny. You said you didn't mind. I thought you liked their company," she said.

Amber and Stevie Nix's furry little heads popped up.

"Mom, I don't want to come here and upset your routines. Just because my life's all blown up doesn't mean yours has to be."

Ursula laid her daughter's head full of short cottony hair in her lap.

"Sunny, this is your home, your bedroom. I can move the dogs to the guest room. They're dogs. They won't care—much," she whispered. "Is that what you want, Baby?" Ursula said to a giggling Sunrise.

"Mom, I love you. But that's not the point, and I know you know it's not.

"I know it's not, but I feel so helpless. I don't know how to fix this one for you, Baby Girl. But I can get you some privacy. You say the word, and your brother and sister are out of here!" Ursula said, reaching for Stevie Nix.

"How about they stay, and I move to a more grown up room?"

"Let me talk to your daddy about it first. He likes having his baby girl back home and back in her old room, with the flowers and dolls. It feels like old times around here!" Ursula teased.

The sun was just high enough to turn Beaux Anderson's home office into an inferno. Overcome by the heat, Ursula walked over and closed the shutters. She leaned against the desk and kissed her husband on his forehead. Beaux folded his newspaper and gave his wife his full attention.

"How's my Sunny Bunny holding up?" he asked.

Ursula sighed and coerced a small smile. She crossed her legs at the ankles and her arms across her chest.

"Not well," she replied. "And it breaks my heart."

"We should have sent her to an HBCU. I knew that WASP of a white boy was going to be a problem. I knew it! Didn't I say it, La La?"

Ursula walked around her husband's desk and sat in one of the brown suede chairs she'd upholstered herself. She stroked its plush arms.

"Beaux, I won't rehash that old college debate," she breathed. "Besides, she met Xander in grad school! We had no control over that; she was an adult."

"An adult looking for her parents to pay for her post-graduate education. Right?" Beaux interjected.

Ursula crossed her legs and clasped her hands in her lap.

"Look, La La. She's our only child. I want her to get better. I want her to feel whole again," he said, shoving a handful of papers into a folder. "That's all. She's my princess. I want to see my baby smile again. And I want her out of that damned room!" he said, pointing upstairs.

"Speaking of that room... she wants to move into the pool house. It's more 'grown up,' she says. So that's progress. Right?"

"It is," Beaux said with a broad grin on his face. "She'll be fine."

Ursula sat up and reached for Beaux. He rolled forward in his office chair and took his wife's hands and kissed them.

"I just love her so much. You know, it's my responsibility to give her a good life. I take that seriously," Beaux said. "I'll never forget that summer evening when Nurse Harper called."

"Neither will I," Ursula said with tears in her eyes.

"We'd only been here for what? three years?" Ursula asked.

"Yes," Beaux nodded.

"I had just come home from a long day at work. I was sitting out on the porch reading the newspaper, and you and your students were inside practicing for the recital," Beaux recalled. He closed his eyes and shook his head softly. "I'll never forget that wail. And the tears..."

"Oh gosh," Ursula said, placing her hand over her face.

"I couldn't make out whether your tears were happy or sad?"

"You came running in yelling, 'La La! Baby, what happened? What's the matter?'"

"Yes. And you were frantic. Your speech was barely comprehensible. I wiped those big brown eyes while the kids stared on—wide-eyed and frightened."

"Poor babies," Ursula said, wiping the tears from her eyes. "I was just so happy."

"You took the phone from me."

"Yes. And it was Nurse Harper. That call changed our lives forever."

"Go ahead, tell me what she said again," the woman beamed. "It never gets old."

"A healthy young lady had had a baby girl the day before and decided to give her up. She'd personally asked Nurse Harper to make sure her baby went to a good and loving home," he said, kissing Ursula's well-worn hands again. "Your eyes were so full of hope. And she went on talking about lawyers, and social workers, and papers. But I was focused on only one thing! We were about to be parents to a healthy baby girl!"

"And two days later, on May 28th, 1984 we brought home our beautiful 7 pound, 8-ounce bundle of joy, and named her Sunrise,"

"The city where I met the love of my life," Beaux said.

"And opened your first federally insured savings and loans bank. The first black man to do so in the state," Ursula sang proudly, raising a finger in the air. "I love you."

"If there is anything I know for sure, it's that you love me and that our daughter is going to be fine," Beaux said, kissing his wife on the lips.

Meet Taliesan

Sunrise lay across her bed clicking through Google images of her soon-to-be ex-husband and his family. She wanted to get out of bed; she wanted to get dressed to join her parents for breakfast in the sunroom, but she couldn't drag herself away from the incessant data mining. The media had laid her and Xander's life out for the public's consumption, and now she'd become obsessed. She analyzed the images and articles hoping they might reveal where she had gone so wrong.

"So I married a WASP, a real live, White, Anglo-Saxon, Protestant," she mused.

Before she met Xander, Sunrise thought that white people were just that--white people, but she quickly learned that not all whites were equal. WASPs were pure British Anglo-Saxon, non-Catholic White people--Mayflower types. And how much money you had meant nothing. If you were Catholic, or Irish, or your last name ended in a vowel, you could forget about identifying as one, much less marrying into a WASP family. And if your family had the slightest blemish to its reputation, there was absolutely no chance.

"Ever the overachiever, aren't you, Sunrise? You had to go all the way out and marry one--complete with blonde hair and blue eyes. That old Greenwich, Connecticut money," she marveled aloud.

"I spent seven long years as Alexander Yates Rockwell Thorpe III's, hippie-dippie black wife. And to think, all the hours of my life I blew at those damned family functions and charity events, and all the balls and cotillions, smiling like a bobble head—constantly checking my reflection to make sure my pressed edges hadn't reverted to a thick mass of kinky waves and coils, exposing my regular old negro ancestry."

She twirled at a patch of thick curls, acknowledging the apology she owed to them.

Xander wasn't the oldest grandson, which made his decision to marry a black girl more innocuous. His birth order ensured that he didn't stand a chance of inheriting the keys to the family fortune, which would have put he and Sunrise over everyone's allowances and trust funds; so his family clenched their butt cheeks and bore her black presence in their purebred family.

"Sunny, Darling. Please call me. Give me an opportunity to explain," a stale Xander cried out from the voicemail she played for the hundredth time. "You know how much I love you. I put everything on the line for you--for us. The least you could do is hear me out."

"Hear you out!" she yelled at the week-old voicemail. "Please explain your cock in her mouth--in our bedroom! It's on a mezzanine you freaking idiot! No walls, Alexander! No walls!" she said, slamming the phone down onto the mattress. A knock at the door startled her.

"Yes, I'm coming." She rolled out of bed and opened the door to find Taliesan standing there with her long sinewy arms outstretched.

"Bring it in, Sunny Bunny," her friend sang. Sunrise smiled and settled into her best friend's embrace. It felt great being in Taliesan's strong, gentle presence again. The friends stood in the doorway rocking back and forth in each other's arms.

"Why do you always smell like a spa?" Sunrise chuckled into Taliesan's neck.

"It's the lavender and peppermint oils," Taliesan chuckled back. "Are you well, my friend?"

"I will be, now."

"Yes. You will be."

Taliesan's visit coaxed Sunrise from her yellow and white ruffled hideaway just in time for a late breakfast with her parents.

Ursula served blood orange mimosas with her signature Belgian waffles and berries. "Champagne before noon on a Wednesday? What kind of sorcery is this?" Sunrise joked.

"It's Prosecco. And don't make jokes about sorcery. I've seen your girlfriend over there," Ursula gestured in Taliesan's direction. "Leaning upside down against trees out back."

They all laughed.

Taliesan sipped from her glass of juice and tipped her head, graciously accepting the jeer. She'd always been different. She'd been a practicing Buddhist and Yogi for more than half her life. And growing up in Atlanta as a black Buddhist in a Baptist household was fertile ground for cultivating a thick skin. Taliesan Pearce Cooper had been the first little girl Sunrise was allowed to have sleepovers with. The Pearce's were their neighbors, and one of only a handful of blacks who lived in the affluent neighborhood of Sandy Springs back then. The girls, along with Taliesan's little brother

Caspian were inseparable. She was only two years older than her brother and Sunrise, but she'd always been much more sophisticated and self-assured.

Sunrise and Taliesan cleared the breakfast table and cleaned the kitchen before excusing themselves. They walked hand in hand alongside the cobblestone retaining wall that delineated the Anderson's property from the Pearce's. Mr. and Mrs. Pearce had both died years earlier, leaving the house to Taliesan and her family. Taliesan was married with two little boys, Kannon and Bodhi. She'd met her husband Ellis when she was only twenty-three years old; they married six months later. He was an Economics professor, fourteen years her senior. Ellis was a warm and spirited man, and his high energy complemented Taliesan's, which was shy and somewhat aloof.

The once Pearce, now Cooper home had changed a lot since they were kids. Taliesan, unlike her mother, kept an immaculate home. The Frank Lloyd Wright-influenced architecture complemented Taliesan's minimalist, and nature-inspired style. The house set high atop a well-manicured hill with large floor to ceiling windows along the entire back and west side of the house. Taliesan slid open the double doors releasing a calming scent of white sage and jasmine.

"It smells like you in here," Sunrise teased.

"I live in here," Taliesan smiled, wrapping her arm around Sunrises shoulder.

Sunrise removed her shoes, following Taliesan's example.

"Oh, you don't have to do that, Sunny Bunny."

"I want the full experience. I want to feel your floors! What kind of floors are these?"

Taliesan smiled and shook her head.

"It's cork. It's good for the boys; it doesn't stain," she said, leading her friend past the kitchen and onto a second-floor deck. "It would be good for your studio, too. It's a natural acoustic insulator," Taliesan said. She immediately tensed and shut her eyes. "I'm sorry Sunny. I wasn't thinking. You're home now."

"It's OK. You don't have to feel weird talking to me about my mess of a life."

"Your mess of a life, right now. This suffering will pass."

Sunrise bowed her head, fighting back the tears pooling in her eyes.

"I know you're right, but I feel so stupid. You know?"

"He's the stupid one," Taliesan answered.

"OK, Tally-Ho!" Sunrise sang in a small shaky voice, trying to lighten the mood.

"Tally -Ho," Taliesan repeated in song with a wide smile on her face. "I haven't heard that in a lifetime. "Tally-Ho!" the two sang in harmony,

"Rise and glow, Tally-Ho!"

"God, I miss Daddy!" Taliesan said.

"Can you call out to God?" Sunrise asked earnestly.

Taliesan handed her a cup of green tea and plopped down in a chair beside her.

"I guess so," she sighed. "In Zen, the concept of God or any deity isn't central." She sat up in her chair and placed her cup on the decorative stump of wood situated between them. "This is not to say that Buddha isn't important--it's just the central theme. Zen is more about the study of oneself—practicing meditation to come to find the humanity of Buddha or God in yourself. Does that make sense?"

"Yes. It does. I understand."

Sunrise sat quietly pondering Taliesan's words.

"Sunny," Taliesan said, interrupting Sunrise's silence.

"Yes, Ma'am."

"Do you want to talk about what happened?"

Sunrise shifted in her seat. She took a sip of the woodsy green tea. She rolled her neck and stretched her legs out before her.

"I don't. But I feel like talking to you about it will somehow give me clarity." Taliesan sat quietly as Sunrise mustered up the confidence to speak.

"Where are the boys?" Sunrise asked.

"They're in school," Taliesan answered evenly.

"You sound like a therapist."

"I do?"

The women laughed.

"I'd spent the night in the studio," Sunrise began. "And I guess it was about seven in the morning when I woke up. The door was locked, and I never locked the door when I was working in the studio, but I was very groggy, so I didn't think about it that much. I got the key from under the pot by the door and let myself in," she said as she pressed the cup of tea to her lips. "That's a cool tree house," Sunrise said, digressing.

"Yeah, Ellis and Cas built it," Taliesan said.

"I walked in, and there they were. She was sitting on our bed with her hands gripping his bright white behind," she said closing her eyes. "They didn't even hear me come in. He kept right on screwing her in the mouth. His eyes were closed, and he was biting on his bottom lip, mumbling, 'we've got to go to the office'"

"Oh no, Sunny! I'm so sorry you had to see that," she said taking her friend by the hand. "What'd you do?"

"I slammed the door shut and stood there. He nearly ripped it off trying to pull away from her. He fell because his pants were down around his ankles. I was so," she struggled for the right word. "I was shocked. All I could do was yell, 'Get out!' and then I went back downstairs and locked myself in the studio."

As Sunrise described the scene, she was surprised that it hadn't brought tears to her eyes. She didn't feel angry either. She looked at Taliesan who had enough tears in her eyes for the both of them and patted her friend's knee. Taliesan dabbed at her eyes and straightened her back. Mussing her hair, she stood and held out a hand to Sunrise.

"Do you want to see my meditation room?" she managed.

"Sure. Lead the way."

James and Camilla

Camilla laughed the moment he said his name.

"Hi, Camilla. James DaCosta here," he stuttered.

"What you stuttering for? Where is Atlanta's top cop? You sound like that nervous twenty-six-year-old I met when I was but an innocent little pup," Camilla cackled.

"Even at sixteen, you weren't innocent," James mumbled under his breath.

James DaCosta was by any measure, a straight-laced, law-abiding citizen. He'd always followed the rules. He finished college in exactly four years, married well, and worked hard to establish a good life for himself and his young wife. He'd made mistakes, just as any other man, but the one that had stayed with him, hanging over his pristine reputation like an anvil, had also produced what he thought of as his greatest accomplishment—his daughter, Camisha.

James was a rookie with the Atlanta Police Department, and his wife was Evangeline Herron of the Atlanta Herron's, one of the most powerful families in the city. He'd met Camilla Robbins at a friend's bachelor party; she was there working as a dancer. Camilla was a striking woman. She had sparkling, greenish-brown eyes like none James had ever seen on a brown-skinned woman. She had long wavy hair that she wore half up in a bun, leaving the other half to hang down around her curvy bottom.

She was both hippy and mouthy. And after a few hours of conversation, and one too many drinks, he took her up on a fateful offer for a "little extra." Six months later, his wife showed up at the Precinct asking him why a sixteen-year-old girl was claiming to be carrying his baby.

Evangeline was accomplished and well educated, with several options for a husband. Her family was not pleased about their first-born marrying a beat cop and didn't hold James in high esteem. If the details of his affair with a teenager became public, it would have certainly ruined his career and reputation.

Faced with this prospect, he quietly accepted the agreement that Camilla laid out. It was an agreement she upheld until she disappeared for several years, only to reappear when Camisha was thirteen years old. She and her mother had ended up living in a shelter for women and children. And true to form, Camilla had gotten the two of them kicked out of the home. When Camilla called James at the Precinct, she offered very few details, "Set us up in a nice place, somewhere near Camisha's school. I don't want her to have to change schools," she said.

Camilla kept James abreast of milestones in Camisha's life, like her high school graduation and her college graduation, but warned him to stay away. James never put up a fight about Camilla's rules. He had aspirations of one day being the Mayor of Atlanta, and mishaps of that kind could prove difficult to overcome. Now that Camisha was an adult, the fear of exposure was no longer there.

When he showed up at Camisha's home for Thanksgiving, Camilla nearly fell out of her seat. He had come as a guest of the Robinsons, Camisha's soon-to-be in-laws. She had no clue at the time that she was hosting her own father. And James gave no inclination that he even knew Camilla. But he hung on Camisha's every word, her every move, no matter how small. The smile on his face could've stretched from Long Island to the San Francisco Bay. He hadn't been in her presence since she was six months old—when he slipped into Camilla's bed a time or two, to be near his only child.

"What can I do for you, King James?" Camilla spewed into the phone.

"Hi, Camilla. How are you? How was your Christmas?"

"As if you give a damn? I've been expecting this call, so cut the bullshit. What do you want?" Camilla said as she sat on the edge of the bed filing her long acrylic nails.

"I want to be a part of Camisha's life."

"So."

"Camilla, please. Be reasonable," James pleaded.

"Be reasonable, huh?" Camilla snickered. "Explain something to me, King James. What the hell do I have to do with you being a part of Camisha's life? She's a grown ass woman now! So why you really calling me?" Camilla rolled her neck, lifting her over-arched eyebrow.

Only silence followed. Camilla looked at the cracked screen of her phone and tapped it.

"Hel-lo,"

"You're right. I'm not sure why I still feel the need to ask for your permission," he sighed. "Conditioned, I guess."

"Well, consider yourself set free! You don't need a damn thing from me. Hell, you're friends with her future in-laws so you can get her number from one of them."

"Future in-Laws?" James questioned.

"Yep! Ali proposed on Christmas Day," Camilla snapped. "As I was saying, you and the Queen of Atlanta popped up at her house on Thanksgiving, so you know where she lives. So I ask you again, King James, why are you calling me?"

James ground his teeth and ran a nervous hand over his head. "You are absolutely right. Goodbye, Camilla. And I hope you have a happy New Year."

"Fuck you, James!"

James sat back in his high back office chair, stroking his chin. Camilla had made valid points. After all, he and her soon-to-be father-in-law were friends. James and Thomas Robinson were old Army buddies who'd reconnected a few days before Thanksgiving. Thomas invited he and Evangeline to share Thanksgiving dinner with his family. The DaCostas arrived to find that the house where their Thanksgiving dinner was being hosted belonged to his estranged daughter, Camisha. James picked up the phone again and dialed his old friend. He smiled at hearing Thomas's voice.

"DaCosta! How's it hanging, Brother?"

"I can't complain, Old Man! I can't. It was good seeing you and Tess for Thanksgiving."

"Likewise. What's up? You don't sound like you're just calling to catch up," Thomas said.

James walked over to close the door to his office.

"I'm calling about Camisha."

"I thought there was some strange energy there that night. You know her?"

"I do. I'm not proud of it, but I'm Camisha's father."

James' confession landed heavily. The men held the line for several moments without words.

"Does Evangeline know?"

"Yes. She's always known. But no one else knows— not even Camisha,"

"How is that possible, DaCosta?" Thomas asked.

"Camille's a beautiful monster," James explained. "She was convinced that Evangeline would take the baby. So she threatened to disappear if we came around. She didn't want Camisha to know anything about us."

"Good night," Thomas drawled. "She is something else."

"That's the understatement of the year, Tommy! You don't know the half. She's always been a beautiful woman, but her bad attitude and dirty mouth made her hard to stomach. And she's still as brash and mean as she was as a teenager--threatening and leveraging our daughter whenever she wanted,"

"A teenager?" Thomas asked.

"I told you. It wasn't my best moment. But, yes. When I met her, she was sixteen years old. But I didn't learn that until she was big and pregnant with Camisha." He took a deep breath and blew it out through his mouth. He walked over to the big picture window of his office that overlooked a busy city street.

"Well, that's a mouth full, brother. You said you were calling about Camisha. What about? My son proposed to her on Christmas day. She's a good woman. She's nothing like her mother," Thomas demanded.

James smiled proudly.

"No, nothing like her mother. And Camille just told me about Camisha and Ali getting engaged. I couldn't be happier. She's marrying into a great family." His chest swelled with pride.

"You know Tommy, when you invited us over for Thanksgiving, we almost declined. We had so many stops to make, but I really wanted to see you and Tess, so we made it happen. When I walked into that room and saw my baby standing there, I knew it was the sign I'd been waiting for. I knew it was time to finally meet my daughter and to let her know that I'd always loved her.

"Camille kept me at arm's length. I watched Camisha grow up from the shadows—viewing her milestones from around corners," he said, his voice trembling.

"So for that my friend, I'll be forever indebted to you. And the fact that our children getting married makes me the happiest man on the planet. Now, I just have to get Evangeline on board."

"Good luck, my friend," Thomas said.

James and Evangeline stood at the front entrance of their home, returning coats and purses to guests after their annual holiday cocktail party came to a close. James could hardly wait to get the last guests out of their Collier Hills home. He puttered around, straightening up, and shutting off lights as the last guests drove out of their circular driveway. He secured the house and followed Evangeline upstairs to talk about his daughter.

James found his wife sitting in front of the television, wiping makeup from her ageless face. He sat beside her and took her by the same slender hand he'd held over thirty years ago when he married her.

"Darling. I want to run something by you," he said.

"Is it about Camisha?"

He sat stunned. "Yes," he mumbled.

"I hoped you'd talk to me about her, and not start the sneaking around again," Evangeline said calmly.

"Go ahead."

"I want to be a part of her life, Lena."

"As you should. She's a wonderful young woman."

James sat quietly waiting for his wife to say more. But there was nothing more.

"Are you sure it's OK with you?" James cautiously asked.

"Yes. But I won't tolerate her mother. And I won't tolerate another round of you and her."

James squeezed his wife's hand. She pulled it away and faced him.

"I know that there was more than the one time, James. But, I'm not a naïve little girl anymore. There will be no second or third chances for you and that woman." Evangeline stood and looked down at her husband. "Are we clear? Camisha only." She took him by the chin, tilting his head to meet her eyes. Once she had stated her conditions, she left the room.

As a beat cop, and later as a detective James had seen many a dead bodies, but none so affected him as his first. His first partner and mentor, Officer Richard Newsome was shot dead by a drunken husband during a domestic violence call. Newsome took the lead. He ordered the rookie cop, DaCosta to go around to cover the back door. James heard knocking on the worn screen door. Newsome yelled out a few commands, then two gunshots. He ran around to where he had left his partner to find him on his back on the rickety front porch, bleeding from the head and stomach.

After James had completed the incident reports and psych evaluations, he headed to Camilla's little one bedroom apartment. Camilla swung the door open, with her hands on her hips, ready to spar. Already deflated, James's shoulders rounded and his eyes glazed over.

"What's happened to you?" she asked, almost reaching out to the anguished man.

"Can I come in?" James asked. Camilla gave the request a moment's consideration and sighed. "Please, Camilla. I need to hold my baby girl in my arms. I need to see innocence and love in someone today. I need to see her smile at me, coo at me, grab hold of my finger. I need to be in her space. Please."

Camilla rolled her eyes as she moved to let him in. He bowed his head and took her hands in his.

"Thank you," he mouthed.

James found his four-month-old daughter sleeping peacefully in front of the big floor model television he'd bought for Camilla's place. He removed his service weapon and wallet and lay beside her on the yellow and white blanket, closing his eyes and breathing in her sweet powdery baby scent. Camilla stood at the door watching him.

"You look whooped. You want something to eat. Or drink?"

James only nodded, keeping his eyes closed. A single tear crept down his cheek.

"Damn. What happened to you? Did the missus kick you out?"

"No," James murmured. He sat up and wiped at his eyes with the back of his hand. "My partner was killed today.

"Damn! In the daylight? That's cold," Camilla said as she sat on the sofa and watched James. "You sure you won't have something to drink. I think you could use a drink after something like that."

"Sure. What do you have?" James asked.

"I got some gin in there," Camilla said, gesturing towards the small kitchen.

"Gin! Why? Camille. Why does a seventeen-year-old have liquor in her house?"

"I guess for the same reason she has a baby in here, a married man in here, and a grown ass cop in here. Because she lives by her own damned rules. I do what I wanna do. Now, do you want the gin or not?" She stood impetuously with a hand on her hip.

"Sure," James relented and followed Camilla to the kitchen, and later to her bedroom.

Sunrise and Camilla

Sunrise sat perched on the high stool trying to stay engaged with the other tellers who were gabbing about the latest episode of Keeping Up with the Kardashians when a spectacle of a woman wearing her face sauntered into the bank. The woman looked to be no older than forty years old. She had long wavy hair that matched her own before she'd cut it off into a cropped, wooly afro; blazing hazel eyes, and rich golden brown skin that also matched hers.

The woman was bold and funny. She was wearing black slacks and a forest green tee shirt with a black apron tossed over her shoulder. Her laughter was quick and easy, as she chatted with the teller two stations away from Sunrise. Sunrise couldn't take her eyes off of her. The woman finished her business in the bank and waved dramatically to the tellers as she sashayed out through the glass doors. When she was out of her sightline, Sunrise approached the teller.

"What was that lady's name?" Sunrise asked.

"Hmmm, let me see here," the young woman tapped away at the keyboard. "Camilla. Camilla A. Robbins, of 2616 W. Enon Rd. in Atlanta, Georgia."

Sunrise looked on over her coworker's shoulder. "Print that out for me, please!"

"Hmmm, no! That's illegal and creepy." The young woman snapped.

"Shhhh! Jesus! OK! OK!" Sunrise ordered.

She returned to her station and frantically typed in Camilla's name and address. She hit the print key and grabbed the paper from the printer. She looked around to make sure no one was watching, and stuffed the paper into her leather shoulder bag.

The days to follow were all about Camilla A. Robbins. Sunrise set out to gather as much information as she could find about her. Her Internet searches didn't render much. But she did learn that the Enon Road address was to a home not far from her father's bank. The home belonged to a woman named Camisha Robbins who was born almost exactly a year before she was.

"Hmmm, Camilla and Camisha. You too must have lived fairly quiet lives," she said aloud. "No judgments, no social media accounts--not even as much as an old MySpace page. This is going to be quite a challenge."

They were nothing like she and her husband. The Manhattan Thorpe's of the Greenwich, Connecticut Thorpe's were all over the Internet. They attended all the balls and nightclub openings in the Hamptons and Martha's Vineyard. Whenever Sunrise played at a club or accompanied a well-known artist, the news was plastered all over Page Six.

During her workday, Sunrise turned around every time the doors swung open. She longed for another glimpse of Camilla. She was convinced that the audacious beauty was somehow related to her, but couldn't muster up the nerve to assume that Camilla Robbins could have given birth to her. She'd always known that she was adopted. Her parents had made no secret of it. She'd grown up hearing how much they'd longed for her--not for just any child, but for her. Her mother had prayed and bargained with God for her. She'd called for her daughter by name--Sunrise. She'd been given to them as a gift from God, and the story of how the nurse had called them and no other couple was irrefutable and absolute evidence.

On the second Friday after her first sighting, Camilla was back – laughing and cutting up with the tellers. She handled her business at the counter, but this time she sat in the lobby for a while.

"I'ma sit in here where it's cool until my daughter gets to the train station. That OK?" Camilla asked the loan officer who sat in the glass office nearest the entrance.

He shot Camilla a flirtatious smile, which Camilla returned.

"Ms. Robbins, when are you going to come in here and apply for your own car loan?" the young man said, joining Camilla in the lobby.

"I don't need no bills. I'm saving up to get out of Camisha's place. You know she's got a man now, and it looks like it's getting serious," Camila explained.

"Really?" he exclaimed. "Well good for her." He moved his chair closer to Camilla's. She smiled and secured a lock of her hair behind her ear.

"Yeah, I guess. So, I've got to get my stuff together. A child shouldn't have to see 'bout her momma. It ain't natural."

"Sure it is. We're supposed to see about our parents. They saw about us," he countered. She laughed, tilting her head back.

Sunrise's eyes were fixed on Camilla.

"Not this soon. Hell! How old do you think I am?"

"I don't think you're old enough to have a grown daughter. I was sure you'd raised your younger sister," he replied.

"Liar. But keep talking," Camilla purred. Her phone rang, breaking up the public seduction. "You ready?" she answered. "Well damn, Camisha! I been sitting out here at the damn train station waiting for you." She jumped up and grabbed her purse. "Well, are you coming home? Is Ali staying the night again? OK, Camisha Ann, I'll see y'all at the house."

"Is everything OK?" The horny loan officer said.

"Yeah, she's getting a ride home with her old man," Camilla answered. "And to think how much damned time I wasted sitting up in here!"

"I hope you don't think all of this time was wasted."

"Not the parts spent with you," she cooed. He stood, offering Camilla his hand and walked her out.

Sunrise glanced at the clock on the wall before she grabbed her things.

"I'm getting out of here. It's pretty slow," she announced as she headed for the door behind Camilla and the loan officer.

"I guess when your daddy's the boss, you can make your own hours!" she heard one of the tellers say.

None of the bank's employees had exactly welcomed her with open arms. But her dad thought it would be good for her to get out of the house and back into the world. So he had Cas, Taliesan's younger brother, find a spot for her at one of the branches. Caspian was her father's heir-apparent. He'd worked for her father since he was a teenager and had returned after college to assume more of a prominent role in her father's banking institutions. Caspian had no interest in following in his father's footsteps as an airline pilot. He was much more suited for a career in finance and took to Sunrise's father at an early age. Mr. Pearce and Beaux Anderson were good friends. Mr. Anderson managed the Pearce's finances and had taken Caspian under his wing after his father died.

Sunrise turned out of the parking lot in time to see Camilla putting her number into the loan officer's phone. He held the car door open for her and watched her pull off. Sunrise followed closely behind, but at a discreet distance.

Camilla and Camisha lived no more than five miles from the College Park Branch of her father's bank. She wondered if her father had ever crossed paths with Camilla. *Or did he know her? Did he know that she was related to her? How could he not have seen his own daughter in her face?*

Sunrise pulled the car over beside a line of hedges and turned off the engine.

The house was atop a long driveway lined with lampposts that reminded Sunrise of the ones in Central Park, not far from the home she shared with Xander. Her heart wrenched as she willed herself to focus.

Camilla's car turned behind the house, and out of Sunrise's line of sight. But before long, she could see Camilla opening the blinds and curtains.

Sunrise had been there for hours, clicking through images of her husband on her phone, when another car turned into the driveway. This time, the shiny black car didn't drive all the way to the rear of the house. No one got out right away, but then, a tall, athletic man rose from the car. He walked around to open the passenger side door for a beautiful brown-skinned woman. She had a head of the shiniest black hair Sunrise had ever seen. She wore it in a shoulder-length bob with long layers framing her perfectly heart shaped face.

Sunrise found them to be an interesting couple. He was wearing a high-end suit, and she was wearing a pair of well-worn khakis and a faded black t-shirt. He helped her with her things before he armed his car, and disappeared into the house.

Something about seeing the young woman tugged at her core, she felt familiar—kindred. She surmised at that moment that she had just laid eyes on Camisha Ann Robbins, who could very well be another relative. After a few more minutes, Sunrise started the car and drove away.

From the open lizard hip stretch, Sunrise rattled off the list of like features she shared with Camilla Robbins.

"I have her eyes and her hair. Hers is still long. She was even wearing it the way I used to wear mine for recitals. Do you remember? With the top half in a top-knot and the back half hanging down my back," she said to Taliesan.

Taliesan moved into a pigeon pose with her knees, thighs, and feet perfectly flat. She gave her friend a warm smile, encouraging her to continue.

"We have the same complexion and the same wide hips!"

"So you really think she's your birth mother?" Taliesan asked.

"I didn't say that she was my birth mother!" Sunrise said. "I said a blood relative."

Taliesan locked eyes with Sunrise until she looked away.

"I'm sorry," Sunrise said. "I didn't mean to snap at you."

Taliesan's smile returned.

"So, have you talked to your parents about her--this blood relative?"

"No," Sunrise answered morosely.

"And why not?" Taliesan asked while keeping her eyes fixed on the modest altar in her meditation room.

Sunrise moved into the downward facing dog. "I don't know, Lucky. I don't want to make them feel uncomfortable."

"Or make yourself feel uncomfortable?" Taliesan said. "They've always talked openly about your adoption. And they may very well know something about your birth mother."

"I don't think so. A nurse said I was left in the hospital. So what kind of information would they have about her?"

"Well, you'll never know if you don't ask, Sunny Bunny."

Sunrise knew her friend was right, as usual. "I'll talk to them," she said.

Boho or Hobo

If the bang on the driver side window didn't startle Sunrise enough, the angry glare in Camilla's honey brown eyes nearly made her wet herself. With a long, red, acrylic fingernail, Camilla ordered Sunrise to lower the window.

"You work at the bank, don't you?"

Sunrise carefully put her cell in the cup holder and nodded. Her eyes were wide with fear.

"Why you following me around? Is Bernard your old man? 'Cause I ain't the least bit interested in his old stinky breath thirsty ass!"

Sunrise blinked with confusion.

"Bernard?" she stuttered. "No. No, Ma'am."

Camilla slapped the door of the late model Mercedes Benz. "Then what's your deal?" Camilla demanded.

Sunrise tried to corral her faculties. "I'm sorry. I mean no harm. I," she paused. "I just want to."

Camilla swirled her pointer finger at Sunrise, hurrying her along. "Spit it out. Or I'ma call the damn cops!" Camilla said as she surveyed the Marta parking lot.

"Please!" Sunrise raised both her hands. She moved to open the car door, but Camilla slammed it shut.

"You better start talking," Camilla said through clenched teeth.

"I – I just want to know who you are," Sunrise whimpered. Her weepy desperation made Camilla wince.

"Why?" Camilla asked, keeping both hands pressed against the car door.

"You look like me," Sunrise whispered, her matching honey brown eyes locked on Camilla's. "We have the same eyes, the same hips, and hair," Sunrise said as she eagerly removed the crocheted cap she was wearing—mussing her soft, thick waves.

Camilla looked Sunrise's up and down. "Sweetie, this is Atlanta. There's a lot of niggers around here who look alike."

Camilla's obscenity made Sunrise cringe.

"You can't be following folks around like this. You can really get yourself hurt, girl," Camilla warned her doppelganger as she moved away from the car. "What do you want to know about me? I ain't nobody important."

Sunrise shrugged like a child. Bewildered, she answered, "I'm not sure. Can we go somewhere to talk?"

Camilla looked down at her fading gold-toned wristwatch.

"There's a little place on the corner, right over the tracks. We can walk over there, but I've only got an hour or so before my daughter gets here from work," Camilla said looking around the parking lot again. "She'll be here around six thirty. OK?"

Hearing Camilla use the term, daughter, plucked at something in Sunrise, sending a tingle up her spine. "Sure," she said as she got out of the car.

Camilla turned her nose up at Sunrise's threadbare baggy jeans, torn hems, and distressed silver Birkenstock sandals. The sleeves of her dingy white t-shirt had been haphazardly cut off. The red cursive letters that spelled out the word WANDERLUST above a galloping herd of wild horses were fading and cracked. Camilla looked puzzled as she watched Sunrise pull a ragged leather tote from the backseat of her Mercedes-Benz S-Class.

"What's up with this girl? And what is she wearing? I can't figure out if she's boho or a hobo?" Camilla mouthed, scratching her head.

"Look, you're a pretty girl, offbeat and all, but I'on know what I can do for you," Camilla uttered, flailing her hands about as they walked along. Sunrise followed a few steps behind her. Sunrise wore shoulder-grazing feather earrings and two bold turquoise rings on several of her fingers; even her thumbs were adorned. She adjusted the gnarly crocheted cap on the back of her head and instinctively moved to tuck the stray hairs behind her ear. Sunrise saw Camilla's wonder at her odd adjustment. " I recently cut my hair," she explained shyly.

The women chose a table on the sidewalk and ordered sweet teas. The small corner café was buzzing with energy--the laughter of tipsy colleagues and melodic bass tunes poured out onto the street every time the heavy wooden door swung open.

"So how long have you worked at the bank?" Camilla asked as she fiddled with the ice cubes in her glass.

Sunrise sensed Camilla's discomfort. She found the usually confident woman's reaction affirming. She forced a small, shy smile at Camilla to put her at ease.

"I don't really work at the bank. I'm actually a musician---and a professor of music theory at Columbia."

"Columbia? They speak Spanish there, right?"

"No. You're thinking of the country. It's a university in New York City."

"A college university?" Camilla confirmed. "Then why are you moonlighting at a bank in Atlanta?"

It was Sunrise's turn to be uncomfortable. She fumbled around with her Thorpe family heirloom opal and diamond wedding ring, before answering.

"I walked in on my husband cheating, so I came home to my parents. I wallowed around for a month or so until my daddy had had enough and sent me to work," Sunrise explained. "He owns the bank, which makes the whole situation all the more humiliating." Sunrise slurped the syrupy sweetness left at the bottom of her glass. "Three degrees and I'm working as a teller at my daddy's bank – and I'm not very good at it either. No one takes me seriously because everybody knows that I'm the boss's daughter," Sunrise droned.

"So, wait a minute," Camilla said. "Yo' daddy owns that bank?"

Sunrise dipped her head.

"And he black?" Camilla asked, leaning in on her crossed forearms.

Sunrise dipped her head again.

"Damn," Camilla crooned, sitting back in the wrought iron chair. "So yo' folks is rich? Like real rich?"

"They've done well; they're retired now." Sunrise shook her empty glass toward a passing server. "Enough about me. Where are you from, Ms. Camilla?"

"Call me Camille. I don't like that country ass "A."

"OK," Sunrise chuckled. "Camille."

Camilla fingered at a tangle in the matching, thin gold chain she and her daughter, Camisha wore.

"I don't even know your name," Camilla said softly.

"Oh my God, you don't. Do you?" Sunrise's tone was feathery and down-to-earth. "I'm so sorry. I've been so focused on what I wanted. I'm sorry. I'm Sunrise, Sunrise Anderson-Thorpe."

Camilla smiled broadly. "What a beautiful name. I really like that." She repeated Sunrise's name joyfully, "Sunrise."

Camilla's delight was well received. The young woman and her smile mirrored Camilla's.

"Thank you," Sunrise beamed. "My parents met in Sunrise, Florida and there you have it--Sunrise."

The mention of her parents drew Camilla back into a defensive posture.

"So what can I do for you, Ms. Sunrise?" Camilla asked pointedly, trying to maintain a cool façade.

Sunrise sat up in the chair and clasped her sweaty hands underneath the shaky table. "I'd like to know about your family. I mean, I think we could be related," she said. Her normally crisp voice cracked.

"So you think we're cousins or something?" Camilla snickered.

"I don't know. Maybe."

"Maybe, huh?"

Camilla glanced at her watch and then out across the street towards the train station.

"I was adopted," Sunrise said, bringing a halt to Camilla's cool act.

"Adopted? When? I mean how old were you? Do you know?"

"Yes. When I was a baby. My parents took me right from the hospital."

Camilla swallowed hard and signaled to their server. "I'ma need a basket of fries and a glass of Riesling. Please," Camilla ordered. "Right from the hospital, huh?"

Camilla's jaw clenched, but she collected herself and looked squarely into Sunrise's eyes. "Well, I don't know much about my family outside of knowing that my momma what'n shit."

The server returned with a chilled glass of white wine. The summer heat sent glistening droplets of condensation running down the stem of the glass, pooling onto the tabletop.

"She was from here in Georgia," Camilla affirmed, "and heard somebody talking 'bout all the good work up North, and took her dumb ass to Connecticut on the first thing smoking. After a year or so, she hooked up with some half-breed nigger and had me." Camilla took a sip of wine from the glass before continuing. "My god momma, Cora claimed that my momma tried real hard to do right by me, but got ate up by the city and didn't know which way to turn. Her name was Irene, and she must've been about nineteen years old when she went up North."

Sunrise listened attentively. She liked the cadence and melodic quality of Camilla's sugary drawl.

"As the story was told to me, she asked Ms. Cora to watch after me until she got settled back in Georgia. She was never heard from again. Outside of that, my daughter Camisha is all the family I know anything about."

Camilla's phone vibrated against the metal chair she sat in. She looked at the screen.

"I have to get going."

"But your fries aren't here yet," Sunrise pleaded.

"Well I guess you can have 'em and pay for 'em, 'cause Camisha's train is pulling into the station."

"I wish I had more to give you, Sweetie and I hope you find what you're looking for, but I've got to get going." As Camilla stood to leave, Sunrise stood with her. She extended a shaky hand to Sunrise. Sunrise wiped her sweaty palms on her jeans and took Camilla's in her own. The women stared knowingly into each other's eyes before letting go. "Good luck finding your kin, Sunrise."

Camilla rushed into the crosswalk and disappeared between the evening commuters on the train platform. She could hardly find the keys to the car from the tears flooding her eyes. When she was sure she hadn't been followed, she lay her head on the steering wheel and let out a piercing howl. The strength of her sorrow called up a torrential downpour of tears.

Camp Creek Parkway was a blurred mess through the stinging of Camilla's tear-strained eyes. She drove towards Cami's house at top speed, wracked with sobs.

"My baby girl," the woman choked and gasped. "After all these years? Why Lord? Why? I've spent more than half my life trying to move past the shame of walking away from my baby. "

"Why now? Lord, you know my heart, and you know that leaving her sleeping in that cold hospital was the worst feeling I'd ever had. You know how many nights I sat up replaying my every damned step that morning; waking up and showering, brushing my teeth and getting dressed...I can't even burn the image of holding her to my breast and giving her what I knowed would be the last thing I'd ever give her."

Camilla crouched over the steering wheel, grabbing her stomach. She nearly missed the turn to Cami's house. She could barely see through her swollen eyes. Her hands were trembling, and she struggled to get the key in the lock. She barely made it down the steps to her bedroom before being overcome.

Camilla's banging headache woke her to dry, burning eyes, and a hankering for a cigarette and ice water. She listened at the basement door for Camisha and Ali, but heard nothing. She filled one of Camisha's fancy glass bottles with crushed ice and water and crept back downstairs. She reached for her phone, but changed her mind and instead reached underneath the bed for her lock and roll storage bin. She took a small key, a loose cigarette, and lighter from the bedside table. Camilla knelt by her bedside and unlocked the bin. It held a baby blanket, two plastic hospital id bracelets, a few journals, spiral notebooks, and some scraps of paper. Camilla held the blanket to her nose and teared up again, she gently folded it and placed it back in the bin. She took out tattered black and white composition notebook, and a Bic ballpoint pen with an eraser on top.

"Why the hell did I agree to go with her? Stupid! Stupid, woman!" Camilla said, chastening herself. She wiped angrily at the lone tear that ran down her face. "You just couldn't leave well enough alone. Could you?"

Camilla lit the cigarette, then pulled the pen's cap off with her teeth. She spat it onto the floor and climbed back onto the bed with her notebook. She took a long drag from the cigarette, and scribbled a few inky flowers and butterflies on the page before penning:

Sunrise. That's a beautiful name. I wanted to call you Cassie, but from the first moment I knew you were there, growing inside of me, I knew that we only had a short time together, so I didn't bother. I knew that I had to do right by you and everybody else.

By the time I made my final decision, I knew what I was doing was the right thing for everybody. It was the mother's intuition that the Lord blessed me with.

I prayed for you, and me, and your daddy, and walked away. I prayed that one day you would understand that it was because I loved you so much, that I walked away.

I thought about you and your adoptive parents a lot. I don't have a whole lot of love to give, but I want you to know that I loved you as much as I loved Camisha. But I knew I couldn't see about you and her. I knew that your daddy didn't mean no harm by being with me again. He was hurting real bad. He was a good man and didn't deserve to have his life blown apart again, because of a real bad situation that was out of his control.

I was always telling you, wherever you were in this big world, that I was sorry. And I still am, if you need me to be. But seeing you again, and hearing about your life is all I need to know that I gave you the best opportunity at a good life.

-Camille Robbins

Meet Caspian

Caspian sat in the middle of the floor playing video games with his nephews. As he struggled to navigate the twists and turns of his virtual raceway, Kannon jumped on his shoulders and smacked the controller out of his hands.

"Lucky, you're raising a couple of cheaters over here on Rocky Hill!" Caspian said to his sister.

Taliesan stood at her sleek kitchen island washing dishes and laughing.

"Come on man. They're six and four! Let them win sometimes."

"Letting them win won't serve them in this mean world, Sis. Am I right, Professor?" Caspian said, pulling his brother in law into the discussion. Ellis sat at his desk reading papers. His kinky twists and curls made his silhouette look like that of a Boondocks character.

"Not at all, Cas," he said without looking up from his work.

Bodhi joined Kannon, and they both double-teamed their uncle.

"Ah, you got me," Caspian yelled out. He loved spending his Sunday evenings with the boys. They played the latest video games, went to car shows, and any other activity the boys took an interest in. He wrestled with them and shot at squirrels from the tree house he'd helped their dad build for them. He loved his nephews and hoped to have his own children one day.

"It's bath time boys," their mother announced to wails and pleadings.

"Awww. But we want to play with Uncle Cas." "Hey. Hey, now! That's my big sister y'all suckers yelling at," Cas said as he tickled the boys. "I'll stay to tuck you in and read you two stories," he said, waving two fingers in their cherubic faces.

"Three stories! Please, Uncle Cas."

"OK, you little tricksters! Three stories. Now go on upstairs and call me when you don't smell like little puppies anymore," he teased.

Their laughter drifted downstairs, making Caspian smile as he swiped through his emails.

"Did you go out looking for your mustang this weekend?" Ellis asked.

"No, Sir. I worked on dad's a little, though," Caspian answered as he moved the heavy wood slab coffee table back to its proper place on the jute area rug.

"How's that going?

"It's going. It's not easy to find parts for a sixty-nine Fastback, you know?"

"Not really. I've never been a car man," Ellis laughed.

Caspian laughed too. Ellis was the stereotypical college professor. He wore cardigans and glasses and drove a faded Subaru Outback outfitted with bike racks.

"It runs, but it's not ready to take out on a track."

"Is that what you're going to do with it?" Ellis turned to face Caspian. "Race it? You've never said that."

Caspian shrugged and flicked the television on to Sports Center. Ellis returned to his work without pushing.

"You can come up now, Cas. The boys are ready," Taliesan shouted.

Caspian jumped at the opportunity to leave the tension-filled family room.

"Hey, you little suckers! Let me see those books!"

Caspian joined the adults downstairs once he'd gotten the boys off to sleep. Taliesan poured green tea into cups, hushing her brother with a finger to her pursed lips. She gestured for him to head out to the balcony. Ellis had moved to the large gray sectional and was softly snoring under an Aztec printed blanket.

"I hope you made mine a grown up cup of tea," Caspian asked.

Taliesan gave her baby brother a once over with a raised eyebrow before handing him the cup. Taliesan was a willowy beauty in a floor-grazing gauzy white maxi dress with brightly colored flowers embroidered down its center. She'd piled her kinky curls neatly atop her head with a colored scarf. She stood beside Caspian looking out over the wooded lot they'd grown up on as kids.

"You can still hear the brook back here," Caspian whispered.

"Hard to believe with all the new development around here."

"Yeah."

The two sat quietly listening to the soft babbling of the cool, fresh water stream that ran through the backyard of their childhood home. As though she could read her baby brother's mind, Taliesan took him by the hand and gave it a reassuring squeeze.

"We made it, Baby brother. And she's at peace now. I know it. Yeah?" Taliesan asserted.

Caspian only nodded and fought back at the lump growing in his throat. He sat down and sipped the hot tea and brandy concoction. Taliesan sat in the chair beside him.

"How's Sunny?" Caspian asked, shifting the conversation.

"She's doing a lot better. You don't talk to her at the bank?" Taliesan asked with her brow creased.

"I speak to her. Of course! But we're not kicking back chatting it up."

Taliesan shifted her head to the side in wait for an apology.

"I didn't mean to snap. Sorry," he said flashing a contrived smile at his sister.

"So is she getting back to herself?" he asked in an airier tone.

"I guess so. It seems like it, but she's been obsessing about one of your customers who supposedly looks like her." Taliesan answered, disarmed.

"Uh Oh, obsessing? That's never good for Sunny."

"Right?"

Sunrise was notorious for digging in when properly motivated. She'd spend weeks examining a potential relationship from every thinkable angle, but once she decided the relationship was worth pursuing, she'd fall hard. When she was in, she was all in.

"Has she told her folks about this lady?"

"I doubt it. I told her to, but you know Sunny. Slow and deliberate."

"Well, give her time, and if she doesn't mention it, I'll find a way to bring it up to Beaux," Caspian said.

"No! Just stay out of it. It's family business."

"Family business!" Caspian barbed. "I run their family's business – literally."

It was true. He'd been groomed for most of his life to eventually take over the banks. Beaux Anderson had been more of a father to Caspian and Taliesan than their own father had ever been.

Caspian was an ideal case study of contradictions. He was secretive, but he was also charming. He was serious about his work at the bank and believed in rules and order, but he was also passionate and daring. He'd spent his summers working alongside Beaux at the banks. He was the younger of the Pearce siblings but was wise beyond his years. What most people had to learn through years of experience, he already knew. During the day, he dressed in suit and tie--every bit the banker. But when night came, he would change into his uniform of oily coveralls, and tinker away at his father's old Mustang.

He was by far the greatest, most fun-loving uncle Taliesan's boys could have asked for, but he could also be moody and vindictive. As much time as the brother and sister spent together, Taliesan knew very little about his personal life. She knew that he liked racecars, she knew that he was straight, she knew about the deeply seated anger he had towards their father, but she knew no specifics. She'd only been to his house a handful of times, and she'd never met anyone he dated.

Caspian didn't spend much time on campus while at the University of Georgia. He hated college; he hated it like a bratty teenager hated curfews. He desperately wanted to attend a historically black college, but their father vehemently forbade it.

Shame On It All

Sunrise couldn't make heads or tails of what had transpired between her and Camilla. She lay in her new bedroom replaying every word Camilla spoke to her, examining every tilt of her head, every glint in her mirror image eyes. "Could she be my birth mother?" The question played on an endless loop in Sunrise's mind. She'd tried to convince herself to stop following Camilla around town, but the question plagued her. It controlled her every move after having sat across the table from the woman with her face.

Stevie Nix hopped onto the bed and rested his furry little body on Sunrise's belly. Ursula had cleaned out the pool house for Sunrise, giving her some sense of privacy and personal space. There was nothing grand about the pool house. There were three rooms--a living area outfitted with a pull out sofa, a small glass coffee table and two wicker club chairs, a mounted flat screen TV, which was a new addition since she'd moved out there, a tall, narrow kitchen table that seated four tall bar stools and a small kitchen with cabinetry installed in a corner. With a private bedroom and shower stall, it was all Sunrise needed. The pool house was at least 150 feet from her parent's back door, with its own small patio and two French Doors. Amber and Stevie Nix had taken to coming and going as they saw fit.

Sunrise was a highly organized individual; she preferred order over spontaneity and routine over adventure. She aligned her days with Camilla's. She left at daybreak to sit outside of the house on Enon Rd. watching for Camisha and Camilla to pull out of the long, steep driveway heading to the Marta station. She followed the Toyota Camry to the parking lot behind the airport, where she watched Camilla board a white and blue passenger bus, which Sunrise assumed took her onto the airport's private property. While Camilla worked, she worked. When she left the bank, she'd grab a bite to eat and head over to the Marta parking lot. She sat in the lot waiting to see Camilla pick up Camisha, and then she'd follow them home. She hated the days when Camilla went off script. She'd weave in and out of traffic trying to keep up with the Camry.

Camilla wasn't a conscientious driver. She drove along the busy roadways making illegal lane changes and tailgating while applying makeup. And once,

Sunrise watched in horror as Camilla steered with what must have been her knees as she removed her bra.

The sun shone against the bright blue sky the morning Sunrise followed Camilla, who had been picked up by a man in an older model car. She looked annoyed while she stood outside arguing with the man. Camilla stepped away from the car and slung a worn black bag over her shoulder. She took a few steps away from the car and angrily waved her middle finger in his direction. Sunrise made out a few expletives and threatening gestures and wondered if she should intervene. But Camilla's combative poses quickly changed to more submissive and almost suggestive ones. She hung her head, appearing to relent as she walked around to the passenger side of the gray Buick Lucerne.

Camilla was an interesting animal. Her moods and actions were capricious and often times, quite volatile. She was a wonder to Sunrise, who'd been raised by parents who were consistent and sensible. She couldn't identify much of Camilla's personality in herself, but the physical resemblance was undeniable, and it drove her incessantly.

The man drove in a more sensible manner, so she easily kept the couple in sight. Traffic was horrendous on Camp Creek Parkway. Drivers zigged and zagged their ways from one lane to another, bobbing and weaving in and out of eighteen wheeler tractor-trailers and SUVs carrying toddlers strapped in car seats. The sun was in the worst place on the horizon for reckless driving. Sunrise craned her neck to get a better view of what looked like tussling going on in the Buick carrying Camilla. The car swerved erratically before slamming hard on the brakes a few cars ahead of hers, sending the closer followers into a colliding, honking frenzy. She thought she saw Camilla's door open, but in the blinding blues, purples, and oranges of the sun rising in East, she couldn't clearly make out the scene. Sunrise's eyes darted wildly around the chaos just ahead of her, trying to spot Camilla. She looked ahead just in time to slam on her on brakes and steer onto the median to avoid the Volkswagen Passat that had also been involved in the pileup surrounding the Buick. Sunrise put the car in Park and got out to see what her car was hung up on when her eyes fell on a bloodied, motionless, Camilla.

The sounds of chatty onlookers and the blaring sirens all meshed together, making Sunrise's heart beat bang uncontrollably in her ears. She sat on the dewy median and laid Camilla's disfigured head in her lap. She took the blue and green cotton scarf she was wearing and wrapped it tightly around Camilla's head to stop the profuse bleeding. She sat as still as possible while more than a few people yelled questions and instructions at her. She was numb and as unresponsive as the woman she held on her thighs. Camilla's blood ran into the tie-dye of the maxi skirt she was wearing, soaking her along with the wet dew from the grass on the median. She sat there silently pleading with God to save the life of who she believed was her birth mother.

"I'll say it! I'll say it, if you'll only save her, Lord. Please Lord, please save my mother."

Sunrise sat there holding her birth mother in her lap until the medics pried Camilla from her bloody hands.

She spent the next hour with uniformed police officers, reporters, and camera crews running from witness to witness asking for their versions of the accident. Sunrise's car had sustained no damage, and there was no evidence that she'd acted negligently or recklessly, so they gave her a business card and told her where she could get a copy of the accident report. Then, they sent her on her way, bloody and all.

Sunrise nervously drove herself home. As she watched the streams of red in the suds from her loofah run down the drain of her shower stall, she decided to go to the hospital to check on Camilla. She quickly dressed and drove to Grady Hospital without a word to her parents.

The days and nights ran together during Camilla's recovery. Sunrise learned a lot about her biological sister and her friends, from the shadows and crowds of the trauma center. She overheard Camisha's angry words to Camilla and to her friend, Oliver about Camilla. She'd listened as they discussed their shared despair and hard times at the hands of Camilla--the promiscuity and alcoholism, and of late, the jealous attempts to sabotage Camisha's relationship.

Camisha and Oliver's private conversations painted an ugly picture of Camilla. Sunrise quietly thanked God she'd escaped the childhood promised to her had Camilla kept her. But there were also quiet moments shared between her, Camisha and an unconscious Camilla, moments when Camisha prayed aloud for her mother, moments when she fought for more loving care from the medical staff for her mother and tender moments when Sunrise would catch glimpses of

Camisha washing her mother's face, brushing her hair or moisturizing her mother's dry hands. Despite the anger and resentment she felt towards Camilla, Camisha loved her mother dearly.

The news of Camilla's passing hit Sunrise like a ton of bricks. She'd missed going to the hospital for two days. Her father had taken ill and required more care than her mother could handle on her own. When she prowled to Camilla's private room, she found an old white man, who appeared to be unconscious and alone. She read the charts that hung on the back of the door and saw the name, *Lawrence Gideon*. She stopped a passing orderly and asked about the black woman named Robbins who'd been in that room days before.

"I'm sorry, Ms. Camilla didn't make it—blood clot," was all she had offered before she went on her way.

"Blood clot," Sunrise repeated.

She left the hospital in a complete fog. *Had she killed her birth mother?* The whole scene was still unclear to her. The investigators had not found fault on her part, and several ambulance chasers had contacted her about the pileup, but none had shown any interest in her as the responsible party. Her head swirled with questions, with guilt. *How had Camisha taken the news? Had she been there with Camilla when she died? Should she reach out to Camisha?* Sunrise felt nauseous and vomited as soon as the morning air hit her lungs.

"Hello."

The singsong quality of Taliesan's voice was much-needed therapy for Sunrise after leaving the hospital.

"She died," Sunrise cried into the phone.

"What? Sunny? You OK? Who died, Mama?"

"No! Camilla, the lady from the bank. The one I told you about!" Sunrise shrieked.

"What? How do you know?"

"I think I killed her," Sunrise cried.

"What! What the heck are you saying, Sunny? Where are you?" Taliesan said as she ran around her house frantically looking for her purse and keys.

"I'm in the parking garage at the hospital."

"What hospital? Have you called the police, Sunny?"

Hearing the panic in her friend's voice, Sunrise tried to steady herself.

"Nothing like that, Lucky. I just want to see you. Are you at home?" Sunrise asked.

"I'm so confused, Sunrise. Yes. I'm home. Are you sure you're all right? Do I need to come and get you?"

"No. I'll be there in a few; just please, don't call my parents. I'm on the way. I'm fine. See you in a bit," Sunrise told her friend.

Taliesan was a ball of raw nerves. She paced her wooden floors barefoot, rubbing her crossed arms from shoulder to elbow. She knelt before the modest altar and wrapped the sandalwood prayer beads around her hands, and recited the vows of refuge to calm herself.

"I take refuge in the Buddha;

I take refuge in the Dharma;

I take refuge in the Sangha,"

She chanted melodiously until she heard a knock at the door. Ending before her one-hundredth chant, she respectfully bent at the waist, in closure, and rushed to the front door. She wrapped Sunrise in a motherly embrace, rubbing her back until their breathing was syncopated.

"What are you wearing on your hand? It feels so nice," Sunrise half- laughed between jerky sobs.

Taliesan laughed with her friend.

"It's my Mala. They're prayer beads."

"Like Catholic rosaries?"

"Sort of, they just help me keep count," Taliesan answered and escorted Sunrise to the living room. She patted an empty cushion beside her and folded her legs underneath her bottom. Taliesan was wearing a white, gauzy cotton maxi, with beautiful embroidery running down the full length of the dress. The turquoise, hot pink, yellow and green flowers momentarily distracted Sunrise from her grief. She reached out and touched them.

Taliesan always admired Sunrise's appreciation for things she found sensually pleasing. She'd always been drawn to the arts--paintings, fashion, music, and dance. It was no surprise to her when Sunrise made a splash in music and patterned her life around performing and teaching.

"Talk to me. What happened to Camilla?" Taliesan asked.

"Camille. She doesn't like the A," Sunrise said. A single tear ran down her cheek. "I mean, she didn't like the A."

She couldn't believe Camilla had died. "She was doing better and looking more like herself; I was sure she'd be leaving the hospital soon," Sunrise said, as her sobs started to regain strength, promising to break her fortitude.

"I didn't even get to know her," Sunrise said as she wept into her trembling hands.

Taliesan remained silent as Sunrise collected herself.

"Sunny," Taliesan said, patting her friend's knee. "Why did you say you killed her? What did you mean by that?"

Sunrise stretched out on the couch and looked up at the ceiling.

"Your ceilings match the floors," Sunrise mumbled. "I think I hit her, during that accident on Camp Creek."

The sobs won out making Sunrise's words incomprehensible. She was inconsolable; she cried herself to sleep on the couch.

"Cas! Are you at work?" Taliesan whispered from the kitchen while she peeked around the bookstand at Sunrise's sleeping form.

"Yeah. What's up? Why are you whisper-yelling at me?" he joked.

"Not now! Listen to me. Sunny is in some kind of trouble, but you can't tell the Andersons anything until I can get her together; she's a mess!"

"Where is she?" Caspian asked.

"She's here, asleep on the couch right now."

"Tell me what you know."

By the time Sunrise awoke, and the boys were home from school, Caspian had made a few calls to his frat brothers on the Atlanta Police Department; they told him the whole story.

Sunrise woke up with a dry mouth and excruciating headache. Taliesan and Caspian were sitting on stools at the kitchen island. Caspian took her a tall glass of water and wrapped an arm around her shoulders. She hung her head and settled on his strong chest.

"You smell good."

"Thanks, Sunny. You OK?" He lifted her chin with a finger and looked into her bloodshot eyes. She nodded and looked away.

"You didn't do anything wrong, Sunny," he said.

"I did, Cas. I stalked her and killed her. I hit her. I know I did."

"That's not what the reports say. They say that you helped her. You wrapped her head and cradled her until the ambulance arrived. Is that how you remember it?" he asked cautiously.

She nodded her head and wiped her nose with the back of her hand. Caspian took the glass of water from her and lifted it to her mouth. She took a few small sips and returned to her resting place on his chest. She was exhausted, and the weight of her head on Caspian's chest revealed just how tired she was.

"I'm going to take you home, and we'll talk more about everything tomorrow. OK?"

Sunrise had forgotten about her parents. She sat up and shook her head wildly.

"No! I can't let mom and dad see me like this. They'll worry, and dad is just beginning to feel better. No! Can't I stay here?" she pleaded.

Caspian looked over his shoulder at his sister. Taliesan joined them in the living room and knelt on the floor beside them.

"Of course you can, Love. But don't you think they'll worry even more when they see the car up here and not you?"

"Yeah. You're right."

"Just go over there and talk to them. Tell them what Caspian told you," Taliesan advised.

"Yes! Stick to what the report says. Don't freak them out with all of that talk about stalking and killing. You understand, Sunny?"

"I'll talk to them tomorrow, but I can't today. I just can't."

"OK. That's understandable," Taliesan agreed.

"Yes. That's probably best," Caspian co-signed. "So here's what we'll do. I'll take you home in your car. You go get cleaned up, and I'll grab us something to eat," he said, pausing briefly. "I'll drop by to call on your mom and dad, while you head back to the pool house. I'll make up some excuse about you not coming in; some female issue kind of excuse, and that way they won't worry.

Caspian turned his attention to his big sister. "Lucky, you check on the boys, they're probably worried. I'll see about Sunny and stay with her until you get your family settled in for the night, and then you can go sit with her. I know you won't be able to get any peace until you see about her yourself."

Things Fall Apart

Sunrise had never been much of planner; she was a dreamer. The five years following the end of life as she'd known it, proved to be an excruciating lesson in perseverance. At the age of thirty-five, she was a completely different woman—awakened and automated all at once.

The ugliness of her divorce only compounded the feelings of betrayal and mistrust Camilla's rejection had planted. The once carefree dreamer was now guarded and wary. Gone were the late nightclub gigs and studio sessions. They had been replaced with uneventful days at work, and quiet evenings with her parents.

She'd bought her own place near the bank--not far from Camisha's home. She carved out at least a half hour every Saturday morning to discreetly watch her sister's family start their weekend. She felt ashamed stalking the Robinson's, but the ritual was out of her control. She needed to see them, to know that they were all right. The act had become habitual--a harmless little peculiarity.

Beaux and Ursula were uncharacteristically quiet as they shuffled between the kitchen and dining room setting the table for Sunday dinner. Sunrise noticed the hushed exchanges and knowing glances they shared whenever she seemed otherwise occupied.

"What's going on, guys?"

Sunrise sat the last glass on the dining table, facing her parents.

"Are you guys fighting or something?"

The elderly couple looked to each other again. Ursula signaled to her husband.

"Sunny, a police officer came here yesterday looking for you," Beaux said.

"Looking for me?" Sunrise said with a furrowed brow. "Did he say why?"

Ursula walked around the table and pulled out a chair for her husband. She stood behind him, clasping onto its back. Sunrise fidgeted as she sat across from her father, holding his gaze.

"Well, he asked about the car. He said it had been involved in an accident a few years back. He said a woman had been killed," Beaux said, looking up at his wife.

"Her name was—Camilla. Yes, Camilla," Ursula added.

Sunrise's eyes darted between her mother and father's weathered faces.

"Sunny, do you know anything about this?" Beaux questioned with a gentle pleading.

Sunrise's eyes filled. She bit her bottom lip, battling the tears pooling in the rims of her eyes. She wound a fringe from her ripped t-shirt around her finger and took a deep breath.

"I was following her," she said as a tear rolled down her face.

"Following her?" Ursula asked.

Sunrise nodded again. Ursula pulled out another chair and sat beside her husband. He put her hand in his lap and gave it a small squeeze.

"Let her talk, La La," Beaux said.

Ursula slapped her hands together and wrung them, but she waited for her daughter to continue.

"I first saw her shortly after I moved back to Atlanta," Sunrise said, wiping her face. "She was a customer at the bank."

Sunrise blinked hard against the vivid image of Camilla's face in her mind's eye. "She looked like me. I thought she could have been," she twisted her mouth and looked down at the velvet chair she sat in, "related to me or something...could I have a glass of water," she said to her mother.

She waited for her mother to return before continuing. She took a sip from the glass.

"Take your time," Ursula said to her.

She took another deep breath before she spoke again.

The Andersons sat around their dining room table digesting everything Sunrise had told them.

"Sunny, why didn't you tell us about the accident?" her father said, reaching across the table for her hand.

"I didn't want to bother you guys. You were battling that upper respiratory infection, and mom needed to focus on taking care of you," she explained. "I was supposed to be here to help you guys, not to add to your load," she said, squeezing her father's leathery hand. "Daddy, I didn't do anything wrong. I wasn't even involved in the accident."

"Then why are they asking about you after all these years?" Ursula asked.

"I don't know, Mommy. Did he leave a card or something?"

Ursula scrambled over to the china cabinet for her reading glasses. After shifting through the drawer where she kept her important papers, she waved a business card.

"Here it is! His name was Chief James DaCosta," she said.

"Chief?" Sunrise took the card from her mother. A look of confusion washed over her face. "Why would the chief of police be investigating a car accident from five years ago?

"Maybe it's not the accident he's investigating," Beaux added.

"Then what is he investigating? And why is he interested in our Sunny?"

"If you recall, he never asked for Sunrise by name. He asked who the car was registered to,"

"But if he had the report, he already knew that it was me who was driving. He already had my name," Sunrise said.

"Exactly," Beaux said. "We'll call Dale in the morning, and schedule a visit with Chief DaCosta."

Ursula put a hand on Beaux's shoulder. "Do you really think we need a lawyer, Beaux?"

"One never knows, La La. But we won't be talking to any cops without one."

The police station was much more modern than Sunrise had imagined. It looked like a cutting edge medical research center with its dark, wooden reception desk, and chrome finishes. There was no dingy gray system furniture, and graffiti scrawled fiberglass chairs bolted to concrete floors as she'd imagined. Instead, there was a shiny chrome and glass staircase that extended to the center of the room, anchored by an elaborate marble inlaid floor medallion of the Atlanta Police Department's emblem.

A plump middle-aged white woman greeted them and checked her computer. Finding the appointment, she smiled at the group and directed them to the empty seats across from her station. Sunrise helped her father into a chair and took a seat beside her mother. The deep, clear voice startled Sunrise as she sat swiping through her cell phone.

"Good afternoon, I'm Chief DaCosta. You can all follow me this way."

Chief DaCosta was of average height, but something in his way spoke to his station in life. He wore his kinky hair closely cropped at his graying temples, highlighting the fine lines around his eyes, which Sunrise thought were from smiling. He led the group to a glass-enclosed conference room with a big screen TV, a small conference table, and six chairs. He took a chair in the middle of the table. Sunrise sat directly across from him after helping her father into a chair at the head of the table.

James was awestruck by how closely Sunrise resembled Camilla. He willed himself to focus on the questions he'd prepared when he got the call from the Anderson's attorney requesting a meeting with him. Sunrise fiddled at the several layers of cowrie shells she wore around her neck. James looked over every inch of her cocoa brown face, her sparkling hazel eyes, her full, perfectly bowed mouth and the larger than life ringlets that formed a large afro around her head. A fatherly feeling tugged hard at him, giving him second thoughts about pursuing Camilla's case. There was an undeniable weirdness in the room.

"Ok, let's get started here," Dale said. "Chief DaCosta, what can we do for you?"

James pushed away from the table. He narrowed his eyes and crossed his legs. "I wanted to speak with Ms. Anderson."

"Mrs. Anderson-Thorpe," Dale said.

"My apologies. Mrs. Anderson-Thorpe."

Sunrise shook her head, never taking her eyes off of DaCosta. "Anderson is fine. I prefer it," Sunrise whispered. She straightened her back and smoothed the edges of her hairline with both hands.

"OK, now that we've gotten that in order," Dale proceeded. "What can we do for you, Sir?"

James could hardly pay attention to anything outside of Camilla's younger face staring back at him. The sparkle in Sunrise's eyes seemed to gently encourage him to continue. He smiled at her. She looked to her parents, confused by the gesture, and shyly returned the smile.

"I just wanted to talk to Ms., I mean, Mrs. Anderson about the day of the accident."

The Anderson's looked around at one another before Dale spoke up again.

"I don't know what more Mrs. Anderson-Thorpe could add," he chuckled arrogantly. "The accident occurred at least five years ago. What's this really about? And you have about one minute to tell it to us straight before we're out the door." Dale said, moving closer to the sliding pane of frosted glass.

"It's personal," James said. He adjusted his cuff links and looked squarely into Sunrise's honey brown eyes. "It's my daughter. Camilla Robbins was her mother."

"She was your wife?" Ursula asked.

"No. No, nothing like that," James said, shifting uncomfortably. He clenched his fists and folded his arms across his chest. "She and I only had the child together."

Dale took a seat at the table and sat his briefcase down.

"I'm sorry for your loss," he offered.

"It wasn't my loss. It's my daughter's," he said, turning his attention back to Sunrise. "So any information or clarity you can provide would be great, for Camisha, that is."

Hearing Chief DaCosta say Camisha's name sent goose bumps up Sunrise's arms. She nervously stroked the big bird yellow pom poms that adorned the hem of her poncho.

"I don't remember much about the day."

"That's OK. Whatever you can remember would be more than we know right now," James said.

A tiny cough escaped her. She rubbed at her neck and asked for a glass of water. Her visible discomfort drew the attention of everyone in the room. James excused himself and left to get her a glass of water.

"Are you OK, Sunny Bunny?" her father asked.

"I'm fine, Daddy," Sunrise said, patting her father's hand.

"You don't have to do this," Dale added.

"No. I want to help his daughter find any peace she can."

Sunrise sat quietly tracing the floral stripes in her bell-bottom pants until Chief DaCosta returned with a small stack of plastic cups and glass decanter filled with water.

"Mrs. Anderson,"

"Please, just call me Sunrise."

"Sunrise. I'd really like to get you and my daughter together. That way you won't have to keep rehashing the accident. I can see it's not easy for you."

His compassion warmed Sunrise and drew her to him even more. She agreed to meet with Camisha in the coming days.

No Kin To Us

You would've thought Sunrise had landed a date with Lenny Kravitz, the way she tore through her closet dismissing one poncho after another. Taliesan and Ursula sat at the foot of her wicker-framed bed watching her.

"I think this is it," she said twisting to see her five-foot, five-inch frame from every possible angle.

"Now what do you call that?" Ursula asked, her curiosity getting the best of her.

Taliesan burst into laughter and playfully poked at Ursula's shoulder.

"Mom," Sunrise said, crinkling her nose at her mother's reflection in the full-length mirror. "It's a cocoon dress! I love this dress! It's nice," she whined. "You told me to tone it down for our first meeting," she said as she spun around to face her critics. "And this is the most toned down thing I own! It's Victoria Beckham."

She turned to give them a full frontal view of the snakeskin printed knee length cocoon dress. She piled on a few chains in varying lengths and stacked a few bangles on each arm. She asked Taliesan to throw her a pair of brown suede over-the-knee boots that lay strewn on the floor of her walk-in closet. Taliesan returned with the boots as instructed and watched her friend pull them on.

"I think you look nice, Sunny," Taliesan said, smiling approvingly. "And very toned down."

Ursula tried to stifle another grin.

"Mom! What?" Sunrise shrilled like a child.

Ursula could only shake her head, as she was overcome with laughter. Sunrise twisted her face and put a hand on her hip. She stood that way until her mother regained control.

"What?" She repeated angrily.

"Now, you just settle down, Missy," Ursula warned. "I find it comical that you are wearing ten pieces of jewelry, not counting earrings, and have the nerve to say it's toned down. I'm sorry! That's not my idea of toned down, Sunny."

Sunrise turned to look at her reflection in the mirror again. She shifted her weight to one leg and tilted her head. She pursed her lips and briefly considered her mother's feedback. She put on a pair of feather earrings and tied a silk scarf around her top knot, allowing her wavy kinks to flow down her back. She turned to her critics again, pointing to her simple headdress.

"Now, if this boring scarf isn't toned down, I don't know what is."

The three women laughed in unison.

"A cocoon dress, you say?" Ursula chuckled.

"Yes, Ma'am. That's what she called it. A cocoon dress," Taliesan sang.

"You sleep in a cocoon bed, in a cocoon bedroom, and wear cocoon dresses. Heck, Sunny Bunny, you make me feel as though I didn't swaddle you long enough."

The women all erupted into laughter again.

Ursula insisted in joining Sunrise for her meeting with Camisha. They'd agreed to meet Camisha and her husband at the police station. When they arrived, James DaCosta greeted them and led them to his private office. Sunrise had rehearsed the expressions she'd use when she finally met Camisha. She wanted to express a believable amount of benightedness. If she came across as too familiar, it might raise suspicion. She couldn't adequately explain how she'd grown to know them over the years -through covert reconnaissance- without being arrested and escorted to a holding cell. DaCosta's office was warm and tastefully decorated. His assistant brought in the same glass carafe they'd used the last time they were at the station, but she had real glasses filled with ice this time.

"Make yourselves welcome, Camisha should be here shortly. They ran into some traffic," DaCosta explained from behind his big desk, managing a tight-lipped smile.

He searched Sunrise's face. The way she was wearing her thick wavy hair made her look even more like Camilla. He let out a deep exhale when the door opened—nearly jumping out of his tall leather chair. He met the couple at the door and introduced them straight away.

"Camisha and Lennox, please meet Mrs. Ursula Anderson and Mrs. Sunrise Anderson-Thorpe."

"Please. Just call me Sunrise," she said, extending an open hand to Camisha. She wanted so badly to hug her. Instead, she shook her hand and then Lennox's. She helped her mother to her feet and ushered her halfway to where the couple stood. Camisha looked petrified. She stared Sunrise in the face without uttering a word of greeting.

Lennox put a hand on the small of her back and gently led his wife to the small round table near the bank of windows in DaCosta's large corner office. Ursula was clearly confused by Camisha's stupefaction. Camisha robotically fell into the chair her husband offered, never taking her eyes off of Sunrise. James helped Ursula over to the table and sat her down. Sunrise sat directly across from Camisha as if the woman's unbreakable gaze was controlling her. The room stood perfectly still as the women felt each other out. The energy was practically audible.

"Thanks for meeting with us, Sunrise," Lennox said, breaking the silence.

"Of course," Sunrise said, tossing a small smile in Lennox's direction.

"I don't know how much you can remember about that day, but any information would be great," he said. Lennox looked at his wife before continuing. "We know nothing other than what was in the report."

"Did you kill my mother?" Camisha said.

Ursula gasped.

"No!" Sunrise exclaimed, looking around the room for help. "I-I don't think I did. Everything was so crazy. Everything was happening so quickly," Sunrise protested. Her green eyes filled up. Ursula patted her daughter's thigh. Sunrise drew in a deep breath and wiped her eyes with the back of her trembling hand. "I thought I saw her jump out of a car ahead of me, just before I swerved to avoid hitting another car in front of me."

"Camisha, we already discussed what happened," James said, reprimanding his angry daughter. "What's gotten into you?"

"Into me? My mother's been dead for five years, and I finally get to face the person who may have very well killed her. Am I not to ask?" Camisha's voice shook. Lennox took her hand in his, but she pulled away. "Did you know my mother?"

Sunrise looked down at the table. James's eyes narrowed. He watched for Sunrise's reaction.

"Answer me! I can't be the only person in the room who has thought about it," Camisha yelled, pounding the table. "She has Camilla's face! Her entire face!" She shook both her hands at Sunrise. "Surely that is no coincidence!"

"What?" Ursula questioned. "Sunny, what's she talking about?" Sunrise's mother stammered. It was Camisha who answered. She took Camilla's driver's license from her handbag and laid it on the table before Ursula. Ursula was stunned by the resemblance. She looked back and forth between her daughter and the image on the driver's license. She wiped her brow and covered her mouth with her hand. The usually composed woman blinked back tears.

"Did your mother ever talk to you about giving up a baby?" Ursula said. "About leaving a baby...in the hospital? A baby girl? In 1984?" she asked, her tone filled with trepidation.

The room fell silent again. Sunrise kept her eyes down. She cried quietly, uncontrollably.

"In 1984?" Camisha repeated softly, shaking her head and looking to her father for help. "I, I don't know. I mean no! She never did," Camisha stood and looked around anxiously. "I, I was just a baby in 1984. I, I was born in 1983," she stammered as she feverishly ran the dates and numbers in her head.

"I kept you! I kept you!" she mumbled. They were her mother's words.

Camisha left the room running. Lennox followed her out, but James stayed seated in his chair. He swallowed hard. After a few seconds, he walked over to Sunrise and handed her a box of Kleenex.

"Mrs. Anderson, please tell me about this baby."

Ursula poured herself a glass of water, and another for her daughter, who had yet to speak another word.

"Sunny was adopted," she said. "We never kept that a secret from her," she said, telling James the whole story.

James was dumbfounded. His mouth moved, but he made no sound--as if he too, was running the dates.

"One last question," Camisha said as she reentered the room. "How long did you know that she was your mother?" Camisha hurled at Sunrise.

"I, I didn't know," Sunrise managed between sobs. "I didn't know for sure," she added. "It was just a feeling," she pouted. "I had lunch with her, and she denied having any relation to me." Sunrise's voice trailed off as she recalled that day. "She told me that lots of black people look alike in Atlanta, and wished me luck finding my kin."

"Well. That's that," Camisha blurted out, cutting Sunrise off. "You are no kin to us. My mother did not leave you or any other baby in a hospital in 1984." Camisha said, clasping her handbag. "Thank you for your time."

And with that, she left James DaCosta's office without as much as a wave to her father, or anyone else in the room. Lennox apologized and followed his wife through the frosted glass door.

The ride home was not easy. Ursula didn't spare her daughter. She wanted to know everything. When had Sunrise first seen Camilla? How had she known Camilla was in a car just ahead of her on the day of the accident? And why had she left out the fact that she knew the woman she'd helped at the scene of the accident. Ursula was both furious and hurt by her daughter's deception. Sunrise told her mother everything that had happened from the moment she laid eyes on Camilla at the bank. She even told her about the Internet searches, and how she had followed Camilla and Camisha. Ursula didn't understand why Sunrise had kept it to herself for so many years. She insisted that Sunrise tell her father everything.

"And don't you leave out a single word of it, young lady!" Ursula ordered.

Unlike his wife, Beaux was more understanding. His heart went out to his daughter. He was not angry, nor did he feel betrayed; he was heartbroken and angered at the way both Camilla and Camisha had shunned his daughter. He vowed to help his daughter find her biological family at any cost. He quickly called their family's attorney to gather her adoption paperwork and birth records.

*****

"Thank God, you answered!" Camisha exclaimed when she heard her best friend's voice on the line.

"Are you at home yet, Oliver?"

"Just walking in, Boss Lady. What's good?"

"Nothing's good, Ollie. Nothing at all. I should have listened to you and just let well enough alone." Camisha rambled on.

"Slow down. Slow down. What happened at the meeting? Was she able to give you any closure?"

"Closure!" Camisha yelled. "Heck no! She left me with a giant stinking gaping hole!" She scrunched her deep-set eyes tight and fastened her long bangs away from her face with an elastic band she pulled from her wrist.

Oliver chuckled at his friend.

"Come on now, Cami. It couldn't have been all that bad."

"Oh really, Oliver?" Camisha exclaimed. "It was bad! She looks exactly like Camilla--hair, eyes and all! She moves like Camilla. She smiles like Camilla, and get this!"

94

"Are you listening to me?" Cami asked.

"Yeah, yeah Cam. Farai just got home. Go on; I'm listening."

"Please apologize to Farai for me. I completely forgot about the time difference."

"Don't even sweat it, Boss Lady. You know we're late night people around here," he assured his friend.

"No worries, Cami. He's all yours, Cheri," Farai added.

"What time is it in France anyway," Camisha asked.

"1:00 a.m. Now back to the meeting!"

"Ollie...she's adopted!"

Neither of the friends spoke right away under the weight of Camisha's statement.

"Did she just drop that on you?" Oliver asked cautiously.

"Her mother did. When I showed her a picture of Camilla."

"Damn," was all Oliver could think to say to his friend.

"When? How old is she?"

"She was born in 1984. Just over a year after I was born," Camisha answered in a distant tone.

"Damn."

"I know. But it gets crazier."

"How much crazier could it have gotten, Cam? I mean, damn," he said once more.

Camisha inhaled through her nose and forcefully pushed the air out through her mouth.

"My dad...he just sat there like he was frozen. I could literally see him counting days and weeks on his fingers! What the hell was that about?" Camisha thought aloud. "And get this...she knew Camilla. She actually had lunch with her! She'd flat out asked Camilla if they were related, and you know what Camilla did? She lied! Flat out lied!"

"Wait a minute. What do you mean Camilla lied? What did she say to her?"

"She gave her some line about black people in Atlanta looking alike!"

"Classic Camilla. So do you think she tried to hurt Camilla?"

"I don't think so," Camisha admitted. "But I don't know her."

Who's That Lady?

"The sun sure is taking its time climbing to its noon position," Taliesan said as she stretched her legs across her brother's bare hardwood floors. Caspian and Sunrise exchanged playful glances.

"I saw that," Taliesan declared.

Caspian and Sunrise collapsed in laughter. Sunrise fell to her knees beside Taliesan and hugged her.

"I'm sorry, Lucky!" Sunrise sang. "He brings out the worst in me."

She winked at Caspian who sat at his kitchen table brushing a car part with a steel wire brush.

"Why can't you just say, this morning is going by so slowly?" he teased.

"I could have, but I didn't," Taliesan shrugged. She patted the empty space on the floor beside her; Sunrise sat obediently.

"Tell us about the meeting."

Taliesan was composed and matter of fact, but always in a nurturing manner. Her direction garnered Caspian's attention, too. He put the part he was working on down and joined his guests in the small living room.

Sunrise squirmed and stretched her legs alongside Taliesan's. She bent low at her waist, placing her forehead against her thighs as she began to recount her meeting with Camisha.

"It was bad," she whispered toward the floor.

Taliesan ran her hand up and down Sunrise's back. "Go on."

"You're OK," Caspian assured Sunrise.

The siblings sat quietly allowing their friend's bouncing knees to settle. Sunrise slowly released her downward facing pose and pushed her back against the linen Chesterfield sofa.

"She asked me if I killed her mother," Sunrise said.

Taliesan gasped, "Are you kidding me?"

"It gets worse," Sunrise continued. "She flat out asked if I knew her mother, and gave my mom a picture of Camilla."

Taliesan pulled her friend closer, but Sunrise politely shook off the kindness.

"Mom was so confused. The way she looked at me," Sunrise mumbled, trying to shake the look in her mother's face from her memory. "I hurt her. I should have told them," she said, looking to Taliesan. "You told me to tell them. You told me to years ago!"

"Don't' do that to yourself, Sunny," Taliesan begged.

"Besides, I told you not to tell them about the accident," Caspian said.

"But I should have told them about my meeting with Camilla. I should have told them everything, right away."

The three friends nodded in agreement--each replaying the poor decisions they'd made.

"Where was the Chief? What was he doing through all of this?"

"Or saying?" Taliesan added.

"Nothing," she whispered. "That is before mom told them that I was adopted and asked if Camilla had ever told anyone about leaving a baby girl in a hospital in 1984."

"What!" The Pearce siblings yelled simultaneously.

Sunrise nodded emphatically.

"Camisha was so upset; she stumbled around and ran out of the room. Then DaCosta spoke up. He asked Mommy to tell him about the baby, but Camisha burst back into the room."

"Oh my goodness! What'd she do?" Taliesan asked.

"She asked how long had I known that her mother was my mother, too!"

The room fell dead.

"Whoa," Caspian said, breaking the stupor. "What'd you say?"

"I told her the truth, partially. I told her that it was just a feeling. I also told her that when I'd met with Camilla, she denied having any relation to me."

"And?" Caspian prodded Sunrise.

The memory visibly pained Sunrise. She winced and rubbed at her temples.

"She said, 'Well, that's that. You're no kin to us'," Sunrise said, mocking Camisha.

"That self-righteous bitch!" Taliesan growled, shocking Caspian and Sunrise.

"Lucky!"

"Now, Lucky. I'm surprised at you," Sunrise said, chiding her girlfriend.

"I'm not sorry! I mean it. Who does she think she is? What gives her the right to treat you that way? You had nothing to do with it. You were left by her mother?"

"Well damn. Bye! Bye! Buddha," Caspian jeered.

"Not funny, Caspian," Taliesan snapped. "I have half a mind to find her and..."

"You sound like Daddy. He's vowed to find my biological family, 'at any cost.' He's already put Dale on the case."

"Of course he has," Caspian said. "Anything for his Sunny Bunny. We really should have told them about this from day one." Caspian said, joining his sisters on the floor.

"This'll all work out for the best, Sunny. You know that. Right?" he said, pulling them into a group hug. She faked a smile, satisfying her friends. Taliesan went into the kitchen and opened the refrigerator.

"This big fancy fridge is as empty as it was the day it was installed."

"Who needs food in there? There is only me, Sis. Remember?"

"Yes, but I was hoping that the leggy light-eyed sister I saw you with at the bank would be sticking around."

Caspian's disapproval flashed across his face. Taliesan quickly dismissed her little brother's scowl with a wave.

"What leggy light-eyed sister?" Sunrise chirped, eager to take the focus off of her family's drama.

"We're not talking about her," Caspian answered.

"Oh, but we are, baby brother."

"Yes, we are!" Sunrise cheered. "Now, who is this woman?"

Caspian relented, seeing that he was clearly outnumbered.

"OK. OK. But let's order something for lunch first."

"I'll order, you talk," Taliesan said.

Sunrise took a seat at the small kitchen table, putting her chin in her hands. Caspian threw a dishtowel at her.

"Grow up, Sunny?" Caspian grimaced. "It's not a big deal."

"Go ahead. I'm a mother. I can listen and order at the same time. I'm ordering Greek."

Caspian joined Sunrise at the table and picked up the car part he'd been working on earlier.

"Her name is Lacey, and she's from Alabama."

"How'd you two meet?" Sunrise chirped like a gossipy teenager.

Caspian scowled at Sunrise and brushed the part harder.

"I met her a few years ago when she came to the bank to discuss expanding her family's business into the Atlanta market. And we kept in touch. That's all."

"That's all? Come on now. Sunrise just bared all."

"Yep! So dish," Sunrise chimed in.

Caspian dramatically inhaled and twisted his mouth.

"I like her. She's cool."

"And?" Sunrise said.

"And she has a kid. And she works too much. And she's cynical as hell."

"He looked pretty captivated by her cynicism and work ethic when I dropped by the bank the other day, Sunny," his sister teased.

"I said she was cool!" Caspian said, defending himself.

"You're being cagey, Cas!" Taliesan said, snapping her fingers at her brother. "Geesh, I'm only kidding around with you; you're so touchy!"

Sunrise laughed at the brother and sister.

"Cas, you know that we'll find out," Sunrise sang.

"Of course you will, Night Stalker." Caspian squeezed his eyes and mouth shut, regretting the jeer as soon as he heard himself say it.

"Wow, Cas," Sunrise said. The corners of her mouth turned downward. "That hurt," she said as she turned and walked out of the house.

Caspian knocked over the chair he'd been sitting in and hurried after his friend.

"Sunny! I didn't mean that. I'm sorry," he screamed, but she didn't turn around. She crossed the tree-lined street and disappeared around the corner.

Taliesan walked out onto the small porch and stood beside her brother. She pressed her lips together and shook her head at him before going back into the house.

"You're a jerk!"

"I know."

"And you need chairs out here!"

"And a trap door," Caspian grumbled under his breath.

Lacey Robinson

Lacey was unlike any other woman Caspian had ever known. She was exceptionally beautiful--tall and curvy in all the right places. She had top shelf taste and the pedigree to back it up. She was socially conscious and business savvy, all at once. But above all, she was sharp. She really knew her stuff. As she'd told Caspian, she'd reluctantly been left in charge of running her family's business after her parents retired, and had grown their small dry cleaners in Alabama to a major chain that spanned four Southeastern states.

When they met, she'd come into the bank looking to buy her first home in Atlanta. Caspian saw her walk through the door dressed in all white, wearing a pair of big frame sunglasses. Her long legs and goldish green eyes captivated him, and just about everyone else in the bank that summer morning. Before he could stop himself, he'd offered to handle her home search personally, drawing questioning looks from his employees.

Lacey and Caspian were fast friends. They spoke the same language. He didn't mind that she was guarded because he was too. He learned a lot about her through her personal finances. He knew that her family was well established and she'd done well for herself, too. There were deposits into her account from a French bank, every month, without fail, telling him that her five-year-old son was well provided for by his father who lived there. Caspian found that both fascinating and relieving.

From a scholarship fund she'd set up in her name, along with Alumni Association dues, he determined that she was educated--and at a historically black university to boot. He secretly envied her. He'd desperately wanted to attend an HBCU, but his father forbade it. His father had an immense desire for him and his sister to assimilate into mainstream, White, America. They had grown up in vastly different homes, but the differences intrigued him.

Lacey had readily shared details about her life, like the fact that she'd been homeschooled until high school, and that she'd grown up on their family's land, neighbored only by aunts and uncles and cousins. As a city boy, Caspian couldn't even imagine a world like the one Lacey described.

"Are you completely locked into living in East Atlanta?" Caspian asked.

"Well, what do you have in mind? I mean, it's the only place I've lived, here in Atlanta," Lacey answered. "My brother used to live in Buckhead. But I don't want to raise my son there."

"You have a brother?"

"Yes. Lennox. He lives here in Southwest Atlanta-- not far from the bank."

"Really? You've never mentioned him," noted Caspian.

"Why would he have come up?" Lacey fired back, flashing a coy smile.

"I guess he wouldn't have."

"Well, Lennox is married and has a daughter. Her name is Lena. She and my son are close so it would be nice to be near them," she said. "So let's do it! I'm open—as long as it's kid-friendly."

Caspian smiled and turned the black Cadillac Escalade onto Main Street.

"What do you think of this area?"

Lacey crinkled her nose at the transitioning neighborhood and the interesting juxtaposition of its abandoned storefronts alongside bustling sidewalk cafes.

"Do you see that? It looks like it's not sure what kind of neighborhood it wants to be when it grows up. Gentrification?"

Caspian nodded.

"Yeah, but now is the time to buy around here. One of the country's most prestigious and diverse private schools is right down this street," he said, as he turned onto what looked like a Division One College Campus.

"This is a private school?"

"It sure is. K-12. This is Woodward Prep."

Lacey typed the name of the school into her smartphone and read silently. She checked the real estate comps in the area and concurred. Caspian's hopes leaped, which confounded him. Lacey excitedly showed him a home on her phone.

"Can we see this one?"

"Let's do it."

"I'll call the realtor," Lacey grinned.

*****

"The house is beautiful, Izzy. You're going to love it!" Lacey gushed.

"How far away is it from here?" Isaac asked, half-heartedly listening as he scrolled through the week's earnings.

"About twenty to twenty-five minutes West," she answered. "It's in the same neighborhood the bank's in, and really close to Lenny and Cami," she gushed. "Oh, and there's a really great school in the neighborhood for Luca."

Isaac looked up from the computer screen and frowned at Lacey, who was perched on the desk beside his laptop, swinging her legs like a six-year-old.

"So this dude just showed you spots near where his job is, huh?"

Lacey rolled her eyes and pushed her crystal and taupe cat-eye glasses up on her nose.

"You're always thinking the worst of people. He knows the city, and he knows what I'm looking for, for Luca," she argued.

"Sure. OK, can we talk about my proposal instead of your new boyfriend?"

Isaac turned his attention back to the computer screen.

"He's not my boyfriend! You're so immature." She slapped at him and focused her attention on business. "What do you have?"

Isaac had proven to have seamlessly transferred his head for street business to any business. The gamble she'd taken on her son's convict uncle, had paid off. He appreciated the opportunity Lacey had given him upon his release from federal prison, and he had thrown himself feet first into all things Dry Cleaning. It had been Isaac's idea to centralize the cleaning facilities rather than have dry-cleaning equipment in every storefront.

His idea to resell the used equipment they no longer needed made her family's company well over $400,000 in his first year on the job. It had also been his idea to use fleets of trucks and vans to go door-to-door to collect soiled garments from time-strapped customers. And now he was hard selling Lacey on the long-term rewards for dry cleaners that were switching to a liquid carbon dioxide cleaning system.

Lacey listened as attentively as her mind would allow, but her thoughts kept going back to Isaac's accusation that Caspian was trying to convince her to buy closer to his bank.

Undoubtedly, she found him very handsome, and she was impressed that a man his age was the president of a black-owned bank. Other than what he did for a living, she didn't know much about him at all.

"Are you listening?" Isaac bellowed.

"What? Yes! It'll be expensive at first, but it would pay off in the long term. I heard you. I heard you." Lacey retorted.

Isaac stared into Lacey's amber eyes and watched as her pupils expanded. He smirked and turned in his chair to face her.

"So you're ready to get back out there, huh?"

"What! Back out where? What are you talking about?" Lacey huffed.

"Don't be sorry about wanting to get back in the game, Lace. It's been long enough," Isaac surmised. "Oliver has moved on, and I think we're good now. Right?"

He placed a hand on her knee. She recoiled under his touch.

"I don't know what you mean," she said as she jumped off of Isaac's desk. "Let's get back to the liquid carbon dioxide."

Isaac grinned devilishly.

"You're the boss," he chuckled.

Isaac had always confused, and often times outright-befuddled Lacey. She was usually in control of her emotions and faculties in general, but Isaac's younger brother, and the father of her son, Oliver

Barnett tested her and taught her a lot about herself in the years they spent together.

He had been her first love, but theirs was a tumultuous, on again and off again love affair. He'd moved to France shortly after the birth of their son Luca, and she'd had a brief and wildly inappropriate attraction to his brother Isaac, shortly thereafter. Lacey counted that lapse of judgment among the lowest points in her adult life. But they'd worked through all of those murky days and were better for it, or so she thought.

"He'd be lucky to have you, Lace."

Isaac turned back to the computer screen and continued on about the innovations in the Dry Cleaning industry.

Running Numbers

Ursula Anderson's pronouncement about Camilla leaving a baby girl at a hospital in 1984 had kept James up the nights following their meeting.

"Could she have gotten pregnant that day?" James muttered. "No! Of course, she had other lovers, but so soon after Camisha's birth? My God, is Sunrise mine?"

James dialed Beaux Anderson and arranged for a time to talk.

Beaux was a strong and lively seventy-seven-year-old man. He'd lived a good life. He was college educated and self-made. He'd only ever worked for one company in his life before opening his own bank by the age of forty-two. He and his wife had indeed lived a charmed life for blacks in the South.

The call from Chief DaCosta didn't surprise Beaux at all; he'd been expecting it. He invited James over for lunch on the day Ursula had her weekly water aerobics class. He counted on her being out for most of the day. James showed up right on time and brought lunch for the both of them.

The men exchanged pleasantries about the weather and marriage, as they ate croissant sandwiches and garden vegetable soup. As James cleared the boxes and cups from the table, Beaux opened the floor for the business at hand.

"Chief DaCosta, I think you're here to talk about my daughter."

James cleared his throat and nodded. He nervously rolled his shoulders.

"I'm not a young man, James. Time is a fleeting resource for men my age." Beaux laced his fingers and gingerly bowed his head, directing James to take a seat.

James sat as directed.

"Now, I understand my wife has already shared with you the details of Sunrise's adoption. Yes?"

James nodded.

"And then you called."

James nodded again. He wasn't sure if it was Beaux's age or his quiet, authoritative demeanor that put him in supreme control of the room. He willed himself to speak up.

"Yes. However, I have a few more questions," he said.

"So do I," Beaux countered.

Beaux was quick. His eyes stayed locked on James,' and he remained perfectly still in his chair. James swallowed hard in the face of Beaux's intensity.

"OK," James stammered.

"Why now? At least five years have passed since the accident."

"Camisha wasn't ready. She's ready now, and I want to give her answers," James offered.

Beaux sat back in the chair and searched James's face for signs of deception.

"Go ahead," he ordered.

"I'm sorry, Sir?"

"With your questions," James clarified, folding his arms.

"Well, they're about Sunrise's birth mother."

Beaux wriggled. It was obvious; he hadn't expected James to inquire about Sunrise's birth mother. "Her birth mother?" Beaux asked.

"Yes. How much do you know about Camilla?"

Beaux shook his head and relaxed his posture.

"I didn't know anything about her before all of this. Sunrise had never expressed any interest in her biological family until she saw Camilla in the bank one day," Beaux explained. "She was a customer at my

College Park branch and Sunrise was working there part-time. It was just after her marriage fell apart; she was in a bad place," Beaux said, crossing his legs.

"So she'd met Camilla well before the accident?"

Beaux was visibly annoyed. He shifted in his seat and rested his index finger over his brow.

"Should I have had my attorney join us, Chief DaCosta?"

"Mr. Anderson, I swear to you, I'm not here in an official capacity," James said, opening his palms to Beaux. "I'm here as a man, as a father. What your wife said in the office the other day has left my daughter reeling."

The older man relaxed his posture. "Not for long. She said that she didn't have the nerve to speak to Camilla that first day," James confessed. "But after seeing Camilla again, she said that she waited to run into her at the Marta station, where she'd seen her go whenever she left the bank. She invited her to lunch, and they talked briefly, but Camilla denied having any relation to Sunny. That's all I know."

"Mrs. Anderson said that a nurse called you all when the baby was left at the hospital."

"Yes. Tammy Harper was her name. My wife taught her child piano. That's how she knew us."

"Is Nurse Harper still around?" James asked eagerly.

"No," Beaux lamented. "She passed some years ago."

The light in James's eyes dimmed. He sat back in his chair, looking up at the ceiling.

"Son, I hope I'm not overstepping, but you seem to be looking for something more than comfort for your daughter. Camisha is her name. Right?"

"Yes, Sir," James answered. "Camisha." James paused, considering his options. "And you're right. You see, I was married when I met Camisha's mother, Camilla, and well, her conception was due to an indiscretion on my part."

"Hmmm, I see," Beaux said.

"Well, I was with her again--just the one time! I was going through something. Well. My partner, he had just been killed. And I...I was so young, and I went to her, to see the baby," James said. "I only wanted to see Camisha; I wanted to hold her and smell her innocence. Do you understand?" James clenched his jaw and put both his pointer fingers to his lips. Beaux bobbed his head acknowledging James truth.

"I've gone over the girls' birthdates over and over in my mind. I haven't been able to sleep or even look my wife in the eyes since Mrs. Anderson's question. Your daughter looks so much like Camilla. I can't come up with an explanation other than the one Mrs. Anderson proposed. Camilla left her; she left her in that hospital. And I may very well be her father."

James twisted, hearing the words aloud. He wrenched and coolly wrapped his fingers around his mouth, but sweat stains grew on his shirt, exposing his anxiety.

James hadn't noticed Beaux leave the table. He was startled when the man touched him on the shoulder, offering him a tall glass of water. He anxiously drank from the glass.

"Thank you," he said.

Beaux sat in a chair closer to James and faced him. "You have to tell your wife," Beaux declared in a fatherly tone. "You sit her down and tell her just what you told me. No excuses. And apologize."

James's eyes glazed over.

"Are you with me, Son?"

"Yes," James mumbled.

"You tell her that you have no details about Sunny, but you wanted to talk to her about it and that you want her to know what's going on--every step of the way. She's going to be hurt, and mad as hell, so I don't anticipate any of this being easy for you, but it is necessary. You were young; you made a mistake by being with that woman again, and an even bigger mistake in keeping it from her for all these years. But what's done is done, and you don't want to keep her in the dark anymore. Right?" Beaux added.

"Right. I don't. I never wanted to hurt her again. And I didn't! I've never tipped out on my wife after that last time. Never," James asserted.

Beaux called up a small, encouraging smile.

"I'm sure of it," he said as he patted the angst-ridden man on the knee. "James you're a good man. I can see that. The fact that you're here, inquiring about a child that you may have fathered, speaks volumes. And I recognize that. It would be much easier for you to get up and walk out of here and never look back, but you haven't made a move towards that door. And son, that's admirable. Damn admirable. So you're on your way. It won't be a cakewalk, but it's something you have to do.

119

There's no turning back now," he chuckled trying to lighten James's mood.

"I'll be here for you, whenever you need me." Beaux stood and stuck his hand out to James. James shook Beaux's hand and thanked him again. "Let me know when, or if you want me to talk to Sunny about you. If you want me to arrange something, you let me know, and I'll make it happen. But right now, you need to talk to your wife. Yes?"

James pressed his lips together and managed another nod.

"Yes, Sir. And I thank you again for seeing me. I'll be in touch."

*****

Camisha had tried everything to busy herself, to keep her mind off of Sunrise, and her face. She threw herself into her work, signed their daughter Lena up for gymnastics classes, and finally set about cleaning and organizing the basement bedrooms that once housed Camilla and Oliver.

"Babe, what should I do with this bin?" Lennox yelled from Camilla's old room.

"What bin?"

Lennox came into the kitchen carrying a plastic box with a locking top.

"Where was that?" Camisha asked, taking the safe from her husband's hands.

"Under the bed in Camilla's room."

Camisha sat the box on the granite countertop and tried to open it.

"Was there a key?" she asked.

"I don't know. I'll check."

She followed him down the bare wooden stairs to the basement. She checked the drawer in the nightstand and found a few pieces of costume jewelry, a pack of cigarettes and a lighter, her mother's torn social security card, and a small key. Her heart lurched in her chest.

"Do you think that's it?" her husband asked, snapping through her daze.

She shrugged and took the key upstairs to the box. She stiffened as she looked at the box. "I'm afraid to unlock it," she said.

Her hands shook uncontrollably. Lennox laid his hand on his wife's and took the key from her. "We don't have to do this right now, Cam," he whispered to her.

"I want to," she said, looking up at him. She took the key from his hands and unlocked the lid.

There was a faded white baby blanket with blue and pink stripes at the edges, and two plastic wristbands folded inside of it. The wristbands were barely legible, Camisha could only make out the date, *05/26/1984*, and *7 lbs 8 oz* scribbled on the smaller wristbands. Her stomach knotted, and her vision blurred under the strain. She inhaled deeply and looked back at her husband who put a hand on her shoulder.

"Wow," he moaned.

Camisha squeezed the wristbands tightly and soldiered on.

There were small notebooks and several scraps of torn paper with Camilla's handwriting on them. There were beautifully bound journals and worn envelopes. They were all covered in her mother's handwriting.

"Camilla wrote?" Lennox asked.

"I-I didn't know," Camisha quivered. She carried the box to the dining room table. She sat the blanket and wristbands in her lap and spread the writings out before her.

"Babe, I'm going to leave you to this. I'll take Lena to the gym. That'll give you some time to sort through all of this. OK?"

He kissed her on the forehead and disappeared down the hall.

The pages smelled like Camilla. The scent of her favorite perfume, J'Adore Dior, mingled with the faint scent of cigarette smoke and talcum powder, brought tears to Camisha eyes. She heard her daughter skipping down the hall, and wiped her face.

"Mommy! Mommy! Daddy's taking me to the gym!" their four-year-old daughter sang as she bounded into the room.

"Yay!" Camisha cheered. "Daddy's the best! I want you to keep your listening ears on, and do as Daddy says. OK, Miss Lena?" she asked as she kissed her daughter's chubby cheeks. She mouthed the words, *thank you*, to him as they headed to the door. Once she was sure they were gone, she laid her face in the pile of her mother's papers.

"So you wrote, did you?" she said aloud. "Well, what'd you write? Poetry? Songs? Rap songs? Were you a rapper, Camilla Ann Robbins?" Camisha laughed.

She spent the next half hour thumbing through her mother's musings. She wrote funny things about guys she met at the airport. She wrote insightful things about current events. She wrote about her regrets and the things that made her angry. But the things she wrote about her own family were what most disturbed Camisha.

Camilla had always told her that her teenage mother had left her in an orphanage, but in her journals, she wrote about being left in Connecticut with a woman she called her godmother.

Her mother had moved to Connecticut looking for work and had been eaten up by the city. She wrote that her mother had left her with a friend saying that she'd be back for her once she settled back in the South, but had never been heard from again. Camilla had come to Atlanta on her own at fifteen in search of her.

The things she learned as she read her through her mother's writings only confused her further. But nothing puzzled her more than the nearly pristine white letter that that sat amongst the old or crumpled pieces of paper. Camilla had addressed it to Sunrise.

In the letter, Camilla said that she had seen Sunrise and had heard about her life. And given the condition of the letter, it hadn't been very far in the past. Camilla hadn't named Sunrise's father in the letter. She'd only said that he was a good man who didn't deserve to have his life blown up again.

Camisha stood up to grab her phone but collapsed under the weight of her thoughts. "How could Camilla have kept this from her? Who was the good man? Was it James again?" she said, nearly gasping for air.

"Oh my God!" Camisha cried. "What about poor Evangeline?" she wailed out to her mother.

"Why Camilla! Why! Why didn't you tell me? Why did you lie to Sunrise? Why?"

She crawled to her phone and dialed her father. She didn't speak right away. She only listened to the cheer in his voice. He was always happy to hear from her. His warm reception always made her feel good. But this call would change his life, and Camisha hated to be the person to deliver the blow.

"Daddy."

There was dead silence between the father and daughter.

"Yes, Camisha," James replied knowingly.

"It's true," her voice broke. "She's Camilla's, and Camilla knew it."

James sat in his office chair, unable to move.

"Daddy, did you hear me?"

"I did."

"You already knew. Didn't you?" Camisha yelled.

James shook at the tone of her voice. He sat up straight in his chair.

"No! Camisha, I swear to you. I know nothing more than you do about any of this," he stammered. "But, I did see your mother again—but just once!" He stood and closed the frosted glass sliding door to his office, and walked over to the window that overlooked the busy street. Camisha sat silently listening to her father's recount of the day his grief drove him into Camilla's bed once again.

"Does Evangeline know?" Camisha finally spoke.

"Not yet. I'm going to talk to her tonight." The corners of his mustache turned down, making him look like a sad little boy. "How do you know that Camilla had another baby? he asked cautiously.

"She kept a hospital blanket and their wristbands," Camisha whimpered. "And there's a letter."

"A letter?" James repeated.

"Yes. She wrote it in a letter. A letter to Sunrise."

"To Sunrise? She addressed it to Sunrise?"

"Yes."

Camisha turned cold. Her voice was distant.

"Do you have that letter, Camisha?"

"Yes, I'm holding it," she answered.

"Where are you?"

"Home."

"I'm on the way."

But before he hung up he asked, "Is she mine, too?"

*****

James called Beaux Anderson as he drove to Camisha's house.

"There's a letter. Sunrise is right, Camilla Robbins was her biological mother."

"And her father?" Beaux asked pointedly.

"The letter didn't say. I'm on my way to Camisha's now. I'll send over a copy of the letter for Sunrise to have, but Beaux, I'm going to need to see her sooner than later."

"I'll arrange it. And James..."

"Yes, Sir?"

"Good luck, Son."

Beaux disconnected the call and said a prayer right where he stood.

Enough

Camisha was not up for a fight after the evening she'd had. She had spent the night combing through her mother's most intimate thoughts, and she was tired. She and Lennox got their daughter into bed and retired in their own room.

"Are we going to talk about Camilla's box?"

She stared at him, listless. "I don't have the energy," she said as she walked into the en-suite bathroom.

"Did you call Oliver?" Lennox pressed.

"No," she tossed over her shoulder.

Lennox's tall, athletic frame filled the doorway. He stood watching his wife brush her teeth.

"Babe,"

"No, Ali." She turned around to look at him. "I can't. Not tonight. Please."

The couple stood staring into each other's eyes.

"Cam, you're obviously upset. And you won't sleep at all unless we get it out right now."

It wasn't like Ali to badger her into emotional conversations, but he was motivated by the depth of her pain.

"You're right," she said, kissing him on the lips.

"Good girl," he teased. "I'll take a quick shower first, and then I'm all ears."

He did as he said and joined Camisha in the tall platform bed. Camisha loved the way he smelled right after a shower. She touched his rippled abs as he crossed over her to his side of the bed.

"Are you trying to distract me, Mrs. Robinson?"

"Kind of," she purred. He kissed her on the lips before settling beside her and pulling her into his powerful arms.

"What upset you so much, Babe?" Lennox asked cautiously.

Camisha laid her head on her husband's bare chest. She closed her eyes against the rise and fall of his breathing. Lennox waited for her to answer.

"Sunrise is my sister."

Lennox sat frozen.

"Camilla kept a baby blanket and ID wristbands from the hospital. You saw it."

"Yeah. But how do you know they were Sunrise's?" he asked.

"There was a letter, too. She addressed it to Sunrise. She wrote to her that she walked away because it was best for everyone involved. She said that her daddy was a good man who was in a bad situation and that he didn't deserve to have his life blown up again."

"Again? What do you suppose she meant by that?"

Lennox lay quietly holding his wife. When he felt her warm tears running down his stomach, he sat her up and hugged her.

"Babe, you don't think James was with Camilla again do you? You don't think he's her father, too. Do you?"

Camisha nodded against his shoulder.

"And so does he."

*****

James swallowed hard against the lump in his throat. He rehearsed his opening lines until he had them memorized. He showered slowly and took his time putting on his nightclothes. He brushed his teeth for the full recommended two minutes, before working up the nerve to enter the bedroom where his wife was watching TV. He sat on the oversized velvet ottoman and put Evangeline's feet in his lap.

"What's eating at you, James?"

Sweat pooled in the palms of his hands. He squeezed his eyes shut and swallowed hard. She leaned to look into his eyes and gave him a warm smile. She lifted his chin.

"Whatever it is, it too shall pass. It always does, and you know that I'm right here for you. So talk. Let's hear it."

He squirmed out of her loving touch.

"Lena, you know how much I love you."

"I do."

"But I am not a perfect man."

"I know," she said.

Evangeline moved her feet from his lap and sat up to look in his eyes.

"James, you're scaring me. What's going on?"

Tears formed in his eyes. He looked as if he was about to choke.

"Oh my God, James. Talk! What is going on? What happened?"

Evangeline's brown eyes searched his face.

"I was with Camilla again," he gulped.

"Camilla? When? How? She's been dead for years?"

James sat quietly. Evangeline stood and slapped him across his head.

"How!" she shrieked. "When, James! When!"

He squeezed his eyes shut, and laid his head in his hands.

"When Camisha was a baby."

Evangeline darkened; her face was marred by confusion. She walked away from the sitting area leaving James alone.

"Why are you telling me this now, James?"

Evangeline propped herself against the antique vanity that had been passed down to her from her great-grandmother. She restored her poise and asked him again.

"Why now, James?"

James looked in the direction of his wife's eerily calm voice.

"There's another child. A daughter, I think."

Evangeline drew in as much air as her lungs would physically allow, and slowly blew it out of her mouth. She tightened the belt of the silk robe she was wearing, and sat at the vanity, looking at the reflection of her glowing caramel face. She saw James move to stand.

"Don't," she warned.

He sat back down and put his face in his hands again.

"How did you find out?"

"During the investigation. The accident--she was the Good Samaritan who helped Camilla at the scene. I found her information in the witness files."

The beautiful woman twisted her mouth as she pored over her husband's words. A sinister laugh escaped her. She closed her sable brown eyes and cackled.

"I asked you to leave it alone. I asked you to let Camisha have some peace, but you couldn't. Could you?" she seethed. "You had to be right. Welp, Chief DaCosta, I hope you found what you were looking for."

Evangeline picked up a hairbrush, then put it down. She sat staring at her reflection before standing again. She walked into the closet and returned with a leather weekender bag. James watched her from his safe space in the sitting room. The flashing light from the television and the laughter from America's Funniest Home Videos in the background only seemed to vex James even more.

"Lena, Darling. Where are you going?" he asked from the ottoman.

"I haven't decided."

"Darling, please. Let's talk about this."

"Not interested," she shot back.

He walked across the room to her side.

"I know you're upset."

"Upset?" she said, cutting him off. "Is that what you think I am, James? Upset?"

She spun around setting him on his heels. He grabbed her elbows and drew her closer, but she snatched her arms out of his grasp.

"Don't you touch me! Don't you dare touch me," she growled through clenched teeth.

She smoothed her hair into place and returned to filling the leather bag.

"Lena, please. It was only the one time. It was the day Rick was killed. On that call, remember?"

Evangeline turned and glared into her husband's eyes. James held his hands up, showing her his palms.

"I'm not using that as an excuse," he fretted. "But that was the day."

Evangeline slipped into a pair of cashmere joggers and removed her robe.

"I was just a kid. I had never seen a dead body," he pleaded. "I only went there to see the baby. I just wanted to hold my baby."

"But you screwed her teenage mother again. Nice job, Chief. Really honorable move."

Evangeline sat on the edge of the bed and tied her shoelaces. James stood in front of her laying out the whole scene, leaving nothing out.

"Sunrise was adopted; she was left at the hospital, just over a year after Camisha was born."

Evangeline threw the packed bag over her shoulder and moved to pass James. He ran to block the bedroom door.

"Lena, please don't do this. Where will you go? Please don't go to your sisters."

She stopped in her tracks upon hearing his request. Her eyes narrowed.

"What difference does it make if I go to one of my sisters, James?"

"I just want to keep this between us," he insisted. "Until we've had time to process everything."

An unfamiliar frown spread across her usually graceful face, and the light in her eyes darkened.

"Process everything? Are you crazy, Man?" She shifted all of her weight to one leg and crossed her arms. "Is this some kind of case for you? Are you the perp? Am I the victim? Is our bedroom the crime scene?" she said, looking around the room. "Or is that little shanty one-bedroom apartment where you knocked up a teenager for the second time, the scene of the crime?"

James flinched at the characterization— strengthening Evangeline's resolve.

"Is this new daughter evidence? Is she the smoking gun? Well, James DaCosta, Chief of Police? Is she?"

His shoulders rounded and the corners of his mustache turned down.

"I'm sorry, Lena. I don't know what else to say."

"You swear to me that you had no idea there was another baby," she huffed.

"I didn't. I swear it, Darling. Camisha found a letter."

She put a hand up stopping him.

"No more. I can't. I cannot. Not another word about this tonight, James. I'll text you to let you know that I'm safe."

He moved to help her with the bag, and she violently rejected the offer, disappearing down the dark staircase.

Lennox opened the door and let Evangeline in. He hugged her as his wife stood beside him. Evangeline's eyes were swollen and red. Camisha took her stepmother into her arms and hugged her until she let go.

"He didn't know," she whispered into the woman's ear.

Evangeline stayed up late into the night reading Camilla's musings.

She had only slept a few hours before she was awakened by the pleas of her granddaughter. She needed the four-year-old's joyful exuberance on the first day of her changed life. She reached for her phone to find several missed calls and text messages from James. She texted him back, "I'm safe."

After washing up and applying a swipe of concealer, powder, and lip gloss, she joined her stepdaughter's family in the kitchen.

"Good morning. How'd you sleep?" Lennox asked, kissing Evangeline at her temple. She shrugged and smiled politely. Camisha handed her a cup of hot coffee and leaned against the kitchen counter watching the older woman.

Evangeline was an attractive woman. She held herself with great elegance and poise. She was always warm, but obviously high class. Even as she sat in the home of the stepdaughter -who was the result of her husband's first indiscretion- she was the picture of grace and calm. Lena pulled herself up on the stool beside her grandmother and asked if she would be coming to school with her.

"Not this time, Miss Lena. Gigi's really tired. And mommy wants to talk to her about grown up stuff. OK?" Camisha said to her precocious toddler.

The child grimaced, but kissed her grandmother and then her mother before heading out the door holding her daddy's hand.

"Maybe we can meet up for lunch," Lennox tossed back over his broad shoulder.

"Maybe. I love you, Sir."

"Love you too, Mrs. Robinson."

Lennox was hardly out of the driveway before ordering his car to, "Call James DaCosta."

"She's at the house with Cami. She came to us last night," he said.

"Thanks, Lennox."

"No problem. Take care."

When Camisha heard the roar of Lennox's Audi drive away, she wasted no time.

"Did you get through the box?"

"I did," Evangeline said, drinking from her coffee mug. "But it doesn't make him right in any of this, Cami."

Camisha raised the mug to her mouth and nodded.

"It doesn't. I know that. But no one is perfect. And no one is all bad," Camisha shrugged. "You want food?"

Evangeline chuckled. "Yes, please. I'm ravished."

"Breakfast coming right up!"

"Did Ali and Lena eat anything?" Evangeline quizzed.

"He does a smoothie in the morning, and Lena eats at school," Cami said, glinting at the woman.

"I was just asking because I don't want you to cook a second breakfast. I would've had whatever was left over," Evangeline explained.

Cami started breakfast. She and Evangeline talked about the letter, and they talked about Cami's meeting with Sunrise at the station. Camisha felt awful about the way she'd treated Sunrise, and Evangeline suggested that she call her. Camisha agreed and asked Evangeline to join her when she met with Sunrise.

"It'll probably be good for the both of us."

"Perhaps it will," Evangeline said as she slid Camisha's phone across the kitchen island.

"What about Dad? You wanna call him?"

"No, Dear. Not today."

Family Business

Lennox spun around in his high back ergonomic office chair, stopping before the spectacular view of the city of Atlanta skyline. He watched as the sun rose over the Bank of America Plaza. "Ah, reminds me of Sonoma County," he said.

He'd gone to college in Palo Alto, and he and Camisha had honeymooned in Wine Country. He loved the region and hoped to one day soon convince his wife to move there. His best friend Kai Beltram had proposed that the two of them go into business. His parents were Sonoma County winemakers. They had made a name for themselves in the organic produce market. Lennox had been working with his friends from Atlanta, making frequent trips to California and Oregon. He'd been waiting for the right time to share the business proposition with his wife, but given the current climate of their family -thanks to Camilla- he'd have to wait for a less tumultuous time. He spun himself around one more time before calling his sister Lacey with an invitation to lunch.

Lacey and Lennox were a strikingly beautiful pair of siblings. They garnered lingering stares from strangers whenever they ventured out together. Both were well-dressed, statuesque figures. Lennox was a hair darker in complexion than his younger sister, and she sported jewel- like sparkling green eyes. For the most part, they looked alike. Lacey arrived first and found a table situated against the rail that separated the cafe from the public sidewalk. She lit up when she saw her brother's shiny black Audi Q7 turn into the parking spot just in front of her. He flashed a similar smile back at her. The brother and sister had always been very close, but as adults, they were undoubtedly best friends.

"Hey, Lenny!" Lacey sang, standing to embrace her older brother. "You look smart."

Lennox was wearing his signature, slim fitted, dove gray pantsuit, and designer aviator sunglasses. His neatly trimmed beard and mustache covered his dimpled cheeks.

"Thank you. Thank you."

He kissed her on the forehead and pulled out her chair for her, before sitting.

A cheerful server popped over to take their drink orders.

"To what do I owe this special treat? Lunch with my dashing big brother in the middle of the week," Lacey asked.

Lennox chuckled and scratched at his beard. He sat back in the chair and rubbed the back of his neck.

"Uh oh, that's not good," Lacey smirked.

The waiter returned with their drinks.

"I'll give you a few minutes to look over the menu," he said.

"What's up, Lenny?"

"Remember the lady we met at the police station?"

"Yes. The one from the accident," Lacey said. She sipped from the glass of sweet tea.

"Well, she's Cami's sister."

Lacey's forehead crinkled and her mouth fell open.

"What?" she stuttered. "How? Wait...what?"

"I told you about the picture of her, right?"

"Yes. She looked like Ms. Camilla, I remember."

"Well in person," he emphasized. "It's eerie. She's like a clone of Camilla."

"Shut up," Lacey gasped.

"Y'all 'bout ready?" the server said with a smile.

Since they hadn't looked at the menu, they went ahead and ordered the specials with side salads.

"I found a box in Camilla's old room in the basement, and there was a baby blanket and hospital wristbands in it. She wrote letters and stuff about the child she gave up."

Lacey looked on astounded.

"How's Cami taking all of this?" Lacey inquired.

"Pretty good. I mean, she feels like crap for snapping on the woman, but she has other things to deal with right now."

"Other things? What could be more important than a long lost sister? Especially for an only child?"

"Well," Lennox drawled. "Get this. The adopted sister..."

"Yeah," Lacey coached.

"Is also Mr. DaCosta's."

Lacey's mouth nearly dropped onto the tabletop.

"Get the hell out of here, Lenny! How is that even possible? How old is the woman?"

"She's a year younger than Cami."

The two sat quietly. Even though he had delivered the news, Lennox looked dumbfounded. There were so many questions surrounding Sunrise's existence.

"Damn," Lacey said, breaking the silence.

"You can say that again."

"How's his wife dealing with the news? Does she know?"

"Oh yeah. She knows, and she's at the house with Cami now."

Lacey clenched her teeth together.

"Ouch! Doesn't she have family here in Atlanta?"

"Yep. I don't know what's going on, Lace," Lennox said.

The server returned, balancing a large round tray with their plates and condiments on it. He quickly placed their meals on the table and left them to their lively conversation.

"The timing is just so bad for all of this," Lennox grumbled.

"How so?"

"I wanted to talk to Cam about us moving out West- -to California." he answered between bites of arugula.

"California? When did you come up with that idea?" Lacey's tone did little to conceal her disapproval.

Undeterred, Lennox told his baby sister all about Kai's offer for him to join their family's new business venture.

Lacey was visibly taken aback. She pushed away from the table, and her eyes narrowed to slits. Lennox shuddered as he watched his sister's eyes turn into kaleidoscopes. He braced himself. Lacey could be brutal.

"So," she sighed, "you want to go work for Kai's family. But for your own family, you had nothing. Our father paid thousands upon thousands of dollars to send your ass to Stanford University, and when it was time to get a return on his investment, you simply couldn't lower yourself to come work for his little operation?" she hissed through her clenched jaw.

"Lacey, that's not fair!"

"Fair? That's a funny word choice, Lennox Ali Robinson," she said as she leaned across the table. "What would you know about fair?" she seethed. "What the hell do you know about fair? All you've ever done is see about your damned self, Lenny!" She sighed dramatically and laced her fingers together on the table. "Don't even get me started," she huffed. "Fair?" She cackled.

"Are you done?" Lennox retorted.

She didn't answer. Instead, she stuffed her mouth with barbecue salmon and glared at her brother.

"I thought Isaac was doing well with the stores."

Lacey balked at her brother's assertion and kept chewing.

"Seriously, Lace. I was never cut out for the dry-cleaning business. And now you all have Isaac. Mom and dad love him! He's like their replacement son," Lennox joked.

Lacey rolled her eyes and pursed her full lips. She ate another bite of the salmon.

"Lace, come on now. I need you to be on my side right now," Lennox pleaded.

She didn't respond.

"What's going on with your house hunting?"

He raised his brows and flashed a smile across the table. Lacey's eyes brightened, and she returned his smile.

"I made an offer on one not far from you and Cami," she said, blushing.

"Really!" he said, standing to hug his sister. "That's great, Lace! When will you know something?"

"Soon. Caspian's been so good for me."

She radiated, warming her eyes and cheeks.

"Caspian's been good for you? In what way?" Lennox teased.

Lacey blushed again and forked at her salad. She shrugged like an ornery teen.

"He's solid. And handsome, and smart, and accomplished,"

"OK. OK. I get the picture," Lennox said. "So have you two entered the dating zone?"

"No. And it's driving me crazy. I think he likes me, but he won't ask me out."

"Honestly Lace, you can be a little hard to read."

"Really? How so?"

"You put off this boss girl image like you don't need anybody," Lennox said, carefully watching her eyes before continuing. Lacey's eyes were revealing. Those close to her knew to watch for the fire.

"Think about it Lace—he does your banking! He knows that you're a boss and a single mother. You should probably make the first move."

"Lenny, please! You know I could never do that. I'm not that kind of woman," she protested. "Maybe. Do you think I can?"

"Of course you can! This isn't Alabama. Go for it!"

"What if he turns me down? What if I've completely read him wrong?"

"No way, Sis. Trust me. I'm a man. And you, my beautiful and talented and ballsy little sister, are a catch!"

"Oliver would disagree," Lacey murmured.

"He would not," Lennox interjected. "And you've learned a lot since your breakup with Oliver. He won't say no; he's going to be relieved. Trust me. Do it!"

Lacey forced a smile. "OK, I'll do it."

She had learned a lot from her mishandling of her relationship with the father of her son. She and Oliver had since made amends and were well on their way to being friends.

"I'll do it! And if he rejects me, you're going to feel my wrath," she laughed. "Lenny talk to Cami about California. There will never be a good time, so just do it. Have you learned nothing about the wife over the years? Don't keep her in the dark; she doesn't like it."

"At all," Lennox added.

Lacey sat in her car, watching her brother make a call from his SUV before he backed out into the busy street. She watched his black truck until it was out of sight. She held her phone in her hand, mulling over her brother's suggestion. She called up Caspian's contact information and stared at it. She bit down on her bottom lip and pushed her glasses up her nose. She secured a tuft of her honey brown hair behind her ear and dialed him. His smoky voice answered on the first ring.

"Hmm, hi!" She spouted, squeezing her eyes tight. She grinned nervously.

"Hmm, hi," Caspian said, mimicking the nervous woman. "What are you up to this afternoon?"

"Just had lunch with my brother," she answered.

"Where?"

"At Cafe Agora. Would you be interested in going out with me?" she asked. "Like on a date. At night."

There was a long pause. Lacey's finger hovered over the HANG UP button on the sleek console of her Porsche Cayenne, but Caspian spoke up.

"I would be interested; very interested."

Knowing Lacey

The knocking on the front door rocked both Caspian and Lacey from their peaceful slumber. Caspian picked up his phone from the bedroom floor and strained to see the screen. He'd missed two calls from Sunrise.

"I'll be right back," he said as he rolled over and kissed Lacey on the cheek. "It's my friend Sunny. "

Lacey smiled and ran her fingertips along his smoky quartz brown skin, savoring the strength of his powerful back and shoulders as he left the warmth of the bedcovers.

"That is a fine ass man!" Lacey said as she snuggled under the fluffy down comforter, and looked around Caspian's stark bedroom. He had greasy car parts on the desk against the wall and books stacked in neat piles. His dresser had rows of cologne bottles and a beautiful mahogany box that held several watches, and a couple of pairs of Ray-Ban sunglasses. There were rows of hats in varying sizes and styles hanging from nails on the wall above the dresser.

"No mirrors in his bedroom. Humph." She rolled over and leafed through the books he kept stacked under his nightstand, "The Art of War," "The Mis-Education of the Negro," "Think and Grow Rich," and "The Chronicles of Narnia: Prince Caspian."

"Prince Caspian," she whispered. "Hmm, now that's interesting."

The sound of a woman's voice cut through her ponderings, drawing her to stand. She slid her feet into her slippers, threw on her silk robe, and crept to the opened door. Lacey was sure she'd heard a woman's voice. She stopped at the threshold and listened.

"I think I want them to come to my house. I bet I'd feel more comfortable there. You know?" the feminine voice quizzed.

"You sure about that, Sunny? How did she sound on the message? Remember, it didn't go well the last time you met with Camisha. Is she bringing her husband? What was his name?"

"Lennox. And I don't know who she's bringing. I haven't called her back. I want to have my emotions in check before I do that. You know?"

Lacey's eyes grew to the size of silver dollars.

"Sunny? Could Sunny be short for Sunrise? As in the long lost sister? The Ms. Camilla look alike? What the hell! I've gotta see this mystery woman!" She fingered her long wheat colored bangs into place, grabbed her glasses from the dresser, and walked into the living room.

Sunrise was sitting in a chair in front of the arched windows that lined Caspian's front porch. He was leaning against the white, painted brick fireplace. An unfriendly glare crossed Caspian's face, darkening his features.

"Hi!" Sunrise sang with Ms. Camilla's warm and engaging smile. The young woman's face plucked at Lacey. Her smile transported Lacey to Cami's kitchen, years earlier, when Ms. Camilla was alive, and buzzing around making Orange Cinnamon rolls and chopping collard greens. Lacey clenched her jaw, keeping the tears at bay.

"Hello. I'm Lacey Robinson," Lacey said as she walked over to the seated woman and shook her extended hand.

"I'm Sunrise, his childhood friend," she grinned. "And neighbor now, I guess! I live around the corner."

Lacey smiled, nostalgia filling her eyes. She moved to pull Sunrise into a hug but stopped herself. The young woman wore her thick, wavy hair the way Camilla often wore hers; half up, but secured with a brightly colored scarf. Her nose was pierced with a small gold ring, and Lacey counted at least six necklaces around her long, graceful neck before taking in the beaded and embroidered kimono that was covering her lady parts as she sat Indian style in the chair. She moved to stand, but Lacey shook off the gesture.

"No, please. I'm sorry to interrupt. I'm looking for my purse."

"It's over here," Caspian answered dryly.

Lacey searched his eyes for clarity but found none. She took her purse from him and told Sunrise that it was nice to have met her. She heard Sunrise scold Caspian for his attitude from behind the closed door.

Caspian returned to the bedroom as Lacey watched a combat boot clad Sunrise bounce down the walkway with her sheer black kimono flapping in the crisp fall breeze. The exuberant young woman had disappeared around a tree-lined corner before Lacey turned to address Caspian.

"What was the cold shoulder about, Cas?"

He stiffly shook his head and walked into the bathroom. Lacey was astonished by how quickly he'd turned cold and off-putting. She threw on her jacket and left without saying goodbye.

Caspian heard Lacey's car start. He peeked out of the tiny bathroom window and watched the white Porsche drive past his front porch. He watched the car until it was out of sight. He twisted his full mouth and leaned hard against the cold, marble vanity. He stared at his reflection in the round mirror.

He liked Lacey, and he was happy that their friendship had grown into a more intimate deal, but he didn't like her imposing herself. He hadn't wanted Sunrise to meet her yet. He imagined Sunrise sitting in her hippy dippy crocheted porch swing gabbing to his sister all about Lacey being at his house this morning. He dreaded having to face the impending inquisition that would be waiting for him at his Sister's house on Sunday. He stood and folded his arms across his bare chest, his scowl softening. He showered and called Lacey. She didn't answer, sending a cocked little smile across his face.

"Saucy," he laughed to himself.

He dressed and went out back to tinker with his father's car.

Seeing Caspian's name and number flash across the digital console sent heated fury burning up Lacey's neck, under her arms and between her breasts.

"Does he think I'm someone to be toyed with? Some average chick? So he thinks he's some kind of prize. A prize for me?"

She could have erupted in her plum and black, custom leather driver's seat. She shifted the car into fifth gear, revving the powerful engine to high speed.

She entered the loft to find Isaac hovering over his MacBook Pro with a large cup of coffee. He barely lifted his head at first, but catching a glimpse of the typically well-dressed woman wearing pajamas and leather jacket, he chuckled.

"Damn, the brother didn't let you dress before putting you out?" Isaac jeered.

Lacey's fire filled eyes shot daggers through him.

"Must you always be so crass?" she shot back as she passed him.

He grabbed her by the arm and pulled her close, sniffing her. She jerked her arm from his grasp.

"What the hell are you doing, Isaac?" Her snarled face marred with anger.

"Take the jacket off," he said, tossing his head towards the staircase, "That way Luke will think you just woke up. In your own bed," he added.

"I'm in no mood for your antics right now, Isaac," she snapped as she removed her jacket and hung it in the coat closet before heading upstairs to look in on her son.

"You're welcome," he scoffed.

"Go to hell!"

Lacey replayed the entire morning at Caspian's as she showered.

"What the hell was that all about? He let her in while I was there. Surely he couldn't have thought that I wouldn't hear another woman's voice only feet away, and in that small ass house!" she huffed. "It's not like I maneuvered my way into his home. He asked, hell! He practically begged!" Lacey closed her eyes and let the hot water beat against her back.

Her phone buzzed against the granite countertop and fell into the porcelain basin. She wrapped herself in a fluffy towel and stepped out of the tall glass stall to answer it. Disappointment crumpled her beautiful face when she heard her brother's voice on the line.

"Hey, Lenny. Let me give you a call back."

"Why?"

"Because I'm just getting out of the damned shower," she yelled.

"What's up with you? You shouldn't have answered the phone!" he bellowed, hanging up on her.

"What the hell is going on with the men in my life this morning," Lacey grumbled as she dried off.

She put on an olive green, silk cargo jumper and yelled down to Isaac for a cup of coffee. She sat at the desk in her bedroom and returned her brother's call.

"I'm sorry, Lenny," she crooned into the receiver. "My day did not start out well."

"Well, I'm sorry that it started out poorly for you, Lacey Baby."

Isaac tapped on the door, peeking in before entering with a steaming cup of coffee and a saucer carrying a toasted cinnamon crunch bagel that he sat it on the corner of the desk.

"Thanks, replacement brother," she joked.

"Is that what I am now?" Isaac said, tossing a sexy grin in the woman's direction.

"You two are unnatural," Lennox said, mocking his sister's relationship with her almost-brother-in-law.

"You're telling me!" Lacey retorted. "Speaking of unnatural," she said, "You won't believe who I met this morning."

"Does everything have to be a riddle with you, woman?"

"Funny. I met Sunrise this morning," she said. "At Caspian's."

She sat silently allowing her brother to grasp what she'd told him. After a few awkward seconds, he asked her for details.

"Get the fuck outta here, Lace," Lennox mused. "What are the odds?" He called out to his wife to join him in his man cave.

"Why are you down here yelling, man? You're going to wake Lena."

"Lacey just met Sunrise."

Camisha walked down the remainder of the steps to where her shirtless husband was sitting on his rowing machine as if being closer to him would provide more lucidity. He toweled off the phone and handed it to her.

"Hey Lace, what's he talking about?"

Lacey gave her the same report, but more concise than the one she'd given to her brother.

"Did you tell her that you're my sister-in-law?"

"No! I just introduced myself and left them to talk. From what I could gather, she's concerned about how you're going to treat her when she sees you again. Did you invite her over or something?"

"I left her a message, but she hasn't called back."

"Well, she's calling back, and she's going to ask you to come to her house. She thinks she'll be more comfortable there."

"That's fine," Cami nodded.

"She lives somewhere near Caspian because she left there walking—In a long t-shirt, a see through kimono, and combat boots, in fifty-degree weather," Lacey laughed. "She's quite the character, but I like her already!"

"You do? That's good," Cami said, lowering her head. "I hope I haven't ruined any chance of getting to know her."

"I doubt it. She seems just as sweet as you are."

Camisha thanked her sister-in-law, and flopped face down on Lennox's gray couch, sending her legs high in the air over the tufted arm. He sat on the rowing machine with his knees to his chest, watching his wife spazz out.

"Oh, Cami. Everything will work out. You want to apologize to her. Right?"

Cami nodded, her face planted between the linen cushions.

"And by Lacey's account, she seems completely nice. And if Lacey thinks so, you certainly will. Lace doesn't like anybody--and you know that! Hell, she's just warming up to you," Lennox teased.

His wife knew that he was right. She nearly split her torso from her bottom half when her cell phone rang. She and Lennox slammed into one another, rushing up the bare wooden steps to the kitchen, where the phone was ringing.

"Hello," Camisha said, panting.

"Hi, it's Sunrise."

All Together Now

Sunrise was a ball of raw nerves. The air was remarkably cold and dry, but sitting on her large front porch swinging in her custom made dream catcher hanging chair always steadied her pulse. She committed to sitting out front in that chair until Taliesan and Caspian arrived. She covered the intricately woven chair, with a faux fur throw and wrapped herself in a cozy cable knit blanket. She closed her eyes and laid her head against a matching pillow, rocking herself back and forth until she heard Caspian's big Escalade turn the corner of her block.

The brother and sister wasted no time preparing Sunrise's large craftsman-style house for Camisha's entourage. Sunrise's home's chief function was for making music; she didn't keep a lot of company outside of her band mates and students. She'd settled into the Atlanta music scene, with no problem. She'd been teaching music theory as an adjunct professor at the Atlanta University Center and was slowly reclaiming her life.

Camisha had called days earlier to let Sunrise know that her husband, her stepmother, and sister-in-law would be joining them for her visit. Sunrise was both excited and nervous. She asked Taliesan and Caspian to join her. She'd mentioned Camisha's visit to her mom and dad but respectfully asked them to let her meet with Camisha alone on this visit. She didn't have the heart to tell them that she'd invited her friends instead.

Caspian moved Sunrise's eclectic collection of deep navy and purple velvets, kelly green painted woods, and brightly colored embroidered furniture into more conversation friendly arrangements.

"This piano is huge!" he grumbled, trying to move the monster.

"Don't move my piano! What are you doing? They're not moving in!" Sunrise shrieked, running over to stop him.

"I'm just moving it back out of the center of the room," Caspian snapped back.

Sunrise considered his motives and relented. She rolled up her sleeves and helped him push the baby grand closer to the wall. Seeing it closer to the flowering vines and bird-covered tiles pleased her. The glossy black finished reflected the yellows, turquoises, blues, greens, purples and reds in the tiles in a notably majestic way. She smiled and put a hand on her hip, admiring the new perspective.

"Sunny, you should probably get dressed," Taliesan said, shooting a look at her brother.

"What!" Sunrise laughed. "My clothes will be fine."

She reappeared minutes later wearing emerald green, velvet burnout bell-bottoms that hugged her curvy hips, and high behind with a matching lightweight velvet motorcycle jacket. The white t-shirt she wore underneath the unzipped jacket was fairly sheer and hung loosely over her full breasts. She opted to go without shoes, without jewelry, and without taming her massive mane of waves and curls. She was an intensely attractive woman, full of quirk and congeniality. The brother and sister smiled broadly at their friend. She glowed, and the light cast from the setting sun danced in her golden green eyes.

"I forget how golden your eyes are sometimes," Taliesan marveled.

"They were her eyes," Sunrise said. "So, do the Pearce's approve? Or should I wear shoes?"

"You're in your house. You don't have to wear shoes," Caspian snorted.

"There!" Taliesan co-signed.

Sunrise's surge in confidence drained at the sound of the doorbell. She combed through her thick hair with both hands and wet her lips while she waited to see Camisha enter the room. Camisha and Sunrise stood at exactly the same height with Sunrise barefoot. The women greeted each other with a clumsy handshake and an abbreviated hug.

Camisha was dressed in dark blue jeans and a tan crew neck sweater with cognac colored riding boots and simple gold hoop earrings. Sunrise noticed the thin chain with the C pendant she was wearing matched the one Camilla fiddled with the day she met with her. A tinge of jealousy surprised her.

Lennox introduced himself, and then he introduced the stately older woman, as Mrs. Evangeline DaCosta. Evangeline reeked of old money and status, turning Sunrise off right away.

"You must be Chief DaCosta's wife," Sunrise said, accepting her outstretched hand.

Evangeline flinched.

Lacey entered the house, adding to the already tense room. She looked electrifying in her signature neutral palette and big sunglasses. Both she and Caspian kept their cool, unaffected facades. Other than the narrowing of his brown eyes, he conceded nothing.

"I think you've already met my baby sister, Lacey," Lennox revealed.

"I have," Sunrise lit up again. "Hi, Lacey! Cas didn't tell us you were the sister-in-law," she sang.

"I didn't know," Cas cut in, never taking his eyes off of the leggy vixen.

The room tightened again.

Taliesan breezed into the room sporting a heather gray, slouchy sweatshirt over a mauve cable knit jumpsuit. Her hair was braided down her shoulder in a single, thick fishtail. Her best effort at a smile was plastered across her angular brown features.

"Now, it's a party," she announced. "Hello everyone, I'm Taliesan, Sunny's best friend."

"I'd like to challenge that assertion," Caspian smiled breaking through the tension.

The guests all laughed nervously as Caspian collected their jackets.

"Lacey, why don't you help me with these," he whispered over her shoulder as he passed her. She took a few jackets and handbags from his arms and followed him up a Technicolor staircase.

Caspian dropped the jackets on a settee and pulled Lacey into his strong arms. He was at least four to five inches taller than she was and he smelled so good her knees threatened to quit on her. He stood as close as he could be, pressed against her. The rise and fall of her breathing thickened his crotch. He bent to kiss her, but she dodged his advance. She didn't move out of his grasp. He bent to kiss her again, and this time she let him.

"Why did you turn so cold that day?" Lacey asked.

Caspian shrugged without letting her out of his embrace. He examined every golden fleck in her honey brown eyes.

"Yes. You do. Tell me," she pleaded, her eyes darting from one part of his painfully handsome face to another. She'd missed him.

"I'm a private person, Lacey."

He sat on the settee and guided her to sit beside him. He kept a hand on her thigh. "And I don't know. I handled the whole situation badly," he easily admitted. "I'm sorry."

Lacey relaxed against him and sighed. She pushed her glasses up her nose and kissed him lightly.

"Please don't be a jerk. Please! I couldn't bear you being a jerk. OK?"

Caspian smiled and kissed her again.

"I'll try, but can't promise. However, I will promise to talk to you, if the situation calls for an explanation. How about that?" He tilted her face to look into his eyes.

She nodded and leaned into his open embrace. He kissed her on the top of her lowered head and patted her thigh.

"Now, let's go introduce you to my sister before she blows a fuse."

"Oh no. You have one of those, too?" Lacey winked.

"Yeah, but she's a pacifist," Caspian joked.

The others had all found places to sit. Between the chairs, floor cushions, the built-in bench, and seating alongside the fireplace, each one had claimed a cozy nook or cranny.

Camisha sat quietly taking in all of the colorful prints and rich textures artfully placed throughout Sunrise's home. She was especially fixated on a ceramic zebra that rested in the center of a green hutch, amidst copper wire planters holding succulents and lush air plants.

"Cam, do you want to give Sunrise the box of Camilla's writings?" Lennox said.

Camisha blinked hard and nodded.

"Yes. Yes," she said—her speech faltering. "I brought this for you. Maybe it will help you to get to know more about her."

Taliesan walked over to stand beside Sunrise, and Caspian joined them.

"But, why?" Sunrise questioned in her childlike way.

Camisha stood and walked toward the lead glass picture window, turning her back to the group and pushing her hands deep into the pockets of her boyfriend jeans. When she turned around, Sunrise's large hazel eyes were glued to her.

"She wrote to you."

"To me? But why?" Sunrise cried. "She said that she wasn't kin. You said so, too."

"I was wrong. And she lied," Camisha tearfully revealed. The sisters stared into each other's eyes, searching for a reasonable explanation.

Sunrise looked up at Taliesan, and then to Caspian, who placed a comforting hand on her shoulder. Evangeline went over and knelt beside Sunrise, covering her hands atop the plastic lid.

"No one can absolutely explain Camilla's reasons, but I think the letter will give you some degree of comfort."

"I'm sorry. Who are you?" Taliesan asked. "I missed the introductions."

Evangeline extended her hand to Taliesan.

"I'm Evangeline DaCosta. I'm James DaCosta's wife."

"Who is James DaCosta?" Taliesan pressed.

"He's the cop, who found Sunny," Caspian answered.

"And what's your role here today?"

Taliesan was dogged in her intention to protect her friend. Evangeline crinkled her nose and straightened her back, but answered the woman.

"I'm Camisha's stepmother; she asked that I be here with her," she said, briefly closing her eyes. "And we think that my husband, Camisha's father, is also Sunrise's biological father."

Everyone turned to stone for what felt like hours. Camisha joined Evangeline and took her by the hand.

"She's right. Camilla's letters suggest it."

Sunrise looked on from her velvet chair, astonished. She opened the bin and removed the baby blanket. Her eyes filled with tears. She removed the plastic wristbands that identified her gender and birthdate, and lastly, she removed the letter. She read it to herself and then handed it to Taliesan. She sat staring out the picture window, then broke into bellowing sobs.

"Why'd she lie to me?" Sunrise cried. "Why didn't she want to know me?"

Camisha moved to her new sister's side. She fought the urge to hug her and patted her on her rounded shoulders instead.

"Trust me, Sunrise. It was probably for the best; she wasn't easy," Camisha testified.

Moving On

The brisk October night air bit at Sunrises bare thighs as she held her front door open, waving Gabriel in. He took the wide concrete steps two at a time, lifting Sunrise into his arms and kissing her. Once in the warmth of the living room, he put her back on her bare feet. She removed the gray skull cap he was wearing freeing his shoulder-length waves. The gold rim around his blue irises made his eyes look green in the light cast from the Moroccan lanterns that lit Sunrise's living and dining areas. She buried her face in his soft chest and ran her hands over his broad shoulders, breathing him in deeply.

"I have missed you so much."

A warm tear streamed down her face. He picked her up, cradled her, and carried her to the bedroom and laid her on the bed. He smiled down at her before kneeling beside her. Gabriel looked around the room noting the changes she'd made since he'd last been there.

"You've painted," he nodded approvingly. "I like it. It feels like you—vibrant and full of life!"

She pulled him into another long, lusty kiss. He kicked off his shoes and climbed into the bed with her. He ran his calloused hand along her back.

"I love the callouses on your hands," she whispered against them between kisses to each of the rough spots.

"You're so weird. I hate them! I think I need new strings," he said.

"You're weird. You should wear callouses like a badge of honor. You're one of the most talented jazz bassists I know, Gabe," she said, kissing his bare chest. "And these battle scars tell the story of your hard work and dedication to the art," she kissed his open hand. "To the music."

"Yeah? Just jazz?" he cooed, in his lowest register.

He unbuttoned the thin brown dress she was wearing and laid velvety kisses on each spot. Sunrise writhed under the warmth of his breath.

"I've gained a little weight," she said.

He put a hand over her mouth and rolled her onto her tummy. A slow grin spread across his face as his eyes traced her cocoa brown skin from the small of her back to the soft mounds of her backside.

"And here I was, thinking these curves could get any wilder or any more outrageously sexy." Gabriel gently and attentively cared for every part of her body.

Sunrise felt perfect. She closed her eyes and let Gabe's touch ease her worries.

Her cell lit up, stirring both she and Gabriel. He stretched, extending his long pale body the entire length of the king size bed. Sunrise hit the remote, raising the blinds on both sides of her bedroom.

"Jesus, Babe!" Gabriel exclaimed.

He snatched the covers over his head and banged his knuckles on the overhead of the cocoon style wicker headboard.

"Goddamit, Sunny! You and this damned bed are going to be the end of my career," he moaned as he rubbed at his scraped knuckles

Sunrise kissed him on the mouth and giggled.

"Using the Lord's name in vain is going to be the end of your career, and your shot at the pearly gates," she shot back as she left the bed.

He reached out for her and ordered her back to bed, but she declined. "No. I'm going to make breakfast."

Sunrise had met Gabriel Beckett when she auditioned to play piano with his jazz band. She got the job and the bandleader. They fell for each other in the medieval town center of Marciac, in Southwest France. At the conclusion of the two-week run at the town's famed International Jazz Festival, Sunrise was back in the saddle, and back in the dating world, but after two years of seeing him, she hadn't introduced Gabriel to her friends and family.

After breakfast, Gabriel helped Sunrise clear the dishes from the breakfast nook and helped her load the dishwasher. He was a gentle giant, the middle child of three, and raised in the Midwest. He'd left home to attend the famed Berkeley College of Music in Boston, but left after only one semester. He found steady work in New York City and started his own band, *The Pre-Apocalyptic Jukebox*. Gabriel was an incredible singer and upright bassist. He was tall and cuddly, with a great head of wavy, chestnut brown hair and gunmetal blue eyes. Sunrise liked being with him and loved the way he made her feel. She never felt the need to slim down or firm up with him. She'd gained weight since she moved back home and divorced. She wasn't exactly fluffy, but she was definitely not the same size six she was as Mrs. Alexander Thorpe.

"Are we going talk about this biological sister or no?"

Gabriel pat the spot next to him on the couch, and Sunrise curled up beside him as Trina Broussard's, "Inside My Love," filled the sunroom. Sunrise bit down her pillowy bottom lip, snuggled closer to Gabriel, and pulled the cable knit blanket up around her neck.

"Her name's Camisha. She goes by Cami," she said as she adjusted herself on the circular couch. "She's beautiful, Gabe."

"You're beautiful," he said.

"And I look just like our mother, Camille. Who was not very nice."

"Was?"

"Yes, was."

Sunrise spent the next hour telling Gabriel about her newly discovered family.

"Gabe. Come on, get up. Let's get you back into bed."

Sunrise shook Gabriel by the shoulders, trying to wake the sleeping man. He'd taken a red-eye out of LA and was exhausted. Sunrise felt her panic growing, as she watched the clock and her driveway for Taliesan's car.

"Gabe, Love. Please. You have to wake up. Taliesan will be here any second now. Gabe, wake up," she begged him.

The groggy man rubbed his eyes and looked across the room at the clock, then at Sunrise, who was wide-awake and dressed.

"What is going on, Sunny? Why are you wearing a hat?"

Sunrise laughed, and pulled all two hundred sixty pounds of Gabriel to his feet, and hurried him up the spiral staircase.

"Why are you still hiding me?" he asked somberly.

He turned to her, and she looked away. The blue in his eyes chilled to a steely gray.

"No one's being hidden. I don't want you to feel like that. Things are just...they're just complicated."

"What can be complicated between consenting adults, Sunny. You're single. And I'm single. So what's complicated about it?"

Sunrise really didn't want to get into the race conversation with Taliesan calling from the driveway, but Gabriel was staunch in his intent to have the discussion. She looked out the window to see Taliesan getting out of her car, and stamped her feet like a child.

The doorbell chimed, sending Sunrise into a panic. Gabriel stood perfectly calm. Sunrise looked back and forth between her lover and the bedroom door, before relenting. She held out her hand to him and smiled.

"Didn't you know I was on my way?" Taliesan asked, before seeing the tall white man standing behind her best friend. She smiled warmly and pushed passed Sunrise.

"Hello, I'm Taliesan. And you must be Sunny's music man," she gushed.

"I hope so, " Gabriel quipped and shook Taliesan's hand. "I'm Gabriel Beckett, and I am indeed a music man. I'm not absolutely sure who I am to Sunny, but I know who I am to the music."

"I like him, Sunny Bunny!" Taliesan smacked at Sunny, who stood quietly watching the effortless chatter.

"So Gabriel, are you joining us for Sunday dinner with Sunrise's parents?"

Gabriel looked to Sunrise for the answer. She smiled, stricken with panic, and asked him if he wanted to meet her parents, to which he answered, "Yes."

Sunrise called her mother to give her a heads up. Her mother appreciated the opportunity to meet the mysterious man in her daughter's life before her husband did. Xander had left a bitter taste in Beaux's mouth for white men who dated his daughter.

Dinner was quite the ticket, as Sunrise brought Gabriel, and Caspian brought Lacey and her son, Luca. Undaunted, the Andersons dressed the formal dining room table and welcomed all of their guests. Taliesan's boys and Luca hit it off right away. They spent most of the evening playing video games in the pool house, leaving the adults to get to know Gabriel and Lacey.

Gabriel talked about meeting Sunrise at the audition and being wholly taken by her look and uncomplicated approach to playing before the intimate room full of strangers.

"She walked in wearing a big floppy black hat, and this long crazy leather braided top thing over tight cut up jeans and what looked like a thousand wood bracelets," he recalled. "I remember wondering how in the heck is she going to play piano with all of those thick bracelets?" He took her hand on top of the table and smiled at her. "But she did it, and went on to play the drums and the every other instrument in the room. She was something, and she was all we could talk about for days."

He leaned over and kissed Sunrise on the cheek. She squirmed, obviously uncomfortable with his open display of affection. Sunrise was happy when the conversation shifted to Caspian and Lacey.

Caspian was as reserved as usual, but he lightened up when the conversation turned to Lacey's new home in Historic College Park. Beaux, who had been largely quiet throughout dinner also opened up more with the talk of the burgeoning neighborhood. He was captivated by Lacey's business acumen. The exchange bored Mrs. Anderson and the others. When the party split after coffee and dessert, Lacey was invited to join Caspian, Ellis, and Beaux in the office for cognac.

Gabriel didn't seem to mind the exclusion; he much preferred talking music with Ursula over more cake and coffee, while Taliesan and Sunrise washed dishes and watched the boys through the kitchen window. Taliesan shoulder bumped her girlfriend when she was sure they were alone.

"Why have you been hiding him," she motioned to the living room.

Sunrise shrugged and dried another plate.

"I haven't been hiding him, exactly. He travels a lot."

"So do you."

"Yes, with him. But he plays gigs outside of the Jukebox. I don't. I teach too, Lucky. You know that."

Taliesan hung the damp dish towel on the rack that hung inside the cabinet door and leaned against the kitchen counter.

"What's that have to do with the price of tea in China? You're so petty, Sunrise."

"Petty?" Sunrise whined.

"Is it because he's another white boy?"

Sunrise pursed her full lips and plopped into a chair. She shrugged her shoulders again.

"I don't know. I don't think so," she frowned. "Daddy can be so, you know. And after everything with Xander, I didn't know how he'd accept another white man in my life." Sunrise explained.

"He's not Xander, Sunrise. And from what I can gather, he's nothing like him."

"He's not!" Sunrise cried. "He's so much easier. He knows exactly who he is and what he wants. I know he's not your typical heartthrob, but he's good to me."

Taliesan grinned.

"Heartthrob," the woman repeated. "And is Ellis your typical heartthrob?" The women laughed.

"Seriously. It's good to see that you're moving on. I couldn't be happier for you."

Taliesan put a finger to her mouth, hushing Sunrise. "You hear that? she said, pointing to the living room. "He makes your mother sing."

Come On Over

Sunrise was wracked with nerves amid Camisha's invitation to join her family for Thanksgiving dinner. The women had spoken only once since the meeting at Sunrise's home, and their last conversation was brief and clumsy. They talked over one another when they spoke, or they sat painfully silent waiting for the other one to speak again. Work and the kids were the extents of their getting to know each other. So the invitation to spend Thanksgiving together had really taken Sunrise by surprise. She accepted without considering what her parents and friends would be doing for the holiday. When Sunrise nervously told her parents about the invitation, Ursula jumped at the chance to see Camisha and her family again, "under better circumstances," she said. Sunrise called Camisha back and asked if she could bring her parents and friends along, to which Camisha cheerfully replied,

"The more, the merrier!"

The joviality in her voice was foreign to Sunrise, as she'd only known her sister to be formal and standoffish.

Camisha loved the holidays, but Thanksgiving was by far her favorite. It brought together some of the things she loved most-- food, wine, friends and goodwill towards others. She'd always hosted a large Thanksgiving dinner she called The Feast for the Orphans. She, Camilla, and Oliver would spend weeks planning the menu and wine pairings, but with Camilla's death, and Oliver's move to France, the Feast as it previously occurred proved to be too much for Camisha to pull off on her own. It had morphed into a much less grandiose affair.

Lennox loved seeing the light in his wife's eyes as she busied around decorating, shopping and organizing for the holiday season. When she shared her idea to invite Sunrise and her family, he couldn't have been more pleased. It meant that she was getting back to herself, and Thanksgiving brought out the best of what he loved about Camisha. She was solid, transparent and altruistic. She had a big heart for helping others, and she loved wholly—once she allowed you into her life. He couldn't help but be hopeful that she'd be more open to his desire to move to California when things were better between her and Sunrise.

Evangeline and James came over early to help prepare. They weren't exactly back together, but they were back under one roof, albeit a seven thousand square-foot roof. The sight of the couple arriving in one car brought a smile to Camisha's face. Camisha met her father and stepmother with a tight hug, enveloping them both at once. James's embrace lingered gratefully.

"Thanks for coming over. There's so much to do," Camisha gushed.

"I'm looking forward to it, Dear," Evangeline said, wrapping a thin arm around Camisha's waist as they walked into the cluttered kitchen.

The counters and kitchen table were covered with market bags, neatly folded piles of table linens, and stacks of white plates.

"Wow!" Evangeline said as she surveyed the room with her hands on her hips. Lennox kissed her on the cheek and helped her out of her quilted jacket.

"This is your first time behind the scenes of the feast. Isn't it?" Lennox chuckled.

"It sure is," James answered as he removed his own coat.

The roar of an engine turned everyone's attention to the rear parking pad. Lacey and Isaac rose from the pristine white Porsche with Lena and Luca bounding behind them. The two looked to be bickering. Lacey's nose was crinkled under her designer sunglasses, and Isaac was wearing a mischievous grin.

"Can you two get along for a few hours?" Camisha teased.

"And to think they work so well together?" Lennox whispered to James, before greeting his baby sister with a hug and kiss on the forehead.

Camisha prepared a simple meal of stew beef and root vegetables for her volunteers, and they all sat out back in their garden gathered around the outdoor fireplace and underneath tall patio heaters.

"Babe, I don't think it's cold enough for the heaters yet," Camisha said as she handed her husband and father a glass of cognac, and Isaac a beer.

She sat down on her husband's lap.

"Izzy, will Valentina and Mix be back stateside for Thanksgiving?"

"Yeah," he flashed a striking smile. "You know how she loves sharing holidays with Luca and Lena." Luca was the only one of her four grandchildren with whom she had unlimited access.

"I'm sure she's bought out half of Europe for him," Lennox grimaced.

"And for Ms. Lena!" Lacey added.

"Of course! She's the little princess," Camisha mocked. "Oliver and Farai won't get here until the day before, but you know he's ordered me to leave the turkey and the twist for him!"

"Ahh, the twist!" The group sang in unison, among big smiles and reflective gestures.

"What's the twist?" Isaac asked. Evangeline and James were equally inquisitive.

"The twist is a surprise side or dessert that my mother and Oliver came up with for the Feast."

"The feast?"

"Yes!" Lacey chimed in. "Camisha, your little brother, and Camilla started hosting the Feast for the Orphans when Camisha bought this house."

"Every year they'd invite folks who had no family or who couldn't afford to travel to be with their families here for Thanksgiving dinner," Lennox finished proudly patting his blushing wife on the thigh.

"So you have no say in the twist?" Lacey laughed. "That man loves his food!"

The mention of Camilla annoyed Evangeline. She left the group and walked into the house to find the children watching cartoons in the family room. Camisha watched her father's eyes as they followed his wife. Lennox rubbed her back and put a soft kiss on her shoulder. She settled into his lap and let him hold her tighter.

"Caspian's coming with Sunrise?" Lennox announced. He raised an eyebrow and stroked his thick beard.

Lacey didn't flinch.

"Did you hear me, Lacey Baby?" he probed.

"I did. And I already knew," she said as she leered at her brother.

"Have you met Caspian, Isaac?"

"What is wrong with you, Lenny?" Lacey yelped.

"What's wrong with you? I just asked the man a question?" he squealed, raising his hands over his head.

Camisha smacked him on the leg. "Stop it," she whispered in her husband's ear.

Isaac raised his forehead and allowed a crooked smile to spread across his chiseled face before he took a sip from the bottle of beer. "I have not. But, I have heard a lot about his banking prowess."

Lacey scrunched her face and narrowed her clear eyes to hardly recognizable thin lines. She leaped to her feet and slapped her brother across the head as she passed him, stomping into the house. Camisha's eyes widened, and she burst into laughter.

"You two are so immature!" she laughed.

Camisha rolled over with a full on smile. The sounds of her best friend's voice in her home the day before Thanksgiving brought back such happy memories. Warm tears flowed. She lay in bed smelling the sweet scents of her mother's homemade orange cinnamon rolls, and freshly brewed coffee the way only Oliver could brew it. Just as she sat up, the bathroom door opened releasing the masculine scent of Lennox's woodsy shower gel and aftershave.

"Good morning, Sleeping Beauty. There are some very special people out front messing around in your kitchen," he smiled broadly, securing the fluffy white towel around his waist. After five years of waking up with the same man, Camisha was still awed by his staggering strength, height, and all around good looks.

"I can smell him," she smiled like a child on Christmas morning. "Come over here," Camisha beckoned.

Lennox obeyed. She tugged at the towel, sending it to the floor.

He blushed as he braced for the immense pleasure promised by the look in his wife's eyes.

Camisha heard her phone ring from the shower and yelled out for Lennox to answer.

He came in holding the phone towards her, covering the mic with a hand.

"It's Sunrise," he mouthed.

Camisha furrowed her brow and tilted her head. She motioned for him to put the call on speaker.

"Good morning, Sunrise. It's Cami. Is everything OK?"

The concern in her voice touched Sunrise. She raised a hand to her cheek and smiled.

"Oh, yes. Everything's great. I - I just wanted to know if there was anything you needed or anything I could do to help you prepare for tomorrow."

Surprise shone on Camisha's face. She smiled broadly and winked at her husband, who stretched his eyes wide mirroring his wife's expression and gave her a thumbs up.

"Not really. Unless you cook," Camisha replied, to which Sunrise answered in the negative with lighthearted laughter. "I only play music and shop," Sunrise added gleefully. "So do you need anything from Theory or Free People?" she joked. "Oh! I could compose something special for the day!"

The women laughed like old friends.

"I tell you what...there are a few musicians here today, so why don't you come by," Camisha said, eyeing Lennox, who agreed. "And maybe you can learn a few things in the kitchen. I'd love for you to meet my best friend, and my in-laws, that way you'll know a few people tomorrow!"

"I'd like that," Sunrise said, tearing up.

"Well, I'll look forward to seeing you around, noon?"

"Noon works."

"I'll text you the address."

Camisha's words struck Sunrise.

"OK," she stuttered. "Oh! Camisha."

"Cami. Please call me Cami," Camisha said, correcting her new sister.

"Sorry, Cami. Do you mind if I bring my boyfriend? He's here for the next couple of days."

"I've told you once, and I mean it. The more, the merrier! Looking forward to seeing you both."

Sunrise gave the news to Gabe, who was over the moon. "Feels good to be included, and without prompting."

Sunrise fought with her hair for at least an hour, before yielding to her old standby style--a neat topknot for the top half, and wild cascades of waves down her back for the bottom half. Gabe sat watching with wonderment from the bed, his long legs crossed in front of him. The look of confusion on his face sent Sunrise into a laughing fit.

"Black girl issues," she noted to her Midwestern, Caucasian lover.

When Sunrise had layered on the last necklace and bracelet, Gabe dressed and went to load his jeep with instruments. He packed his upright bass and Sunrise's guitar; he packed tambourines and Latin cabasas, as an increasingly impatient Sunrise watched on from the porch. He reminded his girlfriend that she offered to compose something in lieu of a food contribution.

"You just love a jam session," Sunrise sighed, tapping her foot.

"So do you!" Gabe shot back, placing a big kiss on her childlike brown cheek.

Sunrise arrived promptly at noon, with Gabe in tow, and to her surprise, Gabe's skills in the kitchen more than made up for her lack. He, Oliver, Lennox, and Mr. Robinson carried on like old college teammates. No one seemed the least bit bothered or surprised that he was white.

Sunrise and Farai were chatting at the kitchen bar while Camisha and her mother-in-law, Tess were chopping and sautéing in the kitchen, when Oliver appeared from behind the basement door. He stood smiling at the scene, and briefly closed his sable brown eyes. He tousled his kinky afro and sighed deeply.

"Wow," he quietly exclaimed, shaking his head. He rubbed the back of his neck and bobbed his head up and down, looking into Sunrise's all too familiar eyes. "You look so much like her."

He turned to an on looking Cami, stirring cake batter and nodding in agreement-- every part the proud big sister.

Sunrise's brow creased.

"I hope my face doesn't make you uncomfortable."

"No! No! Of course not! I loved Camilla. I loved her like my own mom." Oliver said as he walked over to

Sunrise. "Hell, for many years, I loved her more than I loved my own mom."

As if she were cued, Valentina Barnett-Johanssen walked through the front door with her husband Dr. Mikkael Johanssen and her oldest son, Isaac at her side.

"Valentina!" Cami sang as she ran to the six-foot tall supermodel-looking woman.

Valentina was radiant, fantastically chic. She was fit and charismatic. She wore waist-length sterling silver dreadlocks and had the complexion of an onyx gemstone. Sunrise had traveled the world and had never seen such a beautiful human being. Her husband was as equally attractive and sported his thick wavy hair that rivaled his wife's in its silver luster, in a closely cropped clean-cut style.

Valentina and her husband wrapped Cami in tight hugs. Lena tore into the room running behind her mother yelling, "Gigi Valentina and Papa Mix!"

"What a great surprise!" Cami cried. Oliver stood behind his best friend holding Farai's hand. Isaac swooped around the others and lifted his sinewy, baby brother into a bear hug and swung him around like a rag doll.

"What's up, O! You're looking good, Little Bro!" Then he turned to Farai and hugged her too. "I can't believe you haven't dumped this little guy."

Isaac and Oliver broke into a slap boxing match.

"Knock it off, guys! Come on," their mother warned. "Come let me hold you, Oliver."

She wrapped her youngest son in her long arms and held on. She extended a hand to Farai, pulling her into the love fest.

"Mom, geesh. You just saw us in August!"

"Hush now, let me love you," she giggled. "Where's my Luca, Ms. Lena?" She asked the four-year-old girl.

"He's still at home, I bet!" she wagered confidently, before leading her Gigi Valentina to the kitchen. "Come and see! My mommy has a new friend," Lena said, presenting Sunrise like a new bicycle.

Valentina's jaw dropped, and she took a few steps back. Oliver placed a steadying hand on his mother's back. Sunrise stood to greet the woman. She'd grown accustomed to the startled stares.

"Hi, I'm Sunrise Anderson."

"My baby sister," Camisha said, standing beside Sunrise, wrapping an arm around her shoulders.

"We just found out about Sunrise," Oliver added. "We'll get you all caught up later," he winked.

Thanksgiving Mix-ins

Lennox was all pins and needles while he waited for Camisha to come to bed. The clanging of pot lids and the humming of mixers were settling. The laughter and mixture of English and French chatter were subsiding. Lennox had vowed to tell his wife about his California dreams before the sun rose again, and he thought it best to bring it up while her spirits were high. She'd opened her heart to a new family member, and Oliver was in town. He couldn't have asked for a better time.

"Here we go, Robinson," he encouraged himself as he heard her saying her last goodnights to Oliver and Farai.

Camisha closed the bedroom door and collapsed on their bed. Lennox lifted her top over her head and massaged her shoulders.

"That's nice, Husband," she moaned, her face pressed against the plush mattress. "I love you."

"Love you too, Babe. Lena passed out with no back talk or negotiations tonight," he laughed.

"I bet!"

"Cam," he called but kept kneading her back and shoulders.

"That's my name."

"Kai has a proposal for us,"

She rolled over, facing him full on. He bit down on his bottom lip and ran a trembling hand over his head, but went on. When he'd laid Kai's entire proposal out, he was perplexed by his wife's calm reaction. She didn't exactly give a thumb up, but she appeared to be open.

"That's a lot to think about, huh?" Was all she gave up, before kissing him lightly. She took out nightclothes and headed to the bathroom. "Let's talk more about it after tomorrow. Cool?"

"Cool?" His brow creased. He listened for the shower and called Lacey.

"So, I talked to her about California," Lennox didn't wait for his sister's greeting. "And I don't know what to make of her attitude. She was playing it all close to the vest. But it's out there, and I can breathe again,"

"Who's this?" Lacey laughed.

"Ha. Ha. OK, I gotta go, I just wanted to tell you that I talked to her. Love you,"

"Love you, too. Keep me posted."

"Will do! Good night."

"Hi, Mom!" Ursula could hear her daughter's smile through the phone. "So how'd it go today? I think I gave you and Gabriel an appropriate amount of time to get settled in before I called. So! How was it? Were they nice to you?" Ursula fired questions at her daughter, as Beaux lay beside her listening on.

"Yes, everyone was very nice to me. And Gabe was a hit,"

"Of course, I was," he interjected from the foot of the bed. Sunrise hit him in the back with a pillow.

"Her in-laws were there, and her best friend Oliver was there. He lives in France,"

"France?" Ursula crinkled her well lived in face.

"Yes. He's a chef, and he's super down to earth, Mom. His girlfriend is a sister – French-born - and a freaking rapper with freckles!"

"And how about all of that hair!" Gabriel interjected again. "I have never seen so much hair growing from a human head," he marveled.

Sunrise shot him a look. "Do you want to talk to her?" Sunrise pretended to hand him the phone. "Sorry," he mumbled and went into the bathroom.

"Well," Ursula sighed, "I am thoroughly looking forward to tomorrow."

"Me too," she smiled, squeezing her eyes shut and raising her shoulders to her ears. She lay back on a stack of pillows. "How was dad's day? Has that cough gotten any better?" He'd been battling another upper respiratory disturbance, and Sunrise had been tied up with her new family and Gabriel.

"He had a pretty good day. But, that cough's hanging on," Ursula yawned. "He's looking forward to Thanksgiving, too. I think it'll do a lot of good for his spirits."

"I hope so. See you tomorrow, and kiss daddy for me. Love you. Goodnight."

Caspian was looking forward to spending Thanksgiving with Lacey, but he was a little nervous about meeting her family so early in their courtship. The fact that he'd be meeting them as a side story, gave him great comfort. Taliesan and her family had already left town to spend the holiday with Ellis's family in Florida, leaving he and Sunrise alone to navigate the unique family reunion. She worried like a mother hen, calling them several times throughout the drive to Florida.

"What are you taking?" she asked.

"What is Sunrise wearing?"

"Cas, are you nervous? Is Gabe going?"

She called until Ellis made her stop.

Caspian stopped by Sunrise's house while on his morning jog. Taliesan had requested updates on Sunrise and her outfit choice.

He could see Gabriel sitting on a barstool with his beloved double bass leaned against his bare chest, playing a furious bassline.

Sunrise came into sight the closer he got to the teal painted screen door. She was sitting directly in front of Gabriel at her piano—wearing only a men's white t-shirt. He turned to leave, not wanting to interrupt the intimate moment, but Gabriel spotted him and waved him in. Caspian smiled nervously, and paused at the entrance, allowing Sunrise to scamper upstairs to put on more appropriate attire.

"Good morning!" she yelled as she hurried up the spiral staircase.

The men stood awkwardly, avoiding eye contact until Sunrise returned, tossing a flannel button-down to her lover.

"Hey, Cas! What's up?" Sunrise said, hugging her friend.

"I'm here for a fashion check. You know my sister. What are you planning to wear?" he asked reluctantly.

Sunrise and Gabriel turned to one another and laughed.

"Well let's get this show started!" she cheered, clapping her hands together. "Gabe, do you mind putting on a pot of coffee? Oh, and breakfast. Can you make us something to eat?" Sunrise asked, as she headed back up the staircase.

"You cook?" Caspian asked.

"Yes!" Sunrise yelled from the loft. "I learned that little nugget at Cami's yesterday."

"At Cami's, huh? How was that?"

"It was a good time, man," Gabe answered. "That's what we were just working on. Sunny offered to compose a little something for dinner today."

"Really?" Caspian said, peeling off his vest and hoodie. " So you're taking your instruments?"

"Yes!" Sunrise yelled over the balcony. "Lennox and Lacey's dad play, and so does Cami's best friend. And get this! His black, French girlfriend is a rapper! Can you believe that?"

"I cannot," Caspian chuckled, shaking his head at Gabriel, who raised a brow and laughed with Caspian before disappearing behind the kitchen door.

Sunrise descended the staircase in dramatic fashion. She modeled her first option, a knee length Aztec embroidered black suede vest with faux fur lining around the neck, chest, and waist. She wore burgundy coated skinny jeans and black studded ankle boots.

Caspian snapped a few pics with his phone, and sent them to Taliesan, who replied almost immediately, "What else?"

He held up the reply to Sunrise, who shrugged and trotted back upstairs to try again. She returned modeling a black, collared maxi dress with a hi/lo hemline. The dress had a fitted button-down bodice and was covered in peacocks and roses, in shades of red, hot pink, orange, and green. She wore three red tassels as necklaces, along with a pair of oxblood suede knee boots.

Caspian sent the second round of shots to his sister, who approved. He bowed his head and gave Sunrise two thumbs up. She smiled like a child, spinning in a full circle, making the hem of her dress look like that of a flamenco dancer's. Over a breakfast of Applewood bacon, berries, and steel cut oatmeal the trio ironed out their plans for the day.

Camisha had outdone herself. The tables were adorned with tall hurricane vases filled with white column candles and acorns that the kids had collected. There were harvest blends of pumpkins with the words, welcome and thanks painted on them in gold, placed throughout her home. She'd transformed every square inch of living space into dining areas. There were long rectangular tables and smaller round tables. The kid's tables were covered in butcher's paper and crayons. She'd considered everyone.

Farai and Valentina greeted Sunrise and her family at the door. Both of the women looked more glamorous than Sunrise recalled. Farai's mane was braided into two thick goddess braids crowning her chiseled features and sparkling freckles. In the sunlight, they looked bronze. Valentina stood at her soon to be daughter-in-law's side towering over her clad in black from head to toe. Ursula swayed looking up to meet Valentina eye to eye.

Sunrise and Caspian helped the Andersons out of their coats, while Oliver and Lennox breezed by them to help Gabriel unload the Jeep. Both men greeted Sunrise with easy kisses to her cheek. Her face glowed. The simple gesture made her feel at home. Her father noticed it and said a silent prayer of thanks. It was all he wanted for their daughter. After an hour or so Camisha made her appearance with little Ms. Lena on her hip. She looked casual but pulled together in a soft brown sweater dress and tobacco colored, leather-riding boots. Camisha walked right over to her sister and embraced her, before introducing herself to Mr. Anderson.

She knelt at Ursula's side and whispered something in the woman's ear that elicited a tight hug and a few tears between the two. Camisha wrapped an arm around Sunrise's waist, and lead her to the kitchen, where Ms. Tess, Farai, and Valentina were all busy filling serving dishes.

"This young lady needs a proper introduction to the kitchen," Camisha announced with a bump to her sister's hip.

"Oh really? Well, come on in!" The ladies chimed between giggles.

"Well, we can see Camilla in your face, but did any of her cooking skills creep in there?" Ms. Tess teased.

"I-I don't think so." Sunrise crinkled her nose. "But, I can fill dishes! It was the only thing my mom ever allowed me to do, outside of washing them!"

"And for good reason," Ursula added from a stool at the kitchen bar. "Y'all need any help in there?"

"No, Ma'am. You just sit back and relax. You're my guest," Camisha answered, winking heavenward.

"My mother's spirit is here with us, and I know that she is pleased."

The doorbell rang announcing the DaCostas. Evangeline stunned in a full-length mink. Her posture screamed privilege. She and James were a very distinguished couple. Sunrise and Camisha stood shoulder to shoulder at the kitchen island watching them mingle with the guests and with the Andersons.

"Sunny, don't just stand over there gawking. Come and introduce Gabriel to the DaCostas," Ursula ordered.

Sunrise tossed a confused look at Camisha who shrugged. She leaned in and whispered to Sunrise, "Did you tell them about my dad," she said. "I meant, our dad?"

Sunrise squinted, looking into Camisha's eyes. She didn't know what to make of the statement. Nothing had been confirmed regarding who her biological father was. The look registered with Camisha, who apologized for her forwardness. Sunrise went over as instructed, and introduced Gabriel to the DaCostas.

Lacey entered the house cutting through the awkward introductions. She looked amazing in a cream sweater dress and camel colored over the knee boots. Her eyes danced when they fell on Caspian's, and a breathtaking smile spread across her face.

"So he's the new beau," Ms. Tess mumbled under her breath. "Very nice."

Isaac and Luca walked in carrying Whole Foods Market bags. Lacey greeted everyone graciously; she was in full beauty queen mode. When she reached Caspian, she took him by both hands and brought him into the kitchen to meet her mother, Tess before they went downstairs, where the men had congregated.

Oliver came up after a few minutes and was nearly bowled over by his son, whom he swept up in his long, thin arms.

He and Camisha exchanged knowing looks and went out the back door together. Oliver kissed his son and put him down. Kneeling on one knee, he asked the young boy to go help his Grandma and Lena set the tables. Luca ran back into the house without arguing.

"So."

"So. That's Caspian, the banker?" Oliver asked. He crossed his arms and looked back towards the kitchen door.

"It is."

"He's quiet."

"He seems pretty serious. But Sunrise loves him. He's like her Oliver, but he's half of a pair," she laughed. "He has a sister who rounds out that trio."

"So, do you like him?"

"Do I have to?" Camisha shifted her weight to one leg and folded her arms across her chest, mirroring her best friend.

"That would help. I mean, if you OK this dude, I'll feel a lot better about him being around my son," Oliver said.

"I get it." She held out her hands, palms facing Oliver's scowl. "Well, yes. I get a good feeling about him. And Ali likes him," she shrugged returning to her resting stance. "But most importantly, he's clearing up that murkiness between her and your big brother!"

Oliver rolled his eyes and growled. "There is that mess! Cam, you don't think they,"

"Of course not!" Camisha said, stopping him. "Lacey would never, and I don't believe Izzy would either. But, they're definitely very uncomfortable around one another, which isn't easy for any of us. So in my book, Caspian is a good thing. He's solid. He's educated and accomplished. He and Lacey are a good fit."

"Unlike we were,"

Camisha bristled at Oliver's retort.

"What difference does that make now?" She volleyed back. "If I recall, there is a very lovely young woman in there wearing a very expensive ring on her finger, that you put on it," she shoved him in the chest. "So what difference does yours and Lacey's compatibility matter at this point?"

The door opened, breaking up the building argument.

"Y'all OK out here?" Lennox asked from the kitchen door.

"Yep. We're good, Babe."

Camisha left Oliver to ponder her question.

Let's Talk About It

"Tonight was intense," Caspian said, breathing onto the back of Lacey's neck.

"How so?"

She snuggled into the curve of his body.

"I just about met all of your people," he said, kissing her bare shoulders and back. "Your parents, the ex," he drawled.

"And the ex's fiancé," Lacey quickly added as she turned to face him. The color of her eyes was so intense; sometimes they seemed to be lit from within.

"Yes. I'm not tripping. I'm just saying. He was pretty intense. I mean, I felt like I was being interrogated. Your pops didn't even ask that many questions."

"Oliver worries because the last guy I dated after Luca's birth, was not the best decision I'd ever made. But that's a story for another time."

Caspian laid his head on his folded arms. Lacey cuddled against his muscular chest and watched the ceiling fan swirl above them.

"What about your family? I don't know anything about them."

Caspian stiffened beneath her. There was a long pause in the rise and fall of his chest.

"Well, you've met Lucky, my sister."

"I thought her name was Taliesan."

"It is. But we call her Lucky. She kinda saved Sunny's life when we were kids."

"Are you serious?"

"Not exactly," Caspian said with a smirk. "But the doctor said she was Sunny's lucky charm, and the name stuck."

"That's nice," Lacey whispered, repeating his sister's nickname. "Lucky. I like that. And what about your parents?"

His mood turned dark, and she felt it. He turned the room cold in the same way, the day she met Sunrise at his place.

"You don't have to talk to me about your parents if you're not ready," she said to him.

"It's not that," he said, brushing her long soft bangs from her forehead. "There's nothing much to tell. They were nothing like your parents. I can hardly remember seeing them together."

"Are they divorced?"

"No. Well, they're both dead now, but they never divorced."

Lacey kept perfectly quiet and still, allowing Caspian the space he needed

"My parents met in California. My dad was stationed there. He was in the Air Force. And when he left the military, he started flying planes."

"Your dad was a pilot? That's cool."

"Not really. Not for my mom, or for us. It was all he cared about. That, and fast cars--oh and impressing white people. My mom was an actress, but my dad ended all of that when he moved her out here to pursue his dreams. She loved acting, and reading, and singing. She named me Caspian after Prince Caspian from C. S. Lewis's Chronicles of Narnia. She loved that whole series," he said, smiling broadly.

"She was a beautiful spirit, but he changed her when he moved her out here. He pretty much left her. She had no friends or family out here, and we were so young. She was always depressed. She slept and drank for the majority of our childhoods. That's how we got so close to Sunrise's family. They were our neighbors. Mrs. Anderson taught piano lessons from home, so she saw to us getting after school snacks and dinner." Caspian's lips formed a smile against Lacey's back. "Hell, she even saw to our mom eating damn near every night."

Ending on a high note, Lacey turned over, and mounted Caspian, kissing him passionately. He smiled at her effort and showed her how much he appreciated her.

*****

Evangeline kicked off her shoes and rubbed her foot.

The knock on the bedroom door soured her mood. She didn't answer. Instead, she went into the large en-suite bathroom and locked the door behind her.

"I'm going downstairs," James said through the tall double doors. "Can I get you anything?"

She didn't answer.

"Lena? Are you in there?"

"You know that I am, James," she barked.

"Can we just talk about this?"

"James, it's been a long day, bouncing between my sister's house and then Camisha's. The act of keeping up appearances between you and I was back breaking," she sighed and put a glob of cold cream on her face. "And playing nice for Camisha and Sunrise's sake has nearly crippled me. I've spent the last three days hearing about

213

how great that wretched woman was, how talented she was, how much everybody misses her. I barely made it through the day without puking or cussing! The thought of my plush pillow top mattress was all that kept me moving today, so please, just go away."

"Lena, Love. Please. I just want to get through this. I want things back to the way they were before all this mess."

Evangeline's face hardened. Beads of sweat formed on the bridge of her nose.

"You want. You want! You want! James DaCosta wants!" she erupted. "Well Chief, what about me? What about what I want!" she shouted at the top of her lungs. Her voice trembled. She saw the reddened image of her face in the mirrors above the double vanity and was overcome by violent sobs.

"What about what I want, James?" she asked once more. "What about the children I wanted to give to you? What about the ones that died inside of me, James? And you just keep bringing home Camilla's fucking babies for me to accept! Well fuck you James DaCosta!" she spat angrily at the locked bathroom doors. "This time, fuck you!"

Evangeline started bathwater in the Jacuzzi tub, drowning out her husband's voice. He stood at the closed door listening for a few seconds more before giving up and leaving the bedroom. The usually level headed woman sat on the edge of the tub and wailed. James sat at the top of the grand stairwell and wept into his hands.

"I never meant to cause you so much pain," he yelled at the door. "I hate that a moment's weakness from my youth is causing my family so much strife. I'm aching for you, Lena and for my daughters. I haven't forgotten the pain of the losses we suffered! I hate that we weren't able to raise a family together. I wish I could have given you children. I truly do," he mumbled, shaking his head in his hands. "I ache for Sunrise, too. Sure, she was blessed to have Beaux and Ursula, but my daughter was left alone in a hospital, to protect me. And I'm sorry Lena, but I ache for Camilla, too. She committed the ultimate sacrifice to protect me. She gave birth to a child, left it, and hid the secret forever, all to protect my marriage and my career."

His words fell on deaf ears.

*****

Farai stood leaning against the threshold of the bathroom door, braiding her long hair and casting daggers at the back of Oliver's head. He willfully refused to face her, but her resolve won out.

"Is everything OK, Babe?" he asked from the bed.

"Honte à to!"

He hated when she yelled in French. He flinched under the barrage of curses.

"I don't understand. Shame on me for what?"

"Don't feign ignorance, Oli-ver!" She angrily pointed at him with a comb. "I can see the way you behaved to Caspian. How dare you bring me all the way here to play the jealous lover to ton ex-femme!"

Oliver walked over to where Farai was standing, reaching out for her. She stepped out of reach and hurled the wooden comb she'd been using at his head. Her eyes glowed with fury, and her freckles darkened.

"Come on now, mon cherie," Oliver pleaded, reaching for the angry woman again.

"No! You tell me that I am wrong! What is happening, Oli-ver!"

Oliver hung his head and nervously twisted at his kinky coils.

"I - I don't know, Fifi," he stammered. "I guess. I don't want to lose my son."

"Menteur!" Farai shouted.

"I am not a liar, Farai! You know that."

"Je me casse! I'm going! You stay and fight for the woman you love!" Farai snatched the diamond engagement ring from her finger and flung it across the room. "How dare you humiliate me this way!" she yelled. She clenched her fists and stamped away wildly with tears flooding her big brown eyes.

Oliver scrunched his face and bit the inside of his cheek. She was a fiery woman, fiercely independent, and easily offended. Oliver lunged for his petite fiancé and wrestled her to the floor. He wrapped his arms and legs around her until she settled against him. He felt her sobs against his chest and kissed her on the collarbone.

"Farai Sikebo, you know that you are the woman I love. You know exactly who you are to me," he said, kissing her again. "Do I have residual feelings for the mother of my only child? Of course, I do. I probably always will. But you are the only woman I want to grow old with. Comprenez-vous?"

"Your French is getting better," she purred. "You'd better know exactly who you love, Oli-ver. I won't be in second place."

"Vous pourriez ne jamais être en deuxième place, mon cher. Laisse tomber, please." Oliver begged, in broken French.

"You let it go. Let her go," Farai replied against Oliver's crossed arms.

"Done."

"You'd better be!" She slapped his face with a free hand and kissed him on his arm. "Now please let me stand to find my most beautiful ring, mon garçon américain."

*****

Valentina tucked Luca in his bed and joined her husband and oldest son in Lacey's kitchen, where she found them huddled over Tess's apple pie eating directly from the tin.

She loved seeing her husband with her sons, especially with Isaac. He'd spent so much of his life, behind bars, paying for her shortcomings as a mother. He'd done the only thing he could do on the mean streets of Cleveland, Ohio as a child responsible for supporting his younger brothers; he sold drugs.

Valentina had struggled with drug addiction for most of her sons' childhoods, leaving Isaac, the oldest, to care for the family. He'd rose to the ranks of a mid-level hustler when the cops busted their measly townhome in the projects and locked her then seventeen-year-old son away for fifteen years.

"Want some," Isaac eyed his mother, handing her a clean fork.

"Did he give you a hard time?" Isaac asked.

"Not at all."

"As if she'd see it that way," Mikkael teased his wife.

"You've got a point, Mix," Isaac laughed pointing his fork at his stepfather.

Mix excused himself. He placed a gentle kiss on his wife's temple and headed upstairs to bed. Isaac and Valentina took the last of the apple pie into the living room and clicked on the television. The mother and son sat quietly clicking through channels.

"How often do you stay here?" Valentina quizzed. "With Luca?" she added, sensing her misstep.

"Not often."

"Oh. You just seem kind of familiar with things around here," she said.

"Ma, what are you getting at?"

She twisted her face and ate another piece of pie. Isaac stared her down. Valentina forgot how intense her son could be.

"Relax, Isaac. I just want you to feel comfortable staying at the condo."

Mikkael and Valentina had purchased a beautiful two-bedroom condominium in the city when Isaac was released from prison. They didn't make it to Atlanta as often as they had before Oliver left the country, so they'd offered the place to him.

"Look, Ma. I am not banging Lacey!"

"Don't be crass, Isaac Barnett!"

The two bullish Barnett's stared each other down until Isaac looked away and apologized to his mother.

"I know that you would never do something like that. And neither would Lacey,"

It was clear that there was more she wanted to say. Isaac sat quietly drumming on his leg.

"But there is something between the two of you. And things happen."

"Especially when you're under the same roof too much?" Isaac asked Valentina.

"Yes." She sighed. "It doesn't look good, Izz."

"Did O say something to you?"

"No! This is me talking to you. I don't like it."

"Well Ma, Lacey is dating again. She really likes this guy, and she deserves to love again. So I babysit for her once every two weeks," he explained. "She puts Luca to bed and goes out with Ol' Boy. She gets home before Luca wakes up, and I dip. That's all there is. So relax, I'm not banging my baby brother's ex-girlfriend. OK?" He stood so abruptly, it startled Valentina. She hung her head and watched his feet walk away.

"That girl works hard, Ma and she's doing it all on her own, while O's living the high life in France!"

"That's not fair, Isaac. Your brother is a great father to Luca."

"Yeah! For two and a half months out of the year. And Lacey's got it all for the other ten months," he argued. "I care about them, and I want to be here for them. What is so bad about that?" He threw his hands over his head in frustration. "Fuck!"

Isaac picked up the empty pie tin from the coffee table and took it to the kitchen sink. He grabbed his leather coat from the island and tossed it over a shoulder, as his mother looked on from the teal velvet couch.

"Goodnight, Ma. I love you." He bent to kiss her on the cheek and left.

*****

"California, huh?" Camisha said, massaging lotion onto her elbows and hands.

"What's that, Babe?" Lennox looked up from his laptop screen.

"I asked about California. I said we'd talk about it tomorrow, but now seems like a good enough time to hear more about Kai's proposal."

Lennox's stern expression turned to one of confusion. Camisha held her face forward in a steady gaze on his sable brown eyes.

"Well. Do you want to talk about it or what?" She asked, with an air of authority that was palpable.

Lennox ran a hand over the back of his neck and pursed his full lips. His eyes narrowed impetuously.

"What's that look about, Ali?"

"I can see that this conversation is not going to be easy," he murmured and sat up.

He put the laptop beside him on the bed. "OK," his goatee covered mouth turned downward, and he dipped his head towards his wife. "Well, you already know that

I've been working with Kai and Amita on launching the organics for the Beltrams."

"Ahhh, Amita," Camisha dragged.

"Yes. Amita, who you've known that I'd be working with from time to time," Lennox reminded her.

Amita Sawant was Lennox's college girlfriend and on again, off again colleague.

"Go on." Camisha coached.

"Cami, I feel like you're being antagonistic right now. You asked me to talk to you about things that affect our family, and not to just make decisions for the both of us. This is what I'm trying to do right now. I'm including you."

"Are you now?" Camisha shot back. "Are you, Lennox? Are you including little ol' me in the decision making process of moving our family to the other side of the country?" She clasped her hands together and pressed them to her mouth. She closed her eyes and took an exaggerated breath before speaking again. "Do you hear yourself?" She stood and walked over to where he was sitting. "This conversation is not some kind of allowance, Ali. Are you kidding me right now?"

Lennox reached out taking her hand in his own.

223

"Babe, forgive me. I know it's not. I'm trying. Just hear me out."

"I'm listening. That's what's happening here," she said, pointing first to her husband, and then to herself. "But, don't be smug. Don't talk to me as if this conversation is some sort of consolation for a decision you've already made."

"It's not! And I'm not trying to be smug. I feel like you're the one being smug, Cam."

Camisha held up her hands to calm her husband's pending flare up.

"OK. OK. Let's just take a breath and hear each other out. You go first."

She sat on the bed beside him and held his hand in her lap. He kissed her on the cheek and thanked her for the reset.

"Babe, I really want to do this. I think it would be good for us to get a fresh start. And for us to start building our own legacy, for our family." He spoke earnestly.

Camisha listened intently and pat his hand every now and again encouraging him to go on. When he had made his arguments for the move, Camisha posed only one question.

"What about Sunrise? I really want to get to know her," she said. "I have a sister, Ali."

Up Yonder

Sunrise and Taliesan lay flat on their backs with their arms outstretched in a T-shape, palms up, on the cork floors of Taliesan's oversized laundry room, turned yoga studio.

"Now, exhale and drop both knees to the right, stacking them on top of each other," Taliesan instructed in a soft, even tone.

Sunrise complied, taking four deep breaths before switching to the other side.

"I had the craziest dream last night."

"Yeah?"

"There was a jam session at my house. Gabe was on bass; I was on drums."

"You don't have drums in your house."

"It was a dream, Lucky!"

The women turned over onto their hands and knees, dropping their heads and arching their backs.

"Cami's friend, Oliver was there playing the bongos beside my mom at the piano. His girlfriend, Farai was there too. She was playing woodblocks."

"What are woodblocks?"

"Lucky!" Sunrise shouted. "What difference does it make? It was a dream," she said, laughing.

"OK. I'm sorry. Go on!" Taliesan said.

She extended an arm forward, and her leg straight behind. Sunrise followed suit.

"Here's where it really got crazy...Camilla was there, too. She was singing, 'Going Up Yonder.'"

The women looked at one another with matching grimaces. Befuddled, Taliesan asked,

"The gospel song from funerals?"

"Yes!" Sunrise answered. "If anybody asks you," she sang, sending the women into another fit of laughter.

"What do you think it means? Was Camilla religious?"

"I hardly knew the woman. I'm going to talk to Cami about it today."

"Are you seeing her today?"

"Yeah. She and Oliver invited me to the Sweet Auburn Curb Market with them."

"That's a weird date," Taliesan teased. "But if you see any rutabagas, please get me a few."

"Sure thing!" Sunrise sang.

Ursula had the breakfast table set when her daughter walked through the door. Her mother looked tired. Her eyelids were heavy, and her smile lines appeared deeper. The sunlight that rushed in behind Sunrise when she opened the front door made the corners of Ursula's eyes crinkle.

"Morning, Mom," Sunrise said, kissing her mother on the forehead. "Where's Daddy?"

The old woman held on to the small round table to lower herself into her chair. Sunrise took her mother's arm and helped her. It was tough seeing her parents get old. Camilla's untimely death made Sunrise acutely appreciative of her time with them. She often thought of how her divorce from Xander had led her back home. It allowed her to be around to experience Sunday dinners and Saturday morning breakfasts with her aging parents.

"He didn't sleep well last night," the woman said as she sat at the table and watched her daughter wash her hands in the kitchen sink.

"That's the third night in a row, Mom. What'd Dr. Ponder say when you all saw him last week?"

Sunrise set about fixing plates of scrambled eggs and strips of bacon for her and her mother. She sliced the grapefruit in two and sprinkled sugar on her mother's half.

Ursula sat shaking her head in her hands. "The same thing...it's that damn cold, just hanging on. It's harder to shake things at our age, Sunny."

Sunrise joined her mother at the table. She placed her mother's pillbox and a cup of coffee on the table before her. Ursula's eyes were red and sunken like she'd been crying.

"Mom," Sunrise said, leaning toward her mother. "Are you sure that's it?" she said, taking her hand. "You look worried."

"I am, Sunny. Your dad and I aren't as young as we used to be."

"Mom, please. Don't be morbid," Sunrise said, cutting her mother off. "You and Dad are in great shape. You're both still active; he'll be fine. He'll beat this. It's just a common cold."

"Nothing's common in your late seventies, Sunny Bunny."

Ursula put on her best face and got through breakfast with small talk and a bit of gossip. After cleaning the dishes, Sunrise found her mother napping in front of the television in her father's recliner. She took a quilt from the hall closet and covered her mother's legs. She crept down the hall to her parent's bedroom and peeked inside. Her dad was sound asleep, wrapped in bedcovers up to his weathered neck. He was a dignified man--tall and handsome. Sunrise climbed into bed with her sleeping father and lay beside him for a while before she left to begin her day. The sound of his labored breathing stayed with her all the way to her home.

The quiet of Sunrise's house was jarring. Gabriel had been gone for over two weeks, but he'd left the ghost of his presence lingering all over her house. His boots were in the mudroom; his toothbrush and aftershave were in her bathroom. He was always busying around when she left him there. She missed the sound of him humming a familiar tune, and the sounds of pots and pans clanging from the kitchen. And most of all, she missed the sound of him strumming his double bass.

Her phone rang from the inside of her leather shoulder bag, surprising her. She dug around looking for it and missed the call. It was her mother, and she dialed her right back.

"Hey, Mom. That was a short nap,"

"Sunny."

The somber tone of her mother's voice made her instantly weak.

"What is it, Mom?"

Sunrise headed back out the front door. She could hear her mother sobbing quietly.

"Mom! What is it? Is it Daddy?"

She threw her bag in the passenger seat and started the Jeep Wrangler.

"He's gone, Sunny."

"Mommy, no!" she cried. "No!" she wailed. " I'm on my way, Mommy! I'm coming."

Sunrise ended the call with her mother and called Taliesan. She ordered her friend to go over to her parent's house and wait for her. By the time Sunrise reached her parent's house, an ambulance and a fire truck were in the driveway. Caspian's Escalade was parked at the curb. The scene inside the house was eerily composed, with Caspian at the helm. Her mother sat in the recliner where Sunrise had last seen her. She sat there wringing her hands as Taliesan sat on the arm of the chair running her hand up and down the older woman's arm.

Sunrise knelt at her mother's side and kissed her on her folded hands. She followed the sound of Caspian's voice to her parent's bedroom. She was disturbed by the presence of strangers in her parent's bedroom. It felt wrong having them see her father dressed in his nightclothes. "Daddy wouldn't have liked this," she said to Caspian.

He wrapped his arm around Sunrise's shoulders, and the two stood watching the technicians move about with their stethoscopes and clipboards. There were people buzzing around with cameras and voice recorders. Caspian watched as Sunrise's wide eyes darted from one spot to another. When he saw her eyes stall on the black bag at Beaux's bedside, he turned her away.

"What is all of this?" Sunrise asked.

Caspian led her to the sunroom.

"What's going on, Cas? Why are they taking photos? Talk to me!"

Caspian cleared his throat and laid his arms across his chest.

"Your dad had prepared for this. He coordinated everything."

Surprise and confusion registered on Sunrise's face. "For how long? Was he sick?"

"He was old, Sunrise. And he was wealthy and prudent," he explained. "He has a lot to protect, and then there's you and Mrs. Anderson. He wanted to make sure that this time wouldn't be..." Caspian sighed and stuffed his hands deep into his pockets. He looked down at his black wingtips. "That it wouldn't be more difficult than it needs to be, with insurance and bank affairs."

She knew Caspian was right, but it didn't make the reality hurt any less. Her father had come to terms with his own mortality. He had his affairs in order and had confided in Caspian. She wondered if he was afraid. She wondered if he had given up. Had he given up, leaving her mother alone? The thought made her mad.

"Sunny, your dad loved you and your mother more than anything in this world. He would have done anything, bought anything, hell, conjured up anything that could have given him more time! But not even the great Horace Beaux Anderson could beat death. He lived a long, and full life, Sunny."

Caspian walked over and held his friend in his arms until she stopped crying.

The days following Beaux Anderson's death ran together like the dots in a Monet painting. Caspian had handled all of Beaux's business affairs. The old man had been preparing for his demise for years, and he'd entrusted the care of his final arrangements to his protégée, and closest confidant outside of his wife, Caspian Pearce. He'd insisted on making his transition as easy as possible on his wife and daughter.

Caspian delivered the news to Lacey, who in turn informed Camisha and Lennox. Less than two weeks before Christmas, the Andersons were planning the burial of their patriarch.

The sight of a pasty white man answering the door confused Camisha. She took a step back and looked at the turquoise door to check the address plate. Gabriel rubbed at his deep blue eyes and blinked back the long fringes of his lashes.

"Hey, Cami," he yawned. "Come on in out of the cold."

A tight smile found its way onto her ebony face.

"It's good to see you again," he said, hugging her. "I wish it was under better circumstances, though."

Camisha bobbed her head in agreement.

"How is she?"

Gabriel pressed his thin lips into a single hard line and shook his head ruefully.

"Not good. She's been in the bed since yesterday morning."

"I guess grieving processes are hereditary," she mumbled to herself. "Do you mind?" Camisha asked, looking upstairs towards the open loft area.

Gabriel responded, "Of course. Of course. It's the door straight ahead once you reach the landing," he pointed Camisha in the direction of Sunrise's bedroom.

The light drumming on the bedroom door roused Sunrise. She was surprised to see Camisha's face pressed against the threshold of her bedroom. She shot up, bumping the top of her head on the overhanging headboard. "Ouch!" she said, rubbing her forehead.

"You OK?" Camisha asked, taking a step into the dark brown bedroom.

Sunrise managed a polite smile and invited her sister in. She disappeared behind a set of swinging doors, before reappearing wearing a short, colorful kimono and furry boots. Sunrise's golden hazel eyes were bloodshot and foggy. Her cinnamon colored complexion looked dull and ashen. She sat at the foot of her bed, Indian style, and pointed to a hanging acrylic chair with gray cushions. It was anchored by a weathered beam in the ceiling and a thick, steel chain.

Camisha's utter confusion shone on her face, making Sunrise laugh for the first time since her mother's phone call.

"It's very comfortable. And secure," she said, laughing at her sister, as she cautiously held onto both sides of the orb, and backed herself into the odd piece of furniture.

"I'll just stand," Camisha said, crinkling her nose.

"No, don't be silly." Sunrise slid over and patted the bed. "Come, sit here."

Camisha sat beside her younger sister, looking around at the hanging strings of white lights and the purple velvet covered antlers hanging on the opposite wall.

"What can I do?" Camisha asked.

Sunrise fought back tears. She felt her sister's hand on her knee and pat it. She couldn't bring herself to speak.

"It's OK. You don't have to hide from me. I'm here. Tell me what you need."

Gabriel appeared at the bedroom door with a tray of mugs, a teapot and a jar of honey. He laid the tray on the nightstand and pulled two spoons from the pocket of his terry cloth robe.

"Yell if you need anything," he said to Camisha.

Camisha poured two cups of the woodsy green tea and handed one to Sunrise. "There has to be something you need, Sunny. Your mother sent me here to see about you, so I have to do something. Mother's orders," Camisha said, smiling down at her sister.

"I- I don't have anything appropriate to wear," Sunrise said.

"OK. I can believe that."

Sunrise looked up at Camisha, and another big smile spread across her face.

"So, we need to find a dress," she said, clasping her hands together. "Now, we obviously have very different styles, so tell me how you want to look for your dad's...What should I look for?"

"I have no idea," Sunrise groaned as she walked into her closet. "I want to look dignified for him. He was such a dignified man. You know?" She bit her bottom lip and tried to call up an image of her dad dressed for work, in a dark suit and tie, with black leather wing tips. The tears rolled down her face. "Yes. I want to look dignified," she said.

Camisha pulled Sunrise into a tight hug and rubbed her back until the shuddering subsided.

"Dignified it is. I'll take care of everything," she assured her sister.

*****

Camisha leaned in and whispered to her husband, "Oh my God! This place is crazy. It doesn't even feel like we're still in Atlanta."

Lennox patted his wife's hand and held her closer. The space was breathtaking. The marble walls were met by rich wooden lattice covered ceilings and matching beams. Mr. Anderson's stately mahogany casket sat centered before a floor to ceiling, plate glass picture window. The wall framed a cascading waterfall in the midst of unspoiled forest views. And rows of dark leather chairs lined the stained concrete floors.

There were two glossy black pianos positioned at both ends of the casket, along with two of the biggest floral arrangements Camisha had ever seen. The urns looked to be at least three feet wide, filled with lush, evergreen fronds, and large blooms of white roses, Easter lilies, and calla lilies.

Lennox and Camisha were among the first mourners to arrive. Caspian looked every part a bank president in a classic black suit and tie, his beard was pristinely trimmed, and he was wearing black metal

238

framed eyeglasses. He bowed his head, acknowledging the couple, as he went over last minute details with a young looking pastor. He welcomed the couple as they stood over Mr. Anderson, paying their respects.

"Thanks for coming," he said, shaking Lennox's hand, and hugging Camisha. "Lacey's already here. She's in the back with Mrs. Anderson and Sunrise."

"Oh, can I help with anything?"

Taliesan and Ellis entered the sanctuary with Kannon and Bodhi trailing behind. She waved to her brother and to the Robinsons as she made a beeline to the back. Lacey joined the others out front shortly after. Caspian took her into his arms and laughed,

"Mama bear shooed you off. Didn't she?"

"She gave me my walking papers," Lacey said, pouting.

Sunrise and her mother were visions of decorum-- wearing black veils and gloves. Sunrise removed the jewelry from her facial piercings and styled her hair in a perfectly coiffed, low chignon. The dress Camisha bought her fit as if it was created for her body. It hit just below her knee and hugged her hips perfectly. The long black sleeves bellowed as she entered, and the pearl buttons at her wrists added just the right amount of class.

Ursula sat at the closest of the pianos, while Sunrise sat at the other. The pastor took his place in the makeshift pulpit, signaling the guests to take their seats.

"The grace of our Lord Jesus Christ and the love of God and the fellowship of the Holy Spirit be with you all," he said, welcoming the congregation. "At the family's request, Brother Beaux Anderson has been given last rites in the presence of his family along with Holy Communion. For you, his friends and colleagues, I've been asked to read from Matthew 11:28.

'Come to me, all you who are weary and burdened, and I will give you rest. Amen."

He looked to either side of the casket, acknowledging the Anderson women, and stepped down. Caspian took the platform and recited Khalil Gibran's, "A Visit From Wisdom,"

"In the stillness of night, Wisdom came and stood by my bed. She gazed upon me like a tender mother and wiped away my tears, and said: "I have heard the cry of your spirit and I am come to comfort it. Open your heart to me and I shall fill it with light. Ask of me and I shall show you the way of truth."

Caspian was visibly shaken, which looked foreign on Caspian's usually sober countenance. He lowered his head and paused to gather his wits.

"Beaux Anderson was my mentor and my godfather. He was my godfather in every sense of the title. He took the responsibility of caring for my sister and me after the death of our parents," Caspian said, dabbing at an escaped teardrop. "He loved me, and he taught me. He loved so many of you here today, and taught even more of you," he said to the nods among the onlookers. "Beaux and Mrs. Ursula Anderson were more than just a great couple, they were loving parents, dedicated educators, freedom fighters, and above all else they were uplifters. Beaux believed in the importance of uplifting those God put in your lives, and modeled his life around that doctrine. Sunny and Ms. Ursula, he charged me to carry on in his absence, and I intend to honor the man whom I called father--in every aspect of my life. I've got you. I've got you both," he vowed.

The services were fitting a man held in such high regard as Beaux Anderson. All of the participants honored the man's wishes for an understated affair and kept their roles brief.

Sunrise and Ursula's musical tribute to the man they loved was by far the highlight of the service. Beaux's talented pianists were joined by Gabriel, who played his cello. They performed an uplifting rendition of 'Going Up Yonder' that brought their guests to their feet in true celebration of the man's life.

"There are so many differences between Mr. Anderson's funeral and Camilla's," Cami leaned in to whisper to her husband. "There are so many famous people from the city and state here. Is that the mayor?"

The vast space barely accommodated the number of grieving people who wanted to pay their respects to the Andersons. It was in stark contrast to the few people who showed up for Camilla's graveside ceremony. The eulogy and reflections shared by the guests all spoke so highly of Sunrise's father. Camisha frowned from time to time, making her face red with shame.

"Is that my dad and Evangeline?"

She craned her neck to see around Lennox's broad chest. "What are they doing here? He looks pretty upset."

Camisha watched, bewildered by her father's genuine despair.

Lennox, Camisha, and Lacey stood by as Sunrise, Ursula and Caspian thanked each and every guest. There were no limousines or a processional to a grave site, as Beaux was to be committed to his family's private mausoleum.

"I'm very sorry for your loss," Camisha said as she hugged Ursula. "If there's anything I can do for you, please don't hesitate to let me know."

"Just be good to our baby girl. It's what he wanted for her ever since she found you."

Camisha winced and looked up at her husband who offered an assuring back rub.

"I will. I give you my word," Camisha promised.

Caspian laid the plush leather seat of Lacey's car back as far as it would recline and removed his necktie. He closed his eyes and rubbed them between his thumb and middle finger. Lacey caressed his knee, then his face and neck. He shook off the sobs that were rolling up his chest to his throat and kissed Lacey's open palm.

"Do you want something to eat?" she asked.

Caspian shook his head, no.

"Do you want some time to yourself?"

He didn't answer her second question as quickly, but he eventually shook his head, yes.

"That's probably best," he said.

"OK," Lacey said, patting his knee. "I'll call to check on you tomorrow."

But something shifted in him. He sat up in the seat and turned to look at her. The light of the setting sun cast a halo of soft light around her form and illuminated the golden highlights in her wheat brown hair. She smiled and glanced over at him.

"What?" she asked.

"I'd like you to stay. Or come back, if you have to get things settled with Luca."

His abrupt change of heart intrigued Lacey.

"His dad's here, remember? He's with Oliver's family, so I'm all yours."

Caspian leaned over the console and kissed her.

"He really liked you."

"Who? Beaux? I really liked him, too. I'm glad I met him."

"Me too."

The two were hardly through Caspian's door when his phone rang. It was Taliesan calling to invite her brother over for dinner.

"I'm good, Lucky. Lacey's here with me."

Annoyance flashed across Caspian's face, and he left the room. Lacey could hear his voice raised, but couldn't make out what he was saying. He returned shortly wearing navy blue coveralls and steel toe boots. Lacey sat confused, watching the man bang and slam around his kitchen.

"Is everything all right," she asked.

"No!" he snapped. "She'll never stop trying to run my life."

Lacey stood at the arched doorway to the kitchen, watching the capricious man as he looked through drawers.

"What happened?" Lacey asked.

"It's not important. Do you want to go get something to eat? I'm going to go out back for a while," he said, gesturing to his back door.

It was clear to Lacey that there really were no options. She wasn't quite being dismissed, but she was being asked to give him some time to himself, which was a marked improvement.

"OK," she drawled. "I'll go find food and call you when I'm on my way back."

"No. Just take my keys. I'll be out back. Make yourself at home. OK?"

He walked over to where she was standing and pulled her into a passionate kiss. He looked deeply into her eyes for what seemed like minutes, before kissing her again and lightening his grip around her waist.

"We're good. Right, Lacey?"

Weakened by his strong grasp, she could only bring herself to nod.

"Yeah?" he asked for confirmation.

She nodded again, before wiggling from his grasp.

"I'll be back," she said, stumbling towards the front door. When she looked back, Caspian was already in the backyard, unlocking the detached garage.

"Ms. Ursula is staying with Sunrise and Gabe, and Cas is with that Lacey person, so it'll just be us Coopers for dinner," Taliesan groaned.

Ellis wrapped his thin arms around his wife's waist and kissed her.

"Don't sound so disappointed."

Taliesan spun around to face her husband. She tilted her head to look into his eyes; she was saddened by the look in them.

"I'm not disappointed, Ellis. Why would you say that?"

"Taliesan Cooper, I've known you for a very long time. You can't fool me. You're upset."

Her shoulders slumped, and she leaned against the counter. She sneered at her husband before chuckling a little.

"I am." She hung her head.

Ellis leaned against the counter beside her and tapped her shoulder with his arm.

"They're getting their lives together, Lucky. That's a good thing. They have all lost someone very important to them, and no one's crashing and burning. That's a very good thing, Love. Right?" He leaned to see her eyes.

"Yes," she sighed. "It is a very good thing. But, I don't know anything about this Lacey person, and is Ms. Ursula going to move in with Sunny? What's going to happen with the house? I know that Beaux left Cas with implicit instructions, that he's probably sharing with Lacey first!" she cried. "And I lost someone too, Ellis! Who's here with me?"

Ellis was taken aback. His eyes narrowed, and he walked out of the kitchen.

"I am, Lucky," he tossed over his shoulder as he walked up the stone stairs towards the sound of their boys playing in their bedroom.

Lucky sunk to the kitchen floor, filled with regret and sadness. She pulled her knees to her chin and cried. Things were happening so quickly, and she felt left behind. She hadn't meant to hurt Ellis. She loved and appreciated him to no end, but Sunny and Caspian were her people. It had always been that way, but things were changing.

You are the Father!

Sunrise turned onto the cobblestone driveway of the DaCosta home.

"How much does Atlanta's top cop get paid?" she wondered aloud.

"Evangeline is from old money," Camisha answered.

She read the uncertainty on her sister's face and gave her hand a reassuring squeeze.

"You'll be fine. I'm here for you so you won't be outnumbered," Camisha said in an attempt to make Sunrise laugh. "Sunny, look at me. I have been right where you are—with these same people. He was a complete stranger to me. He wanted to be my father, and he wanted to know me."

"Is what I'm wearing OK?" Sunrise asked.

"It doesn't matter what you're wearing, Sunny."

"Says you, the one she loves," Sunrise said running a hand over the silk scarf that secured her wild waves underneath the floppy hat she was wearing.

"I can only imagine how confused you must feel because you already have a father -an awesome one- who loved you. And Sunny, these test results won't change that," she said, squeezing Sunrise's hand again. "James and Evangeline are good people. And, I can assure you, he's doing this for all the right reasons. He won't just let it go. He won't be able to just go on with his life, thinking he has a daughter out here that he hasn't offered his heart to. He's just that kind of guy," she said.

Camisha's words were comforting. They gave Sunrise the motivation to get out of the Jeep, go into the house, and see where the DNA results would lead them.

The DaCosta home was as stunning. The house was decked out in holiday cheer. A large Christmas tree stretched up to the second story of the grand entrance. There were marble inlays on the floors, tall columns, and the most spectacular stairwell Sunrise had ever seen, and she had seen many grand stairwells in her life. James and Evangeline entered from opposite sides of the foyer. Evangeline was a warm as always. She took both of Sunrise's hands in her own and greeted Camisha with an affectionate embrace. James led the women to a room just off of the foyer. There was another, smaller, Christmas tree in the room, along with seasonal trinkets, and porcelain dolls that lined the built in bookshelves. There were pictures of Lena, and some of other people Sunrise didn't recognize.

Evangeline left the room and returned carrying a tray of pastries and fruit, and a silver coffee pot. Sunrise half expected a Latina maid to come in carrying the tray. The sight of Evangeline carrying the tray seemed odd and disingenuous. She ordered herself to stop. *I have to give the woman a fair chance*, she thought. Sunrise was ashamed; she felt that she should have been able to relate to the woman, as she had experienced a similar betrayal. Evangeline's grace amid her husband's infidelity angered her in some way. She surveyed the woman's delicate features for some sign of contention: flared nostrils, a clenched jaw or something, but there was only the polite curl of her lips and a noticeable vacancy in her eyes.

"Sunrise, I'm so sorry for your loss," James said, extending his hand to her. "Beaux was a beacon, and he was very good to me. He was a friend to me when I needed one the most."

The man's declaration befuddled her.

"How'd you know my dad?" she asked.

"Well, I met him when I first opened the investigation into Camilla's accident."

The mention of Camilla's name brought a stillness to the room. The women looked back and forth between one another. Evangeline practically willed herself to stay put.

"After you and Camisha's first meeting at the station went so badly, I reached out to him."

"And?"

"Well, I was in a bad place after hearing about the circumstances surrounding your birth and adoption, and about the way Camisha had made you feel," he said, glancing over at Camisha. "I - I wanted to check on you."

"James cut the crap! You wanted to know how much they knew about Camilla, and about her father--you! Enough of the maneuvering!" Evangeline snapped. "Sunrise, when he learned your birthdate and found out that you were adopted, he figured there was a good chance he was your father too! Why?" she asked, without waiting for an answer. "Because he knew that he'd been with her again after he'd lied to me about being over her. And Sweetie, you look exactly like her."

"Exactly," Camisha parroted.

Evangeline sat the cup she'd been holding on the marble table and walked over to a desk situated in the corner of the room. She pulled out an envelope and carried it to Sunrise.

"These are the results of the DNA tests," she said, waving the envelope. "He was spot on! He is your father too, dear." She sat back down and picked up her cup again. "That's right! My husband has not one, but two beautiful daughters--from the same woman. He slept with the very same teenaged girl, not once, but twice! That we are absolutely sure of!" She crossed her long legs and took a sip from her cup.

Camisha and Sunrise were stunned. James pressed his lips together and shifted his eyes down towards the rich dark floors. He stood up, put his hands in his pockets, walked over to the large windows, and looked out onto his backyard.

"I saw Camilla a few times after we found out that she was pregnant with Camisha."

Evangeline cut her eyes at him.

"What was I supposed to do, Evangeline? She was carrying my child! Right or wrong, she was carrying my child." The pleading in his voice made Camisha want to go to him, but she stayed seated. "There was only the one other time that I was with her," he said, turning to face the women. "I swear it. There was only the one other time...I was so sad. I was sad, Evangeline. I only wanted to see my baby. I needed to see her. I was broken, and Camilla comforted me. She didn't push herself on me. She didn't seduce me. It was nothing like that. She was just nice to me for once. She wasn't snapping at me, or degrading me; she was just nice. One thing led to another, and we were both sorry for what happened," he said as he looked to his wife, his eyes filled with sincerity.

"She was so sorry that she walked away from the evidence, and hid her for the rest of her life, Evangeline! For the rest of her life!"

Camisha put a hand on Sunrise's shaking thigh.

Evangeline broke.

She stood abruptly, dropping the cup she'd been holding, spilling the syrupy sweet coffee onto her polished floors.

"I'm sorry," she stammered and left the room.

"I'll get this cleaned up," Camisha said, leaving Sunrise alone with James.

The man remained in the same spot at the window, staring into space. Sunrise wiped at the floors with the napkins Evangeline had left on the serving tray.

"Leave it," James ordered.

"It's no problem," Sunrise argued.

"Please!" he yelled.

Shaken, Sunrise moved back to the chair where she'd been sitting and longed for Camisha's speedy return. James walked over and sat in front of her.

"I'm sorry. I can't imagine how difficult this must be for you."

His eyes were sharp and clear. He put his knees together and ran his hands up and down his thighs.

"So, I am your biological father," he said, pointing to the envelope that sat halfway tucked in the cushion of the chair. "But I have no intention of imposing myself, Sunrise. I only knew Beaux for a short while, and I know that I couldn't hold a candle to that man. And I don't want to try to be a father to you this late in your life. But I would like the opportunity to be a friend--or whomever you'd like me to be."

Sunrise hadn't expected such frankness from James. It was refreshing, but unnerving at the same time. The sincerity in his tone drew her to him. She offered him both of her hands.

"Thank you. I'm so sorry for all of this. I'm sorry that my presence is upsetting Ms. Evangeline."

"No. Don't you dare!" Evangeline said from the doorway. "It is me who owes you an apology. You've just lost your father, a great man by any measure, and here I am airing ancient grievances as if you or Cami had anything to do with James's betrayal."

Sunrise stood reverently. Evangeline walked over and stood between her and James.

"I am sorry, Sunrise. And I hope you can find it in your heart to forgive my appalling behavior." She pressed her hand to her heart. "I am truly sorry."

For the first time, she recognized something all too familiar in Evangeline's eyes. It was heartache. She lunged towards the woman, wrapping her in an embrace. James stood behind Evangeline and took hold of Sunrise's extended hand.

Camisha and Sunrise rode along in silence for most of the ride home.

"That was intense," Camisha said aloud.

"It was definitely a first for me."

Sunrise pulled the Jeep into her driveway and turned the truck off.

"So we're full blooded sisters. How crazy is that? I have never heard of anything so crazy," Camisha said, shaking her head.

"Never," Sunrise agreed.

"Well, that's Camilla for you! Never a dull moment with that woman."

Sunrise sat debating whether or not to tell Cami about being there, at the hospital and overhearing her and Camilla's conversations.

"So Lacey and Caspian, huh?" Camisha said, bringing a halt to her sister's private deliberations.

"Oh yeah. That seems to be getting serious. Has she started moving into her new house? It's just around the corner. You know?"

"Yes! It's lovely. Ali is excited to have her living so close to us, barring a move to California."

"California?" Sunrise said, facing Camisha, her brows drew together. "What does that mean?"

Camisha rested her eyes.

"Ali wants to move to California."

"But, I - I just found you," Sunrise's said, her lip quivering.

Camisha moved to extinguish the tears shimmering in her sister's eyes.

"It's just talk right now, Sunny. And you travel all the time. Right?" she said with a lopsided grin. "Let's dish about Lacey and Caspian!" She said, widening her eyes. "Do you think Ms. Ursula's up and stirring, yet?"

Sunrise wasn't distracted from her sister's casual announcement, but she gave in and invited her sister in to make brunch.

"Good morning!" Taliesan sang as the women walked through the door. "Oh. I didn't know you were with Camisha."

Sunrise hugged her friend. She was very happy to see Taliesan, after the start to her day. Taliesan made small comforting circles on Sunrise's back and held on until her friend let go first.

"Hey now, what's going on with you, Sunny Bunny?" Taliesan said, adjusting her eyes to meet Sunrise's. "What happened to her?" Taliesan asked. "Camisha?"

"It's been an emotional morning, but she's fine."

"What happened?" Taliesan asked again, as her fingers tightened into a fist.

Camisha shifted her weight to one side and placed her hand on her hip.

"Chief DaCosta is my biological father," Sunrise said, diffusing the situation.

Taliesan's mouth dropped open.

"Oh my," she mouthed. "Does Ms. Evangeline know?"

Camisha and Sunrise nodded in unison.

"That poor woman," Ursula said as she descended the spiral staircase. "I think I'll call her later."

"Mom, you knew?"

"I did," Ursula said, holding out an arm for her daughter's assistance down the last few steps.

"How?"

"James and your father had grown close. He talked with Beaux often, after Camisha told him about that letter she found in her mother's personal effects."

Sunrise helped her mother into her velvet club chair.

"Why didn't you tell me, Mommy?" Sunrise said, crinkling her nose.

"It wasn't mine to tell."

Intentions, Intentions

"Yes, it's too late to back out!" Taliesan laughed. "Why'd you let it go this far? The boys are really looking forward to hanging out with Luca."

Caspian sneered at his big sister.

"When she asked, I was only thinking of the kids, you know? Beaux was like a grandfather to them, and they watched his body carried out," Caspian drawled.

"With a bird's eye view from the tree house," Ellis added as he passed through the room.

Caspian huffed and rubbed his head with both hands.

"A family trip with her ex and his fiancée," Caspian moaned. "What the hell was I thinking!"

Taliesan and Ellis burst out laughing.

"She must really be special," Ellis said, just as Kannon and Bodhi came bounding down the stairs.

The sun was high and giving off a lot of heat in spite of the cool temperature. The lines were long for the makeshift ice skating rink around Atlantic Station, and the kids were bursting with energy. The boys were playing a game of keep-away with Lena, and she was growing more and more agitated. She was outnumbered, and she didn't like it. Farai joined the ruckus to help even out the disparity. Her long, thick hair was sectioned in several rows of twists braided close to her scalp, and she was wearing a loose knit cap to the back of her head. Her freckles and jewel-like eyes were bright with happiness, as she won the children over with her carefree nature.

Caspian liked her. He'd done his research on both she and Oliver. He'd found that she was quite a celebrity in France and in Ethiopia, the country of her parents.

She wasn't filthy rich, but she had amassed an impressive fortune. Oliver was an up and coming celebrity chef in his own right, but Caspian was sure that it was, in part, due to being Farai Sikebo's American lover.

He had read several articles about Lacey's ex and his restaurants. He and Farai often appeared in French tabloids and blogs—arm-in-arm at film festivals, celebrity weddings, and club openings.

"She's something," Caspian said to Oliver, watching his fiancée frolic in her expensive, designer jeans and sneakers.

Oliver beamed.

"She is. She doesn't get this kind of freedom from the paparazzi in France. She's in heaven when she's here." Oliver rubbed his hairless chin.

"I wonder what's taking Lacey so long? I should've gone to help her," Caspian looked around for Lacey.

"If the line for cocoa is as long as this one is, she's probably still waiting. She'll call if she needs help. Trust me." Oliver gave a half shrug. "She has no problem speaking up."

The men laughed uneasily. The smell of popcorn and hot cocoa filled the air, making Caspian regret not eating something before coming out.

"Man, I am starving!"

"When Lacey gets back, I can take you over to this Mexican spot I know. My friend runs the kitchen. It's right across the square." Oliver pointed out the restaurant. "It'll give us an opportunity to talk, without the girls."

Caspian gritted his teeth; his nostrils flared.

"I mean, if you're down with that," Oliver said, holding up both hands. "I think we should get to know a little about each other since you're going to be spending time with my son. That's fair, right?"

Caspian relaxed his posture and shoved his hands in his pockets. He rolled his neck and looked around for Lacey again.

"Yeah. Sounds good."

Lacey appeared carrying two large Thermoses and a small stack of paper cups. Caspian teased that it was her turn to hold the line, while he and Oliver went to grab a snack. She searched his face for clues before suspiciously agreeing to hold their places in line. She grabbed him by the knit scarf he was wearing and drew him in for a light kiss.

"You sure?" She probed.

He studied her face and eyes, before kissing her on the cheek.

"Yes. We'll be right back. Oliver knows a guy."

"Oliver always knows a guy," Lacey mocked and kissed him again.

Farai and Lacey stood watching their partners walk across the square meandering between the crowds until they were completely out of sight.

The restaurant was loud and crowded. A mariachi band was roaming the aisles singing and playing, amid hurrying waiters carrying trays and pitchers. The sounds and smells of sizzling onions, peppers, and beef blended together like a beautiful symphony. Caspian could hardly wait to eat. As promised Oliver took him right behind the bar to the bustling kitchen. He hugged a short, portly Latino man and motioned for Caspian to come meet the guy.

"Hey Cas, this is my man, Augie. He runs the joint," Oliver said.

Caspian shook the jolly chef's hand.

"We go way back. We used to bang at an after-hours spot, that was half restaurant, half club," the man chuckled. "Well, you can use my office." Augie led the men to an office off the side of the kitchen. Hesitance glared in Caspian's narrowed eyes, but Augie's sing-song banter put him at ease, and he followed the men to the little office. Augie left the door cracked and left Oliver and Caspian alone. A young woman appeared carrying beers and a pitcher of water shortly after Augie's departure. She left the room briefly and returned with a black stone bowl of guacamole and another bowl of hot tortilla chips, which she placed on the table between the two men.

"Augie's going to bring us a couple of tacos and shit to take to the kids," Oliver laughed, answering Caspian's unexpressed question.

"OK. Cool. So what's this little sidebar really about, Oliver?"

Caspian adjusted his posture; he straightened his back and leaned forward, lacing his fingers in front of his face. Oliver adjusted in his chair and looked directly in Caspian's eyes.

"What are you doing with Lacey? You don't seem very..." Oliver looked up, searching for the right word. "Open."

"Open?"

"Yeah. You seem guarded. And Lacey doesn't need to be hurt again."

"Again, huh?" Caspian chuckled and pushed his back against the chair. "You have to excuse, me man. But, you may not be the best person to speak on that."

"I may not be, but here we are?" Oliver leaned toward Caspian. "Look, I promise you, man. There is no beef here. None. What Lacey and I had is long gone. But we are Luca's parents, and I get to question your intentions when they directly affect my son. Surely you get that?" Oliver said.

Caspian spread his legs and rested an elbow on his knee.

"I hear you, and I fully understand your concern. I respect that." He sat back and crossed his leg across his thigh. "But I don't like being summoned to your friend's office to be interrogated. And quite frankly, I don't know what I want to happen between Lacey and me. I like her. I like her a lot. And I do think about Luca. He's a great little man. Look, I know that Lacey's a mother. None of that is lost on me. I'm no fool, nor am I a selfish man. I respect that Luca is a major factor in any relationship I pursue with Lacey."

Oliver looked at Caspian's face, then lowered his head and fingered at his hair.

"It's all unfolding very slowly and very deliberately, and that's out of consideration for Luca. I'm sorry, but I don't know what more I can give you than my word. I have no negative intentions where Lacey and Luca are concerned. I am not, nor will I ever lead her on, and I hope she knows that," Caspian said.

Augie and the young lady came back into the room carrying brown bags and more Thermoses. He took the untouched guacamole and chips and returned with them bagged up, too. Caspian thanked the man and his assistant, before stepping outside to wait for Oliver.

"Look, Cas - Can I call you Cas?" Oliver said without waiting for an answer.

"I appreciate your honesty, but it's not enough for me." He held up his free hand. "I get that I don't get to call any shots in Lacey's life—I never really did," Oliver remarked. "But I am going to share this conversation with her—for her own knowledge. She likes you, and she's not the kind of woman who gets into casual affairs. So I think she should know."

The corners of Caspian's mouth turned down.

"That's fair."

"I'd prefer it if you had this conversation with her. I think she'd appreciate having all of the information so she can decide how she wants to handle this thing between you two." Oliver stopped and faced Caspian before they crossed the square. "I gotta keep it one hundred with you, man. I don't like you going on family dates with my son and niece. I mean, considering the fact that you don't know what the hell you want."

The men stood staring at each other, their arms full of brown bags and Thermoses.

"And Cas, you seem like a real straight-laced kind of dude. I mean, you run banks and shit. So I can't buy the whole, you don't know what you want deal. Hell, I'd bet you've known exactly what you've wanted all of your life. You're just not sure you're ready for a ready-made family - the responsibility - the constraints. You like the setup you have with your nephews. I don't blame you! It's a sweet deal, but it's not on the menu. Talk to her before I leave at the end of the month. Please, brother. I really, really don't need the drama."

Oliver's words played on a loop in Caspian's mind. He was completely out of sorts. He felt lost and out of control of his own love life. It was all unfamiliar territory, and he missed his friend Beaux terribly.

The day had ended well. Bodhi and Kannon were passed out by the time Caspian got them home. The sun was sinking, and his sister and brother-in-law were sitting out on the deck when he returned from putting the boys to bed. Ellis offered Caspian a scotch and returned with the bottle and a glass.

"You look like you need this," Ellis said, handing Caspian the glass, filling it half way.

Caspian lay out on the patio lounger beside the ceramic fire pit and gulped down the first glass. Ellis poured him another, as Taliesan looked on, wrapped in a flannel blanket.

"You wanna tell us what's going on, Cas?" Taliesan asked cautiously.

Caspian closed his eyes and covered his forehead with his empty hand.

"I miss my friend."

"Who?"

"I think he means, Beaux," Ellis answered.

"Lacey is serious business," Caspian exhaled.

"Lacey is serious business? Help me out here, Little Brother."

"She's not the casual-affair kind of woman, Lucky." He drank from the glass again.

"No. She doesn't strike me as the type."

Taliesan eyed her lanky husband, who sat beside her on the lounger. Ellis put a finger to his mouth, hushing her. Taliesan tilted her head and pursed her lips.

"I like her," he shook his head but kept his eyes closed. "I mean, look at her. She's special, but she's also a mother."

Taliesan listened without speaking.

"And don't get me wrong, Luca's a great kid, but he's full-time. I can't just drop him off, tuck him in and bounce." Caspian sighed deeply. "They need a full-time commitment. And I don't know if I'm ready for all of that. But, I'm not ready to lose them either."

The beleaguered man sat up and looked for his sister and brother-in-law. He looked startled to find them sitting quietly next to him on the deck.

"Lucky, I'm all messed up. I don't want to lose her, but going any further feeling this way will only complicate matters. What if I decide that I don't want a kid?"

Taliesan could no longer hold her peace.

"What do you mean, you don't want kids? Since when?" She shouted.

Caspian looked away, his sister's eyes bore into him.

"Well?"

"I don't want to make the same mistakes our father made, Lucky," Caspian simpered. "My work is important to me. All of those years, I resented him for putting the work first, and now I'm doing the same thing. But I've been careful to not bring kids into the equation."

"Do you hear yourself?" Taliesan shot upright and spun to face her brother full on.

"Will the work care for you when you're sick? Will the work put your affairs in order when you're at the end of your days? Did you learn nothing from Beaux? Baby brother, time is not promised to anyone. So please don't let the work swallow you up, and let you find yourself all alone—when it's too late. Cas, I'm not telling you to commit to Lacey, or not. I'm only asking that you not take family out of the equation."

"Under no circumstances will your work ever fulfill you like raising a family, baby brother," Ellis added.

*****

Caspian called Lacey and asked her to meet him at his place. The house was dark when Lacey arrived. She used the key Caspian had given her and found him in the garage out back. He didn't stir when he heard the backdoor bang. Lacey had never been on the inside of the detached garage. It was a place that had been off limits because it was the place Caspian retreated to whenever he became cold and out of touch.

She pulled the shawl collar of her coat tightly around her neck, and leaned against the door jam, waiting for him to speak.

"This was my dad's car," Caspian said from underneath the hood of the old Mustang. "He loved this car. He loved this car and flying more than anything. I love my job too, Lacey. I know what to do when I'm there. I know exactly who I am when I'm at work."

Lacey's whole face contorted, but Caspian had yet to look up at her.

"I've strategically avoided starting a family because I promised myself to never put my family after my work. I would never want to make my son feel unimportant. I would never want my son to feel less than a piece of metal!" Caspian said, slamming his wrench against the engine, startling Lacey.

"Caspian, what are you saying, right now? I've never asked you to make Luca and me your family? Is that what you're getting at?"

Caspian winced. He slowly lifted his head looking into her piercing eyes, and walked closer to where she was standing with her arms folded angrily.

"I know that, Lace. I know. But, you deserve that. You don't deserve to be strung along by anyone who doesn't know what the hell they want. Luca's a kid. He shouldn't be getting attached to some dude, who may just decide that this is all too much for him."

Lacey was stunned. She stumbled backward, away from Caspian. She opened her mouth, but no words formed. She stared at a slight imperfection in the painted wood planks of the garage.

"Lace? Are you OK?" Caspian asked.

Lacey shook her head and blinked hard. She formed her lips around phantom words. A tear rolled down her cheek, and she formed her mouth, trying again.

"Fuck you, Caspian Pearce," she whispered.

Caspian wiped his hands on a dirty towel and tossed it across the garage. He moved towards her, and she backed away holding her hand up with her palm facing outward.

"Fuck you for saying that. Who do you think you are? Who do think I am?"

He took another step towards Lacey, and she took another step back.

"My son has a father; he has grandfathers and uncles! Luca Barnett has no void in need of filling," she said, pointing angrily at him.

Genuine regret washed over Caspian's face, and he lunged and took Lacey by the arms.

"Lacey, I'm getting this all wrong. That's not what I mean. I'm trying to be honest with you about my intentions," he pleaded into the curve of her neck.

"Your intentions?" An angry Lacey said as she pushed out of his embrace. "What makes your intentions more important than mine?"

Caspian stood blinking, dumbfounded. He plopped against the back of his father's car, shaking his head.

"Caspian, we're just getting to know each other. The only reason you know my family is because yours is all mixed up with mine! I don't know what I want from this," she said, pointing between the two of them. "I hadn't even considered it. I like you. I feel comfortable with you. I like the freedom you make me feel, even if it's only for a night or two every other week or so. My time with you is mine. I'm no one's mom. I'm no one's boss. I'm no one's heir. I'm just a girl in a t-shirt and panties sleeping in, next to a handsome and accomplished man who has absolutely no expectations of me," she said as tears glistened in her golden eyes. "My immediate intentions for us were to continue on in this non-committed, free from stress and expectations manner until one or both of us had had enough and move on in a mature manner."

Caspian stood watching the strikingly beautiful woman express everything he felt, but couldn't articulate. His crotch stiffened, and he held out his

274

hands towards Lacey. She took them and let him cradle her in his arms. He kissed her on her neck and face and lifted her off her feet. He carried her into the house kissing her passionately. Caspian laid her on the bed and stood, letting her unzip him from the oily coveralls he was wearing. He slipped her arms out of her coat and lifted her silk camisole over her head. He took in every inch of Lacey's creamy flesh before burying his face between her large breasts. The couple made love as heatedly as they ever had.

The sun woke Caspian to find himself alone in his bed with the key he'd given Lacey on the nightstand. He called out to her, but he was alone. His head pounded and his heart thumped in his throat. He frantically looked around for his phone and called Lacey, she answered on the first ring.

"Good morning, Handsome."

The airiness in her voice threw him off guard.

"Where'd you go?"

"I'm turning on Glen Iris right now," she answered.

"Why did you leave Lacey," his voice was hard.

"I'm going home to put up the Christmas tree with my son, Cas."

They were obviously in some kind of battle, and Lacey had the upper hand.

"Why'd you leave your key?"

"I don't want things to get muddled."

"Muddled?" he asked. "Look Lacey I'm not interested in playing games."

"OK. Got it. Well, I'm turning into the parking garage and will probably lose you, so have a good day. I'll try to reach you later. Last night was great, Cas. Thanks for everything."

Oliver watched the mother of his child buzz about hanging ornaments and stringing lights. Lacey's spirits were high, and she was glowing.

"I guess you saw Caspian last night," he teased when he was sure they were out of earshot of everyone else.

"I did," Lacey sang. "What's it matter to you?"

"Lace, I want you to be happy; I just don't want you to get hurt."

She glowered at Oliver.

"I'll ask you again. What does it matter to you?"

She put a hand on her hip and glared at her son's father.

"How you feel affects Luca."

Lacey squinted her eyes and put her hands on her hips.

"Well, Oliver, if you must know, I ended it last night."

He surveyed her face.

"You OK?"

"I am," she nodded. "He somehow got it in his head that I wanted him to be more of a presence in Luca's life." She twisted her full mouth and leaned against the granite counter tops facing Oliver. "I told him that my son had no void that needed to filled, and he said that he understood. But I know that he'd never be the same again."

Oliver cast his eyes down and twisted at his hair. He stood shoulder to shoulder with Lacey.

"How so?"

She shrugged.

"He was for me. You know? Just an escape from the pressures of being me. With Cas, I was just me—not mommy, not the boss, not CEO of anything. He didn't want or need anything from me, and I needed that."

Oliver closed his eyes and rounded his shoulders. "I'm sorry, Lace," he said. "I'm sure he'll come to his senses."

"I ended it. He'll always see me as a bag lady, and that negates everything I gained from the relationship. So I ended it; and all is well, Oliver. So don't worry about me."

"Lace. Please don't give up on love. You deserve it."

"Yeah, yeah, yeah!"

He took her by the shoulders and looked straight into her eyes.

"Promise me," he ordered. "I want our son to see his mommy in love. You're beautiful when you're in love, Lace."

Blood & Water

Camisha felt like crap, but she was really looking forward to seeing Sunrise perform with her band. The sisters hadn't seen each other since Christmas.

Sunrise had accepted a tour with Gabriel's band. She thought it would be good for both she and her mother to get away for a while. They traveled to Detroit, Michigan, West Palm Beach, Florida, New Orleans and Philadelphia before they renewed Ursula's passport and flew to Stockholm, Copenhagen, Mexico, and Canada.

Sunrise sent pictures and postcards to Lena and Luca at every stop. She had taken to her new role as Auntie and loved every minute of it.

Lennox stood with his ear pressed to the bathroom door listening to his wife wretch and heave over the cold toilet bowl. He squeezed his eyes tight against the image of her crouched over the toilet, watery-eyed from the violent contractions. He felt helpless.

"Babe, let me get you something," he pleaded.

"Water," she gagged.

He hurried to the kitchen and was back in a flash. The bathroom door was open, and Camisha was bent over the sink splashing water into her mouth. Lennox walked in and sat the glass on the counter. He rubbed her lower back as she brushed her teeth.

"It wasn't this bad with Lena. Was it?"

Camisha glanced at her husband's reflection in the mirror; she shook her head back and forth. The worry on his face made her feel awful. She put a playful pout on her face and winked at him.

"Ali, I promise you I'm fine. The baby's fine. No two pregnancies are exactly the same. Dr. Stone already told you that."

"I hear you, but it's six thirty in the evening—well past morning. So what's up with the morning sickness? I don't think we should go."

Camisha spun around so quickly she nearly knocked Lennox over.

"Oh, we're going, Mr. Robinson!" She softened her voice and laid her head on his broad, athletic chest. "It's Valentine's day. And I haven't seen Sunny in months."

Lennox raised an eyebrow and smirked, revealing his deep dimples. He picked her up like a child and held her at his eye level.

"If I see one sign of nausea, we're leaving, and if this place is smoky, we're leaving. Deal?"

Camisha dangled from Lennox's six-foot frame. She lifted her chin and saluted her husband.

"Deal!"

He glared at her, and then kissed her on the forehead.

"You really love me," she joked.

"I do."

The accommodations were just as Sunrise promised, and the venue was free of smoke. After they had cleared the VIP entrance, they were greeted by Candace. "I'll be your personal concierge for the evening," she said.

Candace was wearing a short, black dress and very high heels. She led the party upstairs to a plush balcony with eight high back armchairs lined up in four neat rows. There were large floral arrangements at each corner of the space, and partitions, which were drawn halfway, separating their space from the one adjoining. Candace took drink and food orders and left Camisha, Lennox, and Lacey to get settled.

"These seats are nice."

"Right? This place looks nothing like this from the outside." Lennox said.

"It feels like we're here to see an opera."

"An opera in Italy!" Lacey added.

"Good evening."

The deep rasp in Caspian's voice was especially alluring after not having heard it in months.

Lacey crossed her legs tightly, fighting against the arousal of her libido. She took a deep breath, adjusted her eyeglasses, and attempted a smile in his direction. His whiskey colored brown eyes twinkled, and the corners of his mouth crept up reluctantly. He helped Ursula into the suite and sat her on the front row, where everyone greeted her with reverence.

Taliesan and Ellis walked in behind Ursula. Caspian made introductions before disappearing behind the velvet curtain. Taliesan watched Lacey as she watched him leave. She moved to the empty chair beside her.

"Hi, Lacey. It's been a long time."

Lacey shifted uncomfortably and pushed her glasses up her button nose again.

"It has. How are you? And the boys?"

Her face brightened, and sincerity shone in her light eyes at the mention of Taliesan's boys.

"We're great. Thanks for asking. How's Luca? He's a really great kid, Lacey."

Lacey thanked her, quickly turning her attention back to the stage. The band had come on and was tuning their instruments.

"He misses you," Taliesan said plainly. "And he knows that he messed up."

Lacey stiffened. She looked up at the velvet draping above them and then to the back of brother's head. She willed him to turn around and save her from the conversation Taliesan was trying to draw her into.

"I won't push. But, I thought you should know how deeply his time with you affected him."

Lacey remained perfectly still, even resisting the urge to blink.

"You look very nice tonight. But you always do."

"Thank you," Lacey barely squeaked out, before excusing herself.

She practically ran down the hall, bumping into Candace.

"I'm sorry," Lacey said. "I'm looking for the restroom."

Lacey braced herself against the bathroom sink and stared at her reflection, but her expression was unfamiliar. It was flustered, and it infuriated her. She squinted behind the lenses of her eyeglasses and summoned the steady soldier inside of her. She dabbed at the corners of her eyes, powdered her nose and forehead, and left to rejoin her family. Caspian was standing outside of the suite on a call that he ended as Lacey approached.

"Hi, Lacey."

His voice did it again. It effortlessly called up her libido. She looked all over his painfully handsome face and ran her hands over the seascape printed dress that hugged her every curve. Caspian's eyes stalled at her heaving cleavage.

"I'm sorry," he said, shaking his head.

"We already did this part," Lacey said coldly.

"We have. So let me cut to the chase,"

"The chase?" Lacey said.

"If that's what it takes."

Fire flashed in her eyes, but the corners of her pouty lips twitched upwards, encouraging Caspian.

"Is that what I need to do," he said as he reached for her hands.

"No," she said, pulling them behind her back. "Come on, Lace. I miss you."

She leaned in and sneered. "I haven't even heard from you, Caspian Pearce!"

"Have you wanted to?"

Lacey's balled up her manicured hands in frustration. She bit down on her bottom lip and shook her head pointedly.

"No. I'm not doing this, this cutesy stuff with you?" She wagged her finger at him.

Caspian reached for her hands again, but she refused and took another step backward.

"Damn it, Lacey Robinson. You did this!" He raised an open hand and shook it in her direction. "You left me, and then gave me your ass to kiss. You wouldn't take my calls. What was I supposed to do?"

Just as the argument had reached its height, Candace walked into the hallway, interrupting the reunion. Caspian grabbed Lacey by the arm and took her to another corridor, an empty one. He studied her face. It was carefully composed. Her mouth was taut, and her eyes had turned cold.

"I'm sorry, Lacey. I'm sorry," he said, holding out both hands, his palms facing her and his eyes steady on hers. "I'm coming at you all wrong." He lowered his head and ran a hand over it. "We were good. Right? We were great! Then Oliver filled my head with all of that stuff about Luca, and how our relationship could negatively affect him. It called up all of my shit."

Lacey's entire demeanor changed. She blinked hard and tilted her head, sending long soft layers of her hair cascading over one eye. She fingered them away from her face, revealing its full incandescence.

"What does Oliver have to do with any of this?"

"We talked that day we took the kids ice skating. Remember when we walked over to that Mexican restaurant?"

"Yeah. Go on," Lacey said.

"He wanted to talk to me about Luca."

"Wait. So all of that talk about being a father to Luca was planted by Oliver?"

Lacey crossed her arms and shifted her weight to one leg. The fire returned to her eyes and glowed dangerously. Caspian touched her elbow.

"Lace, calm down. He was thinking about his son. Like any loving and concerned dad would. He had every right to know what my intentions were. And he was right. What happens to you, does affect Luca. I'm living proof of that," he gestured to himself. "Seeing my mom sad all the time really messed with me, Lace. And I would never want to make Luca feel a minute of the pain I felt as a kid seeing my mom that way."

Lacey's posture relaxed, and her features softened. Caspian moved closer and unfolded her arms; he held her hands in his.

"I want to be who you need me to be. You want me to be your escape? I hear that. You want to be, just Lacey with me - no titles, no responsibilities, no expectations - when you're with me. I hear that, too."

Lacey felt unbalanced and swayed a little.

"I hear you, Lacey. And I want to be whoever you need me to be for you."

He embraced her and whispered in her ear.

"And if or when things change," he held her face in his hands and kissed her, biting her lower lip softly. "We'll figure it out, together, you and me. We're highly intelligent and capable adults," he joked. "Please, let me be who you need."

Lacey nearly melted under his touch. She squeezed her eyes tight and tried to recall ever being kissed in the way he kissed her. When she looked at him, her golden green eyes shone as bright as the sun. They walked back to the suite hand in hand. Lennox, Taliesan, and

Ursula all beamed when the couple sat side by side and hand in hand.

The band played a set of vintage jazz, and another of popular music, like TLC's Creep played in a 1940's big band style. Sunrise came alive on stage. Something in the music transformed her usual child-like expressions to those of an undeniably sexy grown woman. The smokiness of her singing voice and the twinkle in her eye made her virtually unrecognizable.

It was Camisha's first time seeing Sunrise on stage, and the pride in their faces lit up the club. Their expressions filled Sunrise with emotion. Her eyes glistened from behind the piano.

The atmosphere backstage was so cool. Ellis remarked that he half expected the Rat Pack to come out of dressing rooms marked with glittery stars, but it was Sunrise who walked around the corner.

Gone was the sultry songstress and back was the fresh-faced thirty-something in bare feet and toe rings.

She rushed into her big sister's outstretched arms.

"Sunny! You guys were amazing! And you," Camisha rocked her back and forth. "You were stunning. Stunning! And you look so different under the bright lights. What are you thinking about when you're up there?"

All of her guests looked on with wide eyes and bright smiles, anticipating her answer. She shyly raised a shoulder. A half grin tugged at a corner of her Cupid's bow mouth.

"I'm not thinking. I only see the music. You know? The meters and rhythms, the half and quarter notes, the rests and clefs," she savored the images.

Only Ursula related, and she beamed proudly.

Gabriel came around the corner carrying a chair. He kissed Ursula on her cheek and helped her get comfortable.

"Hi, Gabe! You're looking rather dashing," Lacey said.

"Well, I try. The bright lights can be unforgiving," Gabe joked, hugging her.

He was dressed in classic black slacks and suspenders, a tuxedo shirt with a bow tie undone and hanging freely around the open collar. He'd rolled his shirt sleeves up to his forearms. In his usual manner, he boisterously greeted the rest of the small group. He'd lost a few pounds and looked more fit.

"Gabe Man!" Lennox said, dapping him up. "You're looking strong; what have you been doing out there on the road?"

Gabe laughed proudly.

"Thanks for noticing. Thanks. Thanks." He flexed his developing biceps. "Hey Man, being around the bunch of you fit models got me off of my fat behind and into motion."

The men all laughed and congratulated Gabe on his hard work.

"Now that's a first for me," Ellis said. "My physique has never inspired anyone. But I'll take the compliment!"

They all laughed again.

Camisha invited everyone over to their home for brunch the following day. She and Lennox had some news that they wanted to share with the group. The announcement caused Sunrise's stomach to ache.

"Could you come over a little earlier tomorrow," Camisha asked as she hugged her sister once more.

The group said their goodnights and headed their separate ways—Lacey with Caspian, and Taliesan with Ellis.

*****

Sunrise was greeted by the scents of breakfast food in the afternoon, intermingled with quick banter and children's laughter. She drove the jeep to the rear of the house like a regular. Camisha waved energetically from the covered carport while Sunrise unpacked the bags and casserole dishes Gabriel had sent ahead with her. Camisha helped unpack Sunrise's things and asked her to join her in the basement.

Sunrise had never been to Camilla's bedroom, and it felt weird being among her things. There were still half used perfume bottles and a beat up old cosmetic bag on the dresser. Her gaudy clothes and bent high heels filled the closet. Camisha sat on the bed and pointed to a chair in the corner, which Sunrise declined, sitting beside her sister on the bed instead.

"I wanted to talk to you about a few things. I want you to hear it first—I'm pregnant!"

Sunrise's jaw dropped, and she hugged Camisha enthusiastically.

"Congratulations! I'm so happy for you guys!"

"Thank you. We're really excited. But there's more."

Camisha pushed her hands together and put them to her mouth. She took a deep breath.

"Sunny, we're moving to California in the spring."

"The Spring?" Sunrise said, her eyes filling up with tears.

"Late Spring. May," Camisha said.

The sisters sat quietly holding hands.

"It's a great opportunity for Ali, and I'll get to help him build something from the ground up. I'll finally get to put my Masters in Finance to use. And you're traveling again," she added.

Sunrise wiped at her face with the back of her hand.

"I'm happy for you guys. What part of California?"

"Sonoma."

"Wine Country. It's beautiful up there."

"It's where Ali and I honeymooned. We'll be launching an organic wine and producing a line with a group of his college friends."

"Wow. Now I'm really happy for you guys. Black folks making wine," she said, attempting a bit of humor.

"OK, so I'll have to put the West Coast on our gig list. West Coast swing," she remarked to herself. "It'll be good."

"Sunny, there's one more thing I want to discuss with you. And if I'm overstepping, just say so, and I'll shut up. OK?"

"OK," Sunrise drawled.

"It's about my Dad. Our father,"

Sunrise took a pillow from the bed and held it against her chest.

"He'd really like to get to know you. He'd like to spend some time with you—when you're ready, of course."

Sunrise shifted on the bed and pulled her legs underneath her bottom, but said nothing.

"I don't need another father. I've already had the best."

"I know. I don't think he wants to try to replace Beaux. He cared a great deal for your dad."

"He hardly knew him," Sunrise snapped.

Camisha took a brief break to let Sunrise cool.

"Look, I get what he means to you, but I don't want him. I don't need him. I don't mean to be a jerk about it, but it's how I feel. You and I aren't the same. You represent a youthful indiscretion—a character building misstep. But me, I am the result of a willful betrayal. I represent his uncontrollable desire to be with Camilla," Sunrise's said, her voice quaked. "I am a painful manifestation of Evangeline's inability to give her husband children. And she can't stand to see me; she won't stand for it."

Camisha wrapped her arms around her sister's trembling shoulders.

"You don't know that, Sunny. Give them a chance. Evangeline is a wonderful person, loving and kind."

"She told my mom."

Camisha narrowed her eyes and tilted her head to look into her sister's red-rimmed eyes.

"She told your mom what?"

"That she wouldn't stand for me, so there it is. I won't push. I don't need a father figure."

Sunrise unfolded her legs and neatly placed the pillow back in its original spot on the bed.

"Is there a bathroom down here? I don't want Mommy to see me this way. She doesn't need to worry about me."

"Sunny...I invited them here today."

Sunrise nodded and left the room.

Camisha's homemade biscuits had become one of her best recipes. They rose tall and fluffy, with golden brown tops. She sliced them open and gave them a place of honor at the makeshift brunch buffet. She sliced country ham and fried eggs.

She sat out Gruyere and cheddar cheeses alongside peach jam and raw honey for the breakfast sandwiches.

There was fresh, cut fruit and creamy stone grits. She loved feeding her family.

The tables were set, the coffee was brewed, and everyone had arrived. Looking around the room at all of her family brought up many emotions, but most of all gratitude. Camisha had spent most of her life an only child, and then Oliver came along. And until she met Lennox, it had only been her, Camilla and Oliver. A few short years later, her home was brimming with people who loved her and called her family; it made her heart full.

The big sister in her wouldn't let her simply revel in the warmth. She couldn't block out what Sunrise had told her about Evangeline's flat-out rejection. *Had she forbidden their father from having a relationship with Sunrise? Did he know that Evangeline had spurned her sister—his daughter? How could she maintain a relationship with her stepmother, knowing that she'd turned away her own flesh and blood?*

The questions flooded her and boxed around with her good feelings. She kept her attention on Evangeline and Sunrise for any signs of discourse, but there were none. Evangeline was as pleasant and unassuming as she was the first day she and James had shown up at

Camisha's house for Thanksgiving, as guests of Lennox's dad. If nothing, the woman was the picture of grace.

Lennox clinked his water glass and called for everyone's attention. The chattering subsided as his family all turned to him and Camisha as they stood arm in arm, all smiles.

"As you all know, we have a couple of major announcements we'd like to share with you, our loved ones,"

"Mom and Dad aren't here," Lacey shouted.

"They already know!" Lennox shot back.

"Of course they do,"

Everyone laughed at the bratty exchange between the Robinson siblings.

"OK," Lennox looked down at his wife. "We're expecting baby number two!"

Camisha glowed, and Lennox couldn't have been more proud, amid the pats on the back and handshakes.

Lena twirled around singing, "I'm going to be a big sister, just like my mommy!"

"There's more," Camisha said, rubbing her hands together. She inhaled as much air into her lungs as possible and let it out slowly. Lennox gave her hand a gentle squeeze and motioned for Lena to join them.

"We're moving to California in May."

The California news didn't go over as well as the baby news. Mouths hung open, eyes shined with tears, and there were a few barely audible congratulations.

Sunrise pouted like a baby and Ursula wrapped a thin, wrinkled arm around her daughter's shoulder. Lacey sat wide-eyed, but silent as Caspian rubbed her back.

Evangeline stood and hugged the couple.

Camisha asked if she could have a word with her afterward, to which Evangeline agreed.

"I know you've considered all the important things, and have made this decision because it's what you think is best for your family. I'm proud of you, Son," James whispered to Lennox, shaking his hand.

He turned to his wife and respectfully asked if she were ready to leave.

"No!" She snapped and returned to her seat without another word to James.

Camisha and Lennox noticed the icy exchange and returned to their seats, too. They spent the rest of the meal cuddled against one another, answering questions about the new addition and the move to the West Coast.

Gabe pulled his thick wavy hair into a man bun and cleaned the last of the dishes, before taking Ursula and Sunrise home. James lingered around with Lennox in the basement, at his daughter's request.

"Do you know what that's about?"

The older man gestured towards the closed basement door, where they'd left their wives.

"I do," was all Lennox offered and clicked on the TV.

Camisha fretted about, wiping counters and folding kitchen towels.

"You want to talk to me about Sunrise."

Evangeline's matter of fact tone rattled Camisha.

The regal woman held out her hand, inviting Camisha to sit beside her on the couch. Camisha joined her stepmother but struggled to look at her. She'd always been wowed by the woman's style. Evangeline had a luminosity about her; she was fabulously chic and exuded refinement, but at that moment, all Camisha could see in the woman she so admired, was unkindness.

"I've expected this conversation, so I'm ready. Give it to me."

Evangeline sat patiently, allowing Camisha all the time she needed to express herself. She loved Camisha.

She'd never had a moment of ill will towards her husband's lovechild, and over the five years of getting to know her, she'd grown to truly love her. The perplexity in Camisha's eyes tore her apart.

"Did you tell Ms. Ursula that you wouldn't stand for Sunrise?" Camisha's voice was small.

Evangeline crossed her long thin legs at the ankles. She tucked a sparkling strand of silver hair behind her ear. She twirled the pearl earring she was wearing in her ear.

"Cami, I love you...and, I've always known about you. Your mother was carrying you when she came to my office." The woman touched her own stomach. "But you already know all of that. Camilla kept us at a distance, so I was able to move in this world, to stay in my marriage because you were out of sight. Your conception was a character building obstacle for our marriage, a youthful indiscretion."

Camisha flinched at hearing the "youthful indiscretion" characterization again.

"I justified your father's night with Camille as a one night stand, a one-time thing. We were newly married. He hardly knew me. He didn't love me enough yet."

Evangeline tapped at the pooling moisture in her eyes and rubbed her hands together.

"When we walked into your house that day, I saw James in your eyes. I saw James in your manner. It was James in your voice, not her. But Sunrise," her voice broke. "She is all Camille. She is irrefutable evidence that on my husband's worse day, he turned to her...again. Sunrise is irrefutable evidence that I can't give life," she said as tears flooded her soft brown eyes. "I couldn't give my husband a family, but she could. When my family sees you, they see James, but her?"

Evangeline shook her head wildly.

"No! No! I'm sorry, Cami. I can't. I can't!"

Camisha hugged Evangeline tightly. She held on until the woman fell calm against her shoulder. The intense pain Evangeline emoted cut straight through Camisha, confusing her even more. How could she not understand Evangeline's deep-seated hurt?

"I gave him my whole life! And one look into her eyes and he wanted her. He wanted her!

He smiled when he read the DNA results. He was discreet. He probably doesn't even know that I know, that I saw him. I saw the twinkle in his eyes," Evangeline looked pleadingly at Camisha. "He has to see Camille when he looks at her. Hell! We all do. And I know it's not her fault. I know that! But if I have to sit across my goddamn table looking at her," she said, pointing angrily to her chest, "I can't stay married to him. And if I don't stay married to him, then what were all these years for? Camille Robbins has been around for my entire marriage! And then she was not. She was gone! And now, here comes Sunrise wearing her face. It's like that woman will never leave my marriage! I can't. I won't. I'm sorry, Cami. I love you, but I have to be done with your mother."

Evangeline's words haunted Camisha. She turned the situation over and over in her mind. She considered it as a parent and as a daughter. She considered it as a wife. She considered it as a sister, and as a friend. She'd barely survived the force of nature that was her mother, but she hadn't realized all the other lives that were left in Camilla's wake. Her mother's path of destruction was as wide as tornado alley, and the damage inflicted continued to maim those unfortunate enough to have been an intimate part of her life. Taking into account all of the things Camilla had kept secret - for whatever reasons, and all of the lives she had affected, Camisha considered herself one of the lucky ones.

*****

"That was James again," Lennox said, looking down at his wife.

Camisha and Lena sat in the middle of wrapping paper and moving boxes, in the little girls' pink and white bedroom. Lena was over the moon about her family's move. They'd gone out to Sonoma twice, and on the last trip, they'd taken Luca along. The kids loved running freely through the acres of fruit groves and rolling hills.

"Cam, you're going to have to talk to him."

"I know. I'll call him from the road," Cami giggled.

Lennox crouched beside his wife and kissed her on the cheek.

"Cam."

"I know. I know," she argued. "I'll call him back today."

"Good. You can call when I take Lena over to Lacey's."

Lacey had moved into her new home in Historic College Park and was all settled in. She and Caspian were growing closer, but still very cautiously. Lacey and Sunrise were also developing a relationship. Lacey gushed about the way Sunrise lived, and how much she admired her carefree spirit and genuinely loving nature.

She and Sunrise spent a lot of time with the kids. Ursula had moved into Sunrise's large Craftsman style home and was giving Luca piano lessons, much to Lena's dismay. But her parents promised to get her lessons when they got to California.

The day went by in a haze, and Lennox reminded his wife to call her dad as he fastened Lena into her booster seat.

James picked up on the first ring.

"Hi, Stranger. I was beginning to think you were going to leave without saying goodbye to your old man."

Guilt tugged at her Camisha for having avoided her father the weeks following her and Evangeline's conversation.

"I'm sorry, Dad. It's been crazy around here with all of the packing and this big belly. How are you and Evangeline?" she asked half-heartedly.

"I won't lie. Things aren't getting much better. But she hasn't left me," James said, mustering a small chuckle.

Camisha didn't know how to respond to her father's remark.

"Dad."

"Yes?"

"She won't deal with Sunrise."

"I know."

"What are you going to do?"

Camisha plopped down on the couch and listened to her dad breathe over the phone.

"I don't know. Right now I'm just waiting her out and praying she has a change of heart," James answered.

"I don't know, Dad. Sunrise's face tears her apart." Camisha said, putting her feet up on the couch. "She knows how Evangeline feels about her, and she doesn't want to push. You know how sweet she is. She doesn't want to cause anyone an ounce of pain."

James knew that Camisha was right. When he'd called Sunrise, she tearfully asked him to not contact her again. The sorrow in his daughter's voice ripped at his heart. She didn't deserve any of the rejection she'd experienced at the hands of the women in his life. He wanted nothing more than to make it all right for her.

He recognized her resilience and felt proud of her. Although she'd lived a privileged life, the last few years had thrown her a few nasty curveballs, all of which she handled with great poise. And through it all, she maintained her light and humanity.

"Dad, I want you to know that I love you and Evangeline both very much, but I love my sister, too."

"I want you to," James interjected.

"I'm sure you do. So I say this at great expense to my love for Evangeline. But you cannot let Sunrise live knowing that her biological father is in the same city and has chosen to not know her. You have to find a way to have a relationship with her, or you will regret it. And I will regret it."

James took in everything Camisha said to him.

"What do you suggest I do, Cami?

He sounded like a child, begging for an answer.

"I don't know. But, I know that you can't give up - on either of them. Promise me."

"I won't give up."

"Then I will employ every resource at my disposal to help you get through to them," Camisha promised.

Mocktails and Swallows

Sunrise stood on her front porch greeting her guests with a large wicker basket.

"Cell phones in the basket," she instructed with cheerful hellos, and I'm glad you made its. The women gladly surrendered their phones as they entered Sunrise's converted living room.

Camisha had misgivings when her younger sister called her with the crazy idea of throwing a sleepover in her honor, as a farewell party. One night while chatting on the phone with Sunrise, Camisha shared that she'd never had a birthday party as a child, or even been invited to one. The story made Sunrise sad, and she asked in disbelief,

"So you never got to have sleepovers or anything?"

Camisha laughed at the absurdity of her sister's question but never thought she'd be inspired to give her one. Camisha didn't have close women friends, and she'd never heard of grownups having a slumber party. But Lennox loved the idea and convinced his wife that it would be a good experience for her. She'd grown up an only child and didn't have many friends. While other little girls were at slumber parties, she was probably at home alone waiting up for her mother's return from a wild night out and worse. He painted images of sisters having slumber parties in their pretty pink bedrooms and painting each other's nails between their matching twin size canopy beds. A childhood Camisha would have loved, she admitted.

"Well, Sunrise is making it happen for you. Do it! Go, have a great time with your little sister," he smiled. "Go on, be a good big sister, Cam."

Lennox's little speech changed her entire mood and excited her about a farewell slumber party.

Sunrise had turned her already eclectic home into a blanket and pillow constructed fort that rivaled the souks of Marrakech. Blankets and quilts were suspended from the staircase and second-floor loft, covering the ceiling and walls. Strings of globe lights were draped around the room. Sequin throw pillows, oversized bed pillows, and colorful sofa cushions covered the hardwood floors. Taliesan brought three fitness balls and a sparkly disco ball that hung from Sunrise's antique lantern light fixture. There was a gourmet pizza station set up in the dining room. There were bowls of popcorn and smaller bowls of candy and nuts, and an elegant display of tall glasses of milk in champagne flutes and topped with giant M&M cookies. Camisha stood in the middle of the room taking in all of the loving details Sunrise had put into the slumber party she'd never had. Stacks of magazines, bowls of nail polish and face masks helped get the party started.

"I know that Cami's preggers, but we all aren't," Lacey said. "Please don't tell me there's no alcohol at this shindig."

Sunrise laughed and disappeared through the old west style kitchen doors. She returned carrying three miniature bottles of Moet with gold straws in them.

"For you, Mom." Ursula took a bottle from her hand. "And for you Lacey."

She sipped from her own bottle and held it up to her guests.

"Everyone grab a glass."

Taliesan handed a glass of milk to Camisha and clarified which was soy for her.

"I want to thank you all for coming to Cami's very first slumber party!"

They all cheered and clapped.

"I want to congratulate her and Lennox on their second baby, and ask her to please let me name my new niece or nephew," Sunrise smiled and bowed to Camisha. "I want to wish her great success in their new business venture and most sadly, bid her a fond farewell."

They held their bottles and glasses up to toast Camisha and said, "farewell" in unison. Lacey and Sunrise's eyes filled with tears, as they hugged their big sister.

The night was full of junk food, games, and laughs. They painted their nails and sang songs from their teenage years. As it got later, the women all picked out sleeping spots and settled in. Taliesan stretched her muscular thin legs and gracefully reached for her toes.

"Miss Lacey Robinson, what's my little brother been up to?" She asked casually.

Lacey adjusted a shaggy white throw pillow on her back.

"Work, as usual," Lacey answered. "Oh! He finally bought that Mustang after spending several of my and Luca's weekends at car lots all over the state. Luca, of course, loved the test drives, but I was bored to death. So I'm glad that's finally over."

"Really?" She looked up at Lacey and smiled broadly. "So he finally bought his own? Well, that's great news!" Taliesan gushed. "Great news!"

Curiosity spread across Lacey's face.

"What's so great about it? It's just a car."

Ursula, Taliesan, and Sunrise exchanged knowing looks.

"Our dad was into race cars. And he loved that old Fastback that Caspian keeps in the garage in his backyard, but he died before he finished restoring it," Taliesan explained.

"He never let Caspian work on that old car with him. And he knew how much that child loved that car and how much he needed to spend time with him," Ursula inserted.

"So after dad died, Beaux put the car in storage for when Caspian wanted it. He got the car, but it took him years before he restarted dad's restoration work on it."

"Haven't you noticed that he only went out there when something was bothering him?" Sunrise said.

"Or when he was mulling something important over," Taliesan added.

The three women nodded in agreement.

"So him getting his own means a lot," Camisha noted. "I get it. He's stepping out of his father's shadow. I totally relate to that."

"Yeah. And he's really looking forward to racing it, once it's all ready for that."

"Racing it!" Taliesan and Sunrise asked at the same time.

"Yes." Lacey noticed their surprise. "You do know that he races cars? On the weekends. He's taken me a few times. It's very scary. But, he comes alive out there," a thoughtful smile crossed Lacey's mouth. "He's a completely different man when he's at the track."

"How did I not know that about my brother? He is full of surprises."

"A man of mystery," Sunrise joked. "Your turn, Cami!" Sunrise nudged her sister.

"My turn for what?"

"We've heard what Lacey and Caspian are up to, so what are you up to these days?"

Camisha moved her hands over her belly.

"Well, you all know that I'm growing a life in here, and let's see. You all know that I'm moving to California,"

"Boo!" Lacey cried out, sending the ladies into wild laughter. "Tell us about how you're feeling about working with your husband's ex-girlfriend."

Camisha squeezed her eyes and lips shut. She crinkled her nose at her sister-in-law.

"You're such a brat, Lacey!" She laughed.

"You're going into business with your husband and his ex-girlfriend!" Ursula screamed. "Are you sure you're moving to California and not Utah?"

They all laughed again and waited for Camisha's explanation for the odd arrangement. She got comfortable and drank from her milk.

"Ali and Kai are both Ad men, and they started working with Ali's college girlfriend, Amita a few years ago. They were working on rebranding Kai's family's line of wines. Well, that effort morphed into starting their own line. Amita's a sharp businesswoman, and she'll handle the business end. And, I will handle the money," she proudly explained. "Believe it or not, we've been working very well together. She values my input, and together we keep the boys in line. They're dreamers, and we ladies," she put a hand to her heart, "are the brains behind making their ideas a profitable business."

Sunrise looked on admiring her older sister. She couldn't have been prouder. Camisha was a self-made woman, who'd beat the odds stacked against her, all while maintaining absolute humility. And now she and her husband were stepping out on their own terms to build their own legacy.

Lacey crawled over to Camisha and hugged her.

"I am so proud of you, Cami." She squeezed. "Gone is the nervous little girl my brother fell in love with, and here sits his new Chief Financial Officer!"

Camisha laughed and returned her tipsy sister-in-law's tight hug.

"Thank you, Lace. I think it's someone else's turn," she squeaked under Lacey's death grip.

"I'll go!" Ursula raised her hand.

"What do you have going on, Mom?"

"I'm moving back home," the woman blurted out.

"Mom, what are you talking about," Sunrise whined. "You can't. You can't be there alone."

"Why not?" Ursula snapped. "I'm elderly, not indigent!"

Sensing the building tension, Taliesan spoke up.

"I'm right next door, Sunny."

"But, I'm not!" She shut Taliesan out. "What will you do there all day?" Sunrise glared at her defiant mother.

"Teach."

"Teach! Mom really!" Sunrise shook her head. "You can't have strangers in and out of the house, while you're staying there alone. No! That's not happening."

Ursula struggled to her feet and put her hands on her narrow hips.

"I'm not asking for permission, Sunrise. I am telling you that I am going home, to my house. The house where I raised my family with my husband." Ursula asserted. "I miss teaching kids, Sunny. I need this."

Taliesan stood in between the feuding Andersons.

"Let's talk about it later. We're here for Cami."

"We're done. I'm going back home, next week," Ursula said and sat back on the couch, crossing her arms.

"Fine! Will you still go out on the road with me when I tour?"

"I will!" Ursula shot back, with her head held high. "I love being out on the road with you."

Everyone laughed again.

"Well Ms. Sunrise, I believe it's your turn," Camisha sang.

"No, I want to go last. Lucky, let's hear it. What's going on with the Coopers?"

Taliesan clasped her hands together and pressed them to her lips.

"Well, my neighbor's coming home," she beamed, then turned to Sunrise and mouthed an insincere apology. "And she's teaching piano again, so Kannon will be starting lessons. And let's see," she paused, "my baby brother and best friend are getting their lives on track and needing less of me, so I think I'm going to plan a spiritual getaway for me and my husband - to Tibet, to visit the Lhasa Jokhang Temple."

"Wow!" Sunrise exclaimed. "I'd like to help you guys with that. I know how long you've wanted to go there, and I'm sure it's an expensive trip. What will you do with the boys?"

"Their Uncle Cas will be on the hook - This is your warning, Lacey," Taliesan laughed.

Lacey bobbed her head, sending her thick bangs into her eyes, behind her glasses and giving Taliesan a playful thumbs up.

"So that's it for me. Sunny, you're up."

Sunrise sat her cell phone down to jeers and moaning.

"You cheated. No cell phones!" Her guests shouted.

"It's part of my last surprise for Cami! I'm sorry - I had to use it!" She yelled back at them. "Chill out. Now it's my turn," a tight smile appeared, and the rims of her golden eyes sparkled. "I have a sister."

Her emotion warmed the room. Sunrise covered her crying eyes with her ring-covered hands.

"And she's more than I could have ever dreamed of. She's dependable and easy to talk to," Sunrise lifted her eyes to face Camisha, who was also crying. "Ours is a relationship we worked at - like a successful marriage. There was no love at first sight. There was no magical moment that bonded us, it was all DNA and desire to be each other's sister that has us all here, celebrating this fantastic woman," she clapped in Camisha's direction. "I love you, Cami, but you know that."

"I love you too," Camisha replied with a wink.

"My mom is moving on, which I am not totally on board with, but she's always been an ornery one, and I love her for it. She stood by me and lifted me up during the worst year of my life. She took care of my daddy and me and never complained. They both afforded me the luxury of living out my dreams, and for that, I owe her anything she needs to be happy. Gabe and I are working on West Coast gigs for this year because I can't be an absentee Auntie."

The doorbell rang interrupting Sunrise, to her delight. She clasped her hands together again and leaped like a child on Christmas morning.

"I have a surprise for you, Cami!" She cheered as she hurdled over pillows and the legs of her friends and family to answer the door. The others craned their necks in curiosity.

Two exotic looking women hugged Sunrise and walked in carrying black cases and card tables. The women waved and greeted the group. The first introduced herself as Marissa and the second said her name was, Prisha. Marissa had long, straight witchy black hair. She wore little or no makeup but shiny black lipstick and feathery false eyelashes. She wore a black vest with no shirt, boldly framing her full burnt umber tone breasts and tattoo-covered arms. She sat down the case she was carrying and asked if everyone was ready to get "tatted." There were a few audible gasps and dropped jaws. Sunrise laughed heartily, slapping her knee.

"Don't scare them, Marissa!" Sunrise introduced Prisha, as Atlanta's premier Henna artist and led the women through their makeshift fort to her music room. When she returned, she was still laughing.

"So, I wracked my brain for the right gift to give you, Cami. I wanted to give you something that you would use because you're so practical. And I wanted it to be something that would make you think of me and smile whenever you looked at it."

Camisha's brow furrowed listening to her sister.

"Don't be afraid," Sunrise smiled.

"I am. I'm terrified!" Camisha wrapped her arms around her tiny baby bump.

Sending everyone into another fit of laughter.

"Sunny what are you up to?" Ursula asked.

"OK, OK." She inhaled dramatically. "I want us to get matching tattoos."

Camisha's eyes grew to full moons, her mouth flung open.

"Absolutely not!" She yelled, getting to her feet.

"Are you crazy, Sunny?" Taliesan yelled.

Sunrise laughed uncontrollably. She mimicked her sister and wrapped her arms around her belly, too.

"Oh my God! You guys are killing me!" She howled. "Look I'm getting the tattoo, and Prisha is here to give Cami a matching henna one."

Relief washed over Camisha's face, and she stumbled back onto the couch next to Ursula, who put a soft, wrinkled hand over the young woman's.

"But, when I come out for the baby's birth, you're getting the real thing!" She jabbed a finger in Cami's direction. "Deal?"

"Where does this tattoo have to be?" Camisha asked.

"On the inside of our wrists, just under the thumb," Sunrise said, pointing to her own wrist.

Camisha twisted her mouth and looked up at the draped lights and blanket overhead, before nodding.

"OK. Deal!"

"What!" Lacey screamed. "I can't believe this! Who is this adventurer?" She chuckled. "Lenny is going to freak!"

"You only live once!" Camisha winked at her sister.

She stood and hugged Sunrise. "So let's see these tattoos."

Everyone gathered around Marissa as she unfolded the thin sheet of wax paper with the ink rendering of three swallows in flight—the first in black, the next in a darker blue and the third in royal blue. The women inhaled collectively.

"This is beautiful," Camisha teared up and wrapped in arm around Sunrise's curvy waist. Sunrise laid her head on Camisha's shoulder.

"I'm glad you like them."

"How big will it be?" Lacey asked.

"Just about two and a half inches or so along their wrists," Prisha answered.

Prisha looked like a beautiful gypsy. Her dark olive complexion made her emerald eyes scream from underneath her dark, heavy brows and thick eyelashes. The part she wore in the middle of her thick dark brown hair made a straight line through her thin nose, uneven lips and dimpled chin. Her face was marked with faint scratches that added more interest to her mystifying look.

"Why are there three? What does it mean, Sunny?" Camisha asked.

Sunrise looked into her sister's eyes and took her by the hand, as she sat in the chair across from Marissa. The tattooed woman took Sunrise's free arm and started drawing out the three birds on it. Sunrise looked down at the drawing and nodded to the artist. Marissa opened packs of fresh needles and laid out three little caps that she filled with the black, blue and white inks. She assembled her tattoo gun and snapped on a pair of black latex gloves. Sunrise winced a little and squeezed Camisha's hand, as her mom and friends looked on.

"One is for you, one for me and the other is for Camilla." Camisha stood astonished. She bit the inside her cheek, fighting against the lump lodged in her throat. Lacey walked over to her sister in law and pat her on the back.

"The swallow symbolizes a lot. They represent freedom and hope—freedom from the secrets that kept us apart and hope that our family continues to heal and grow."

Ursula stood beside her seated daughter and placed a hand on her shoulder. "And most importantly, they signify the return home. Because, wherever you and I are together is home - be it in California or in Georgia, we're family."

Runaway to Wine Country

-The Next Year-

"Sunny you have to talk to the man," Taliesan said. "Gabe's a great guy, and all he wants to do is hear from you."

Sunrise held the line.

"Sunny, you there?"

"I'm here."

Taliesan breathed in deep and mussed her long, wild locks.

"Will you at least tell me where you are?"

"I'm still in California."

"You can't hide out there forever. Your mom needs you."

Sunrise curled into a tighter ball underneath the crisp bedcovers. She groaned. "Why'd he have to mess everything up, Lucky?" she whined. "I mean, everything was good—real good! The music we were making was outrageous and," her voice waned. "And then he started trying to change me."

"Change you how? Tell me exactly what happened out there?" Taliesan ordered.

Things between Sunrise and Gabe had always been friendly. They had their intimate moments, but overall, theirs was a relationship built on their love for the music.

He'd helped her through her divorce and the loss of her father—two of the worst times of her life. They lived together whenever Gabe was in Atlanta, which worked well for Sunrise because he was often on the road. But for the past two years, their home was more often than not, a nice hotel suite in between gigs.

"You know what happened, Lucky! He pulled me on stage and got down on one knee in front a club full of strangers and asked me to marry him," she cried.

"Sunny, it couldn't have been that surprising. I mean, four years is a long time to be with someone,"

"We weren't together, together. We were convenient and easy, and fun, but not together—not like a real couple," Sunrise argued. "And every since he started losing the weight, he was all over me about what I was eating and staying after me about working out. One day he pinched my waist, and I slapped his hand away. Do you know what he said to me?"

"What'd he say?"

"He said, 'If you don't want me touching your muffin top, get rid of it. Do something about it, like get out of the bed and on a treadmill,'" Sunrise said imitating Gabe's sardonic tone.

"I'm sorry, Sunny. I didn't know."

"I didn't tell anybody because it's not like he was cruel about it. He was just always making these little comments, you know? It'd be something about straightening my hair, or buying me something to wear on stage."

"Something more mainstream?" Taliesan said.

"Exactly! Just the way Xander started slowly chipping away at me," she mused. "Don't misunderstand me. I know the Gabe's not Xander. I know it. He's nothing like Xander, and I'm nothing like that twenty-year-old girl who married him. I won't do it again, Lucky. I won't ignore the red flags this time. I don't need it. I've worked hard for my independence, and let me tell you something; I've never felt freer! I'm sorry that I hurt Gabe. It was never my intention to humiliate him. I only wished he knew me well enough... to not have put me in that kind of situation. What was I supposed to do?"

Taliesan laughed.

"I can think of at least three better ways you could have responded to his proposal, and none of them include vomiting on him and running away,"

Sunrise laughed, too. "Not my finest moment."

"So what are you going to do? When are you coming home?"

"I don't know," Sunrise said, kicking the covers off. "I think I'm going to Cami's for a few days. Seeing my nieces will do me good."

"Sounds good! You're always in a better place after a few days in wine country with them."

Sunrise smiled and climbed out of bed.

"I'll call Mom, and tell her where I'll be. Maybe she'll come out, too. She loves spending time with Lena and Tennyson."

Yeah, and since you've set her back another two years on being a grandma, she'd probably appreciate it," Taliesan teased.

"You're a jerk, Lucky! But, I love ya."

"Love you, too. Get some rest, and bring your behind back East. I miss you."

"Will do!"

*****

The engine's roar ejected Cami from her office chair. She let out a yelp when she banged her knee against the L-shaped desk she and her husband shared in their home office. The smile on her face and the light in her eyes forced Ali to smile, too.

"He's here!"

She tore through the limestone arches of their 1950's California ranch house to greet her best friend. Oliver had recently moved back to the United States after living in France. He had settled in Atlanta with his fiancée. Ali quietly followed his wife through the formal living room to the front door.

"Boss Lady!"

Oliver wrapped Cami in a warm hug lifting her off of her feet. The two stood holding hands on the gravel driveway as Ali stood watching from the thin metal French doors.

"What's up, Ali," Oliver said over his friend's shoulder.

Ali waved him into the house and hugged him as he walked through the tall doors.

"Damn y'all! This is hot!" Oliver looked around the couple's dream house in awe. "Y'all didn't defer a damn thing in this dream."

Ali beamed with pride. He picked up Oliver's worn duffel bag and led him down the hall. "Your room's this way."

Cami and Oliver followed Ali around the corner of the two L-shaped wings that made up the outdoor courtyard, and past the aluminum storefront system of windows and doors that led to bedrooms. The home was a brilliant mix of both Cami and Ali's aesthetics. The converted, mid-century ranch had a decidedly contemporary exterior composed of two copper-roofed gabled wings that connected at a sunscreen made of reclaimed grape stakes from their sixty-acre vineyard. In contrast, the interior was more country formal, with classic details, rustic materials, and perfect siting. The Robinson's dream house was a timeless beauty with lots of personal touches, capturing all of the couple's passions.

Oliver unpacked and joined his friends in their state of the art kitchen. He took in every high-end nook and cranny. The kitchen showed off striking views of the vineyard and the surrounding hills, a Sub Zero refrigerator built into custom Shaker style cabinets, and a floor to ceiling wine refrigerator that the couple designed, separating the dining area from the formal living room.

"Damn, Cam that's a lot of wine—even for you," he teased.

Cami shifted her head downward. A small smile spread across her delicate features.

"In wine country, you wind up with a lot of wine bottles; it's my business now," she explained. "It just happens!"

Ali wrapped an arm around his wife's waist.

"The refrigerator stores up to four-hundred bottles, and we're building a wine cellar!"

"By yourselves?" Oliver asked.

"Well, we're designing it, but a company here in town is building it."

"Nice," Oliver beamed. "Man, it is so good to see you guys!" He wrapped his long arms around his friends' necks.

"Yeah, man! It's going to be so good working together," Ali said. "And I know my wife misses working with you." He took Cami by the hand and gave it a gentle squeeze.

Tears brimmed in Cami's eyes as she smiled at two of her favorite men.

"Where are Lena Bean and Tennyson?"

Cami dabbed at her wet eyes.

"Lena's in school and Tennyson is at the sitter's," she answered. "And we've gotta head to the airport to pick up Sunrise; so make yourself at home and we'll be back in an hour or so."

"Sunrise's coming? Cool. You didn't tell me that."

"She's out here touring," Ali said, handing his wife her purse. "She comes and hangs out with the girls whenever she's on the West Coast."

"Ha!" Oliver exclaimed. "Auntie Sunrise is making her move for that top spot! I better step up my game!"

Ali and Cami laughed at his claim.

"She's coming for ya, Uncle O! I'm telling you," Ali tossed over his shoulder as they left the room.

The sound of giggles and a piano woke Oliver from his jet lag. His face brightened when he heard his niece's laughter. He washed up in the en-suite bathroom and set out looking for Lena. Oliver had ventured in and out of several rooms before he found his niece and her aunt in her playroom. Its chalkboard painted walls, and brightly colored cabinetry was a sure tell. He tapped an elaborated drumbeat against the door jam.

"Uncle O!" The child shrieked as she jumped up from the piano bench.

Lena was growing up quickly. She'd added at least four inches since he'd last seen her in Atlanta. She was full of personality and had her dad's serious eyes. At only seven years old, she'd become quite the pianist.

"You're good on 'em keys, Baby girl,"

"Thanks to Aunt Sunny," Lena sang.

Oliver swept the little girl up into a wild, spinning hug. Lena wrapped her little arms and legs around her uncle, burying her face in the crook of his neck. Her tears surprised the both of them.

"What's the matter, Baby Girl?" Oliver asked, trying to get a look at her face.

Lean fought against his efforts to loosen her grip.

"Awww, Lena Bean. Why are you crying," he asked again.

Sunrise stood beside the piano looking on.

"I miss you so much," the little girl sobbed. "Is Luca here too?"

Oliver put the little girl down and ran a hand over his kinky hair. "No. Not this time, but I'll bring him out real soon. I promise. OK?"

Lena nodded against her uncle's long legs and smiled up at him. She drug him to the piano bench. "Do you remember my Auntie Sunny?"

"I do," Oliver said, extending a hand to Sunrise, but she pulled him into a hug.

"It's good to see you, Oliver! Cami's so happy to have you here," she gushed.

Oliver smiled broadly. "Yeah, I should have gotten out here a long time ago."

"Well, you're here now! And I heard you're back in Atlanta. I'm sure Luca's pleased about that."

A half grin crept across his face.

"I hope so. Being separated from him was hard. Real hard. It's why I had to move back to the States," Oliver gulped. "He's eight now and growing closer and closer to...to Caspian."

Sunrise shifted all of her weight to one leg and looked away.

"Where's Tennyson?" Oliver asked looking around for the baby of the family.

"She's out on the property with mommy and daddy!" Lena answered.

"Really now? Out on the property? How rich," Oliver teased. "Well, I guess I'd better start dinner."

He leaned over and tickled his niece again before leaving the two ladies to finish their lesson.

"My mommy said that he'd say that," Lena whispered to her aunt with a giggle.

The smells from the kitchen beckoned the Robinsons from the vineyard. Oliver couldn't wait to get in his friend's spectacular kitchen and wine collection. He prepared a gourmet meal of grilled pork tenderloin, morel mushrooms, and cannelloni beans to be served with one of Cami's regional Cabernets.

He made a rice pilaf for the children.

"Wow, man. It's good to have you here, brother!" Ali dabbed up his houseguest. They all disappeared to wash up before dinner while Oliver set the large dinner table in the formal dining room. The adults chatted about the promising project they'd all be working on together when Ali excused himself to take a call. He returned after a few minutes, asking Cami to join him in their shared office. Oliver and Sunrise exchanged curious glances. When they rejoined the others, Cami was visibly upset. She plopped down in her chair and snapped her napkin across her lap.

"Are you OK?' Sunrise asked.

Cami twisted her plump mouth, took a sip from her glass of wine, and glared across the table at Ali.

"Babe, this could be huge for us," he said.

"I know. But the timing stinks."

"Is anyone going to tell us what's going on?" Oliver interjected.

"Right!" Sunrise agreed. "What's up? Should I take the girls out?"

"No. No. It's nothing like that," Ali explained. "We have an opportunity to pitch to a resort in Lake Tahoe. That was Amita calling. She and Kai are in South Africa and can't take the meeting, which leaves Cami and me."

Amita Sawant and Kai Beltram were the couple's business partners, who handled the travel side of their winemaking venture, while the Robinsons managed operations and finance. It allowed Ali and Cami to stay close to home with their young children. The arrangement had worked out well.

"That's awesome!" Sunrise yelped, clasping her hands together. "But I don't understand why you look upset, Cami."

"When do you guys have to be there?" Oliver asked, eyeballing his best friend.

"Friday," Cami answered.

"Like tomorrow!" Oliver exclaimed.

"Yep."

"Well it's a good thing me and Sunrise are here," he said, turning to Sunrise.

"Oliver's right!" she chimed in. "In fact, why don't you guys leave first thing in the morning, and make a long weekend of the trip. Lake Tahoe can be very romantic."

"But we already have meetings and tours set up for you, Ollie," Cami argued. "And the girls have school."

"School! Tennyson's barely walking. What are you talking about?" Oliver chuckled. "I'll be here, Cam. Don't worry about me. Our deal is a sure thing. Farai's in the studio, and the contractors for the restaurant are off for the next two weeks, so I'm good. We can get the girls back and forth, and I'm sure you two could use a break. The girls will be fine with us. Right, Sunrise!"

"Right!"

The two high-fived each other, and Lena cheered from her seat at the table.

"We're going to have so much fun! Right, Tenny?" The child pinched her baby sister's chubby cheek.

"And Lena makes a consensus!" Ali grinned. "Babe, they'll be fine. Sunny and Oliver are responsible adults.

Come on, Cam," he said kneading her thigh. "Everyone's on board. Let's get away while we have the opportunity."

"Well, I can see that I'm outnumbered," she sighed. She and Ali packed, got the girls settled, and left before daybreak.

The next morning, Sunrise dressed the girls and got them off to school. When she returned, she sat in the driveway, watching Oliver as he cleaned the kitchen. Sunrise recalled all of the things her sister had told her about him. He was self-made, and he'd run away from Ohio at thirteen, moving to Atlanta on his own. He made a name for himself in after-hours cooking competitions around the city, where he met his mentor, the famed Chef Stephen Black who sponsored his formal culinary training in France. After inheriting an established kitchen from another mentor, in the South of France Oliver opened two more restaurants in the region.

Oliver fidgeted around Sunrise, and largely tried to avoid her. She was the spitting image of Camilla, which he found unsettling. It was something he had discussed with Ali when he called to check on the girls.

"I've just never met a woman like her. She always so damned happy and upbeat," he said.

"What's wrong with that?" Ali chuckled.

"Nothing! I mean, I like her energy, but she can't be real. Being that happy all the time makes her seem – I don't know, magical—in the unicorn sense," the men laughed.

"Seriously, Bro. What kind of sister can't cook and has no real practical skills?

"That you're aware of," Ali said.

"And she's completely unbothered by it!" Oliver said, shaking his head.

The sound of her unlaced combat boots flopping against the wood floors startled him. It was eerily quiet out there in the middle of nowhere. Sixty plus acres of privately owned property didn't allow for any neighbors or noisy traffic. Sunrise tossed her canvas and leather shoulder bag on the counter as she passed the kitchen.

"I'm going to shower, and I'll be right back. We can catch up and maybe take the four wheelers out to explore the Valley and vineyard," she said, not waiting for his response. "Black folks making wine," she remarked as the bedroom door closed behind her.

Oliver turned the television volume down to listen more closely to what he thought was dull banging. He frowned when he heard Sunrise's muffled cries, and jumped over the back of the large sectional couch.

He called out to her and followed her voice to her bedroom on the East wing of the house. He knocked on the closed double doors.

"Are you alright in there?"

"Not really," she whimpered.

"Are you hurt? I'm coming in."

Oliver cautiously opened the doors and looked around for the woman. The room was empty. She called out to him from behind another set of tall double doors. He knocked.

"I'm so embarrassed," she said in her childlike way.

Oliver pressed an ear against the door.

"What happened? What do you need?"

"I slipped, and my ankle hurts really badly. I can't stand on it!"

Oliver could hear her crying softly.

"Sunny, I'm coming in. OK?"

"No!" The woman shouted.

"Then how can I help you?"

"I don't have a towel in here. Can you find one for me?"

Oliver went off to find Cami and Ali's linen closet. It wasn't easy, but he returned quickly and lightly drummed on the bathroom door.

"I found one," he said. He opened the door a little and held the towel out.

"Hold on. This bathroom is frigging huge," Sunrise grumbled.

"Jesus, Sunrise! You're being ridiculous! You're obviously in pain. I'll close my eyes and help you up. OK?"

She didn't answer right away.

"Hello?"

"OK," the woman relented. "But please don't look at me. I'm so fat."

"Are you kidding me? You're fine as hell, Girl."

The two were struck silent. Oliver squeezed his eyes shut and held the towel opened wide in front of him.

"Are you standing or what?" he asked.

"I'm on the floor."

She held out her hands until he walked into them. She grabbed hold of his ankles to stop him. Oliver knelt down, wrapped the towel around her, and helped her to her feet. The woman slipped around and fell flush against Oliver. Her full breast pressed against him and his body responded. Sunrise felt his crotch stiffen; she froze in place. The two stood holding on to one another without saying a word. Oliver shut his eyes hard, willing his cock down. He adjusted himself against Sunrise and profusely apologized.

"Sunny, I am so sorry. I don't mean anything by it. It just happened."

Sunrise clenched her lips and closed her eyes. She shook her head back and forth, squeamishly. Oliver straightened his shoulders.

"If you can't put any weight on this ankle, I'm going to have to pick you up."

"No! Please, don't. I'm too heavy," she cried.

He stood paralyzed. Too heavy? Is that her biggest concern? Not my rock hard dick jammed into her naked body?

"Whatever, woman! Here we go. Hold on to me," Oliver instructed.

Ignoring her pleas, he lifted her into his arms and carried her to the bed. Sunrise tightened the towel around her.

"You don't have clothes out?" he asked. Oliver rifled through her things and picked out a dress and a poncho.

"I need underwear," Sunrise said, barely loud enough for Oliver to hear. "I'm so embarrassed," she whined, covering her face.

"Don't be. You're hurt. And that ankle looks bad, Sunny."

She winced with every move she made. She had loads of lacy things in sultry dark colors.

"Please, don't be scared, Sunrise. You are perfectly safe with me. I hope you feel that way."

"I do. Oh my gosh!" She covered her reddened face again. "I feel totally safe with you. I'm just in a bit of pain, and well I'm so out of shape," she shuddered. "I'm sorry. I don't know why I said that."

Oliver shook his head, dismissing her apology. He tossed a bra and panties on the bed and left her to dress.

When she called for him again, he'd assembled an ace bandage, a heating pack, and alcohol.

"Where'd you find all of this stuff?"

"Ali's an athlete. Athletes keep stuff like this around. Let's get your ankle wrapped, and we'll look for a hospital."

"Hospital? No!" Sunrise argued. "I'm sure it's just a sprain."

"Are you a medical doctor? I mean, I know you're a doctor, but of music. Right?"

The two laughed.

"Can we just call one?"

"Oh yeah!" Oliver exclaimed, raising a finger. "I'm sure there's a house call doctor or concierge type of dude around here with all of these rich people."

"Exactly!"

The doctor arrived and treated Sunrise in much of the same way Oliver had. He wrapped her ankle more securely and left her with pain pills, a pair of crutches, and instructions to keep her ankle elevated.

Oliver made it his day's mission to make Sunrise's convalescing as pleasant as possible. She was humiliated when he found her in the bathroom.

He had another four hours before it was time to pick-up the children. Oliver made Parmesan popcorn, prosciutto wrapped melon and bruschetta. He made a pot a green tea for Sunrise and uncorked the remainder of the Cabernet he'd used for dinner the night before.

"You sure do cook a lot," Sunrise, said.

"It's my go to," Oliver acknowledged. "You need to eat. It's almost time for another painkiller."

Sunrise sighed but took the plate Oliver offered. He smiled and plopped down beside her on the couch. He flipped through a few channels, before stopping at Spike Lee's, Mo' Better Blues.

"You should like this movie," he smiled at Sunrise.

"I don't know it."

Oliver sat up in the chair and stared wildly at the alien black woman.

"Are you fucking kidding me? You're a jazz player, and you teach it! So how can you be telling me that you don't know, *Mo' Better Blues*! Now that's some serious fuckery!"

"You sure do use that word a lot?"

"Which one?"

"The F- one."

"Do I?"

Sunrise popped a piece of melon into her mouth. Oliver turned his attention back to the screen and propped a few pillows under his head. Sunrise quietly munched from the snack tray and watched along, glancing over at Oliver every now and then.

"Sunny. Can I ask you something?"

She didn't answer right away. But, Oliver was undeterred.

"Does Gabe make you feel," he hesitated. "Unattractive?"

"What!" Sunrise shrilled. Her face reddened.

Oliver held up his hands in surrender.

"Of course not! What does he have to do with anything? Why would you ask that?"

Oliver pursed his lips and twisted at his hair. He paused but didn't withdraw the question.

"I want to understand why you felt so insecure about the way you look."

"Who said that I felt insecure?" Sunrise barbed.

"Back there," he gestured to the bathroom. "You called yourself out of shape, a few times."

Sunrise shrunk a bit.

"And grant it, I don't know what shape you think of in your mind's eye, but the shape I remember and the one in front of me right now is far from too heavy. In fact, it's pretty damned nice. Very, nice."

Sunrise blushed and looked back at the television.

"Thanks," she said. "But I'm the heaviest I've ever been."

"Then maybe you were too thin before," Oliver shot back.

She smiled again.

"That's something I've never heard."

"Do you think it's because of the world you've been living in?" Oliver asked cautiously.

"What world? The white world, Oliver?"

He frowned.

"I guess so. But it's not a judgment! Hell, I've lived in France for years!"

"And yet, you're marrying a black woman," Sunrise said, cutting him off.

"I guess I am."

The room filled with tension just as Clarke the jazz singer's pain-filled voice rang through the television, cutting through the awkward standoff between Oliver and Sunrise. The two turned their attention back to the woman's haunting performance of "Harlem Blues." Oliver put a hand on Sunrise's elevated leg.

"I'm sorry if I offended you. I didn't mean to. Your life choices are none of my business. I just think it's a shame for a woman with as much as you have to offer to feel at all insecure. You're accomplished, easy-going, and sexy as hell—in a pure way, you know? You're not out here flaunting your sexuality - and trust me, you have it to flaunt, but you don't. And forgive me for saying so, but that's sexy as hell, Sunny."

The two held each other's gaze until the movie interrupted them again.

"Do you mind telling me about Camilla?"

Oliver's brow furrowed; he tilted his head. He turned to face Sunrise full on.

"Sure. What do you want to know about her?"

"How was she? To you, I mean?" Sunrise stuttered.

Oliver smiled and laid his head against his folded arms.

"She played an integral part in my life. She was like a mother to me, in the absence of my own drug addicted one."

Surprise registered on Sunrise's face.

"Yep, Valentina was a drug addict when we were kids. And Camilla was by no means a saint, but she was there. She may not have stayed the night under the same roof with Cam and I every single night, but she never left us, and we never went without," he said, glancing over his arm at Sunrise.

"When Cam found out about you, the idea of Camilla leaving you as a newborn in the hospital, it, it was just unbelievable—I mean, it made no sense. I spent much of my childhood watching Camilla sacrifice for Cami and even for me. I saw her work hard and make tough choices in order to provide for us, and I wasn't even a cousin," he shook his head and huffed. "I still can't make any sense of how she walked away from you. But I know it wasn't easy for her."

He put a hand on her extended leg.

"Trust me Sunrise, you were better off. You had great parents with money, who wanted you. I ain' never known a black woman as carefree as you. You live your life directed only by your dreams. I can't even wrap my mind around the fact that you travel the world playing and teaching music. You're truly a modern day, African-American, Southern born gypsy – with the wardrobe to prove it," Oliver chuckled.

He stood and patted her on the leg again. He walked away with the dirty dishes. Sunrise sat wringing her hands, trying to decipher Oliver's words, and the feelings they stirred up inside of her. Her ex-husband had never called her sexy, and Gabe had often referenced her "curves, " but they were never "sexy curves." She was flattered and confused.

"I guess the four wheelers are out of the question, now," Oliver said from behind the couch where Sunrise was sitting.

"Lightening the mood, Uncle O?"

"I'm trying."

"I appreciate it. Come around here so I can see you," Sunrise said.

Oliver walked around the couch and sat where Sunrise patted. He nervously twisted at his hair again. Sunrise put a hand atop of his free hand.

"Thanks for everything today. I'm really glad I wasn't here alone when I fell."

"It would've been pretty bad, but I'm confident you would've figured your way out of it," Oliver chuckled, and reached for her teacup. Sunrise rested her hand on his.

"Oliver, I'm trying to say thank you for the food, and the movie and your words. They meant a lot to me."

"Cool," Oliver said and hurried back into the kitchen.

Oliver stood over the deep farmhouse sink running dishwater. He squinted. "What the hell just happened?" he asked himself. "Surely it's not. She's Cami's sister.

That makes her my sister. Right? And I'm engaged to be married—well eventually—at some point. Right?"

He heard the bump of Sunrise's crutches on the floor and turned to see the woman limping down the hall.

"If you need anything, just holler," he called after her.

"Will do! Thanks."

Oliver smacked a sudsy hand against his forehead.

"What the fuck, O! Control yourself, man! Damn, I do use that word a lot."

Lena begged and pleaded for her aunt and uncle to build a fire out back in the courtyard after Sunrise woke from her nap. She wanted S'mores and wouldn't take no for an answer.

The adults acquiesced, wrapped up baby Tennyson, and headed out back for dessert by a fire.

"Ali and Cami called to check in," Oliver said. "The meeting went well. Ali's pretty sure they'll close an exclusive deal with the resort."

Oliver assembled a S'more and blew on it before handing it to Lena.

"Cami's worried about your ankle," he said, looking over the fire at Sunrise. "But she relaxed after she heard the girls laughing and playing in the background."

"Boss Lady is a long way away from the Genesis House Shelter for Women and Children," he whispered. "These views are spectacular."

"Is that where you two grew up? In the shelter?" Sunrise asked.

"Yeah. And I don't think either of us could have imagined that the future would be this good to us."

He stood up and scooped Tennyson in his arms. "Lena Bean, let's get ready for bed."

Sunrise struggled to her feet.

"Let me help," she said.

"I have them. You keep that ankle elevated,"

Oliver put the girls down to bed and rejoined Sunrise in front of the hillside fire pit. He poured himself a glass of wine and brought a pot of tea for Sunrise. He lowered himself into the teak lounger and put his feet up beside hers. The two sat quietly looking out at the expansive sky.

"The sky looks so close out here in the mountains."

"Yes, it does. I'm always in the city, either in Atlanta or in Marseilles," Oliver said. "The stars never look this close."

"It's the lights of the city. They're too many of them, and they're too bright, " Sunrise explained, matter of factly. "My daddy told me that."

"Man, your dad was so cool. You must really miss him."

"All the time," Sunrise sang. She poured a cup of tea and let the steam from the cup warm her face.

"What's Farai working on?"

He shifted uncomfortably and took a sip of the Cabernet.

"She's doing a few features, but you know that we've moved back to Atlanta. She's testing out her appeal here in the U.S."

"Wow! That's awesome. I'd love to collaborate with her one day."

"You two should hook up when you're back in the A. Do you still live there?"

"Yes. It's home for me. Remember? Besides my mom's still there. She's touring with me less and less," Sunrise smiled. "She's hanging out with her friends a little more, and she started giving piano lessons again. That's why she's not out here with me now."

"That's good. Right?"

"Yes. Oh my gosh! I'm happy for her. She's resilient. Much more so than I."

"Don't go there, Sunny," Oliver stopped her. "Why can't you see yourself? You're a lot like Cami, you know."

Sunrise balked.

"Not in the obvious sense, but in ways like your resilience. You'd had a rough few years when I met you. There was the divorce," Oliver counted off on his fingers. "Then you found your biological family, who didn't exactly welcome you with open arms, and then your dad died. But, when I met you, you were all smiles and joy. Just pure, you know? There were no signs of the hell you were going through. That's how I always think of you—the happy go lucky one!" Oliver laughed, and playfully pushed Sunrise's shoulder. She took him by the hand. Oliver recoiled but then relaxed into it. They sat there silently holding hands and counting stars.

The low humming of Sunrise's slumber woke Oliver. He watched her sleep for a while.

"You look so much like her," he said as he brushed a piece of hair from her shoulder. "But you're so different. Camilla was calculating and brash. And you're sweet and open. You definitely have all of Camilla's womanly charms, but you're so uncomfortable with them, or are you simply unaware of 'em?" Oliver asked the sleeping woman.

He knelt beside her and kissed her lightly. Sunrise kissed him back. She pulled him on top of her and kissed him deeply. Oliver didn't resist. She slipped out of the beaded kimono she was wearing; Oliver helped her out of her thin t-shirt dress. Heat sprung from her center, and she held him against her skin.

Her large breasts heaved in the burgundy and black lace bra, and her taut nipples threatened to rip the seams of the delicate material. Oliver was rock hard against her; she lifted her womanhood towards him.

"Are sure about this, Sunrise?" he asked between wet kisses to her neck and chest.

She only bobbed her head and unbuttoned the cut-off cargo shorts he was wearing. She pulled at his boxers, freeing his full erection and slipped it into her wetness. Oliver ripped off the faded t-shirt he was wearing and tossed it somewhere over the hillside. He

352

thrust and grinded hungrily against the warmth of his best friend's sister, but wouldn't look in her face.

"We shouldn't be doing this," he said.

"We're adults," Sunrise panted.

"I want you so bad."

"I'm right here."

"I've wanted to feel the softness of your skin against mine. I've wanted my hands all over your hips and titties ever since I picked you up from the bathroom floor."

Oliver kissed her neck and chest.

"I need to know every sensuous curve of this body that you keep covered up in all those crazy ass clothes. I haven't been this hard in years, and I feel awful about what is happening between us. So bad! But so good, too," he whimpered.

Sunrise had never felt so free, so in charge. She had made up her mind the moment Oliver called her, "sexy as hell," that she wanted to be that for him. She wanted to be the alluring woman he saw when he looked at her, the woman whose naked body elicited an involuntary erection from a man of his considerable experience.

He'd been with the audacious, leggy stunner, Lacey Robinson, and the exotic, French beauty, Farai Sikebo, and yet, he found her uncontrollably enticing.

She'd noticed him watching her, she felt his restraint while caring for her and it made her feel alive and sophisticated, the way music made her feel. The way John Coltrane's *A Love Supreme*, made her feel and she wanted that feeling against her bare skin. She wanted that spirituality inside of her; she wanted to be consumed by it. Their lovemaking felt to her like a musical narration of a devotional psalm. Their bodies locked and swayed effortlessly.

"Oliver," she breathed against his ear, "You are indeed a gifted lover."

In his arms, she felt as safe as she could ever remember. She didn't want to think about the moments after, and she shushed him with a finger to his lips.

"I only want to surrender to this intensity."

Oliver obliged.

I Ain't Sorry

The morning sun shone brightly through the large glass windows. Oliver groggily rolled out of bed and vowed to call Cami to find out how to operate the window shades. He looked down at his flaccid penis and shut his eyes tight.

"Fuck you, O!" he cursed himself. He hung his head and covered his face. "You fucking heel! What kind of dude takes advantage of a family friend when she's vulnerable?" He looked around for his pants and jumped when he heard the knock on the door.

"Just a sec!" Oliver pulled his pants on and then pulled a wrinkled t-shirt from his duffel bag. He slipped the shirt on and opened the door, bracing himself for Lena to bounce into his arms. But it was Sunrise, dressed in cut-off jean shorts and an Aztec printed poncho. Her hair was all pulled up into a messy bun, and her bright eyes sparkled against her fresh face. A half smile turned up the corner of her mouth, and she looked down. She squeezed her crutches, and he touched her on the shoulder.

"You don't have to say anything. We're good," he assured her. "Friends?" He extended a hand to her. She took it.

"Friends," she agreed.

"You wanna come in?" Oliver opened the door wide. "The view from this room is sick."

"The view from all of the bedrooms are; they sited the house for that purpose."

She always spoke in such a matter of fact tone, but she never sounded like a know it all. Oliver smiled at her as she hobbled past him. She sat in the small leather love seat situated at the foot of the bed and propped her foot up.

"How's that ankle feeling this morning?" Oliver asked while checking his cell phone. "Jesus, it's super early!"

"Yeah. I'm sorry for waking you," Sunrise moved to get up. Oliver stopped her. "No, you didn't. I was already awake."

"You couldn't sleep either?" Sunrise asked.

"I slept fine, I think my body's just still on Eastern Standard Time."

"Oliver, I know you said that we don't have to talk about last night, and I appreciate that. But, I want you to know that I'm not sorry about what happened. And I don't regret being with you,"

Concern marred Oliver's face, and she moved quickly to calm him.

"There will be no grand overtures or expressions of love on my part, I assure you,"

The tension in his shoulders eased.

"But I don't want you to feel like you somehow forced the situation because you were a perfect gentleman. I wanted you last night, and I went for it."

Oliver remained pressed against the large armoire with his hands deep in his pockets.

"And I want you now."

Oliver swayed, and he hardened against the seat of his pants. He walked to the bedroom door and locked it. A vein in his neck pulsed. He took off his t-shirt and walked over to where Sunrise was sitting.

"Are you sure?" He could hardly speak against the beating of his heart in his throat.

She bit her thick bottom lip and nodded. She pulled him down to kiss her, then pulled herself over the back of the loveseat onto the bed.

"I am," she breathed.

Oliver obliged Sunrise over and over again until they were awakened by the ringing of his cell phone. It was Farai, and Sunrise quietly slipped out of bed and left.

Oliver later appeared, showered and dressed again to find Sunrise scrambling eggs, while the girls looked on. He lured them away from the kitchen with cartoons in the great room. He perched himself on a bar stool and watched Sunrise clumsily move around the gourmet kitchen.

"I thought you didn't cook," he said to her.

"I can scramble eggs, Chef."

He bit at his top lip and rubbed the back of his neck. Sunrise felt his discomfort from across the large room.

"Oliver, please don't say anything. I know what we did wasn't right," her small voice broke. "But I'm still not sorry about it."

His cognac-colored eyes narrowed and a half grin set up on his face.

"Sunrise,"

She raised a hand stopping him.

"I know. It can't happen again. It's all just so wrong. And so complicated. It's almost incestuous. I know," she inhaled dramatically and exhaled evenly.

"Trust me, I know. No one deserves this—especially not Farai,"

"Or Gabriel," Oliver mumbled.

"That's over," Sunrise said.

Oliver tilted his head, then nodded. "I see," Oliver mumbled. "Then that's it. We're good."

"We're good!" Sunrise agreed, showing her palms to Oliver.

Oliver nodded and hopped off the counter.

"I'll make coffee and set the table for these eggs you cooked," Oliver said cheerfully.

"Sounds good."

It was a spectacular Sonoma County afternoon, and the group ventured into town for some shopping and sightseeing. It was Oliver's first time in the region, but Sunrise had become a regular since her sister's move out West. A few of the shop and restaurant owners knew the girls and greeted them warmly.

Lena proudly introduced her uncle Oliver, "the chef who lived in France" to everyone she knew in town. She was bubbly like her aunt Sunrise and sharp like her mother. She walked with her back straight, and her head held high. Tennyson was eighteen months old, and already displaying the serious attitude of her father. Her smiles were hard earned and shared sparingly, but on the rare occasions when she laughed, it was all encompassing and well worth the wait. The laughter from her small, chubby body filled all four thousand square feet of their home.

Again, there was no awkwardness between the adults. They spent the afternoon in each other's company as naturally as they had before they'd seen each other in the nude. There were no stolen hand grazes and no flirtatious glances exchanged—Just Uncle O and Aunt Sunrise out sightseeing and having lunch with their nieces. They snapped pictures and texted them to Ali and Cami throughout the day.

Sunrise took a call from her mother and laughed easily with Ursula about spraining her ankle and having to call out to Oliver to rescue her from the slippery, bathroom floor. The day went along peacefully, without incident. When Tennyson started to get a little fussy, they took the girls home, bathed them and put them down for their naps. They made love again, twice more, and started dinner.

Oliver held Sunrise's hourglass figure tightly against him, wrapping his arms around her tiny waist and kissing her shoulders. She pulled a remote control from the bedside table and pointed it towards the bank of windows, sending the sunshades down.

"Damn it, I couldn't figure out how to get those things down," he laughed. "I kept intending to ask Cam about them, but never thought about it when she called."

Sunrise snuggled closer.

"You should've just asked me. I've been right here with you all weekend." She kissed his fingers that were laced with hers. "I'd better get out of here before your Lena Bean wakes up."

He squeezed her tighter.

"Just a few more minutes," he pleaded against her bare back. "They'll be home today, and then it's back to reality," he grumbled.

Sunrise smirked and kissed Oliver's arms.

"Yep, back to reality."

She rolled over to face him and looked over every inch of his angular face. She took his face in both of her hands and kissed him on the mouth.

"I want to remember you just like this," she mouthed against his parted lips. "I have something for you. I need your email address."

"My email address? I hardly ever use that thing."

"Well, you're going to have to use it to get my gift."

"OK," Oliver reached for his phone and clicked around looking for his email address.

"Give me your phone. I'll just download it for you."

He handed her the phone, and she fiddled around with it for a few seconds before stopping. She pursed her full lips into a tight line and handed the phone back to Oliver.

"Farai says, she loves you and can't wait to have you back in her arms,"

She rolled out of bed and slid her dress on over her thick mass of waves. Oliver read the text message, then watched Sunrise put her furry boots on and grab her crutches. He reached out for her, but then stopped. She left the room without as much as a glance back. He stretched his long, lanky legs to their full length, rolled over and pressed his face into a pillow. It smelled of Sunrise's airy perfume. He growled into the pillow.

"I'm not this kind of dude. And I know better. There is no good way for this shit to end!" He growled again and turned over. He lay back against a stack of pillows and looked up at the uncut redwood beams that lined the vaulted ceiling. "Now what are you going to do? How are you going to face her and how about Cami? Damn it, man!"

Sunrise stood in the huge shower stall letting the rainfall showerhead drench her from head to toe. The hot water mixed with her warm tears and swirled down the drain. *How had she let this thing with Oliver go so far off the rails? She knew his fiancé, she liked her; she wanted to work with her. And what about Gabriel? He'd been so solid for her over some of the worst years of her life, and she'd just leave him hanging? He wasn't exciting and romantic, but he was definitely a great friend to both she and her mother - who also knew and liked Oliver. What would her sister say, and what about Lacey and Caspian?*

"What kind of monster are you, Sunrise Nicole?"

Sunrise was certain of a couple of things; for one, she couldn't ever let anyone know about the weekend she and Oliver had shared, and above all else, she couldn't let her feelings get out of hand.

For the large part of the day, Oliver and Sunrise avoided each other. Oliver made breakfast for the girls, while Sunrise set up arts and crafts for them in their playroom. She ate while he saw to them brushing their teeth and washing their faces. She dressed them while he cleaned the kitchen. At lunchtime, he prepared lunch while she worked with them to finish the art projects for their parents. They ate out back in the courtyard with Uncle O, while Sunrise ate alone at the kitchen counter. And by two o'clock, Ali's SUV was driving up the long, dusty driveway, much to Sunrise's relief. She hoped that having Ali and Cami back in the house would normalize the atmosphere and keep her otherwise occupied. She'd made up her mind to leave earlier than she'd originally planned since Oliver was indeed there on business.

After the last dinner dishes were washed and put away, and after the girls had gone down to sleep, the adults gathered outside around the hillside fire pit for cocktails. The night sky was clear, and the air was brisk. Sunrise and Cami shared a blanket and a lounge chair. They'd grown to be as close as any two sisters who'd been raised together. They sported matching tattoos on their wrists and shared just about everything.

Oliver beamed watching the new layers to his childhood friend. He made small talk about their trip, and winemaking operations, but Cami watched his hands move about more than usual, and watched him fidget with his hair, incessantly. She watched him

364

closely throughout the night. When she was sure they were alone, she quizzed him on his behavior.

"What's up with you, O?"

She pulled him by the ear, as she passed him. He laughed nervously. "You know me all too well." He was ready with a well-rehearsed explanation about the state of he and Farai's engagement. It wasn't a completely fabricated issue, it was something they'd discussed and were indeed at an impasse about. He took a seat at the kitchen island and rubbed his face between his hands.

"I talked to Farai today. I asked her about setting a date again," he said.

"Why today? While you're out here?"

Cami was quick. He twisted his mouth and looked away.

"Damn! I don't know Cam. It was on my mind, and I asked her."

Cami narrowed her eyes at her friend.

"Why are you snapping at me? We're just talking."

"I'm sorry," he smirked. "She so complicated. She was raised in a strict Nigerian home, but when it comes to marriage, she's all French,"

"All French? What does that mean?" Cami sat on the stool beside Oliver.

Sunrise heard the friends talking and stopped just out of their eyesight.

"She's not very religious, you know?"

"Neither are you,"

"I know, but I believe in marriage. And I don't think Farai believes in it as strongly. She calls it, 'happily ever after' which she doesn't believe in. Whenever the conversation comes up, she grumbles, 'everything is great between us, Oli-ver.'"

"When do you want to do it?" Cami asked pointedly. Sunrise leaned in to hear his answer.

He shrugged. "I don't know, Cam."

"Then why the heck are you all the way on the other side of the country fidgeting about it? None of this makes any sense to me, Ollie Dollie."

His friend patted him on his shoulder.

"You still sound as confused as you've always been when things get real between you and a woman."

"That's fucked up, Cam."

"Old habits die hard, Ollie. But, I'm exhausted so can we finish this tomorrow?"

"Yeah," he drawled and kissed her on the cheek. "Goodnight."

Sunrise watched her sister cross the great room and turn down her and Ali's wing of the house before she hobbled from her hiding place. She leaned against the kitchen counter, staring at Oliver, who only stared back at her.

"How much of your story is true," she asked dryly.

"All of it."

"Is that right? And being engaged isn't enough for you anymore, Oliver?"

Sunrise's once ingénue like wonder had morphed into something sultrier. Her voice possessed a smoky quality that visibly aroused Oliver. His eyes traced her buxom breasts and her curvy thighs. His crotch thickened under the island. He tried rubbing the thickness away.

"Cami can never know about the past few days."

"Why not? We're adults."

Oliver shook his head vigorously. Sunrise took a few steps towards him.

"Look, I know she loves me, but we ain't blood. And I watched her with you tonight; she loves you something serious."

"And I love her," Sunrise countered.

"You know what they say about blood being thicker than water, and I don't want to find out on which side of the equation I'll come out on if she chooses."

"She won't find out. I promise," Sunrise said, crossing her heart, never taking her eyes off of Oliver's. "Come to my bed tonight. I'm leaving in the morning."

His eyes widened, and his mouth dropped open, but he nodded. He sat alone in the kitchen for a few more minutes talking to himself, appealing to his more logical side,

"Don't go, man. Don't do it. Just let her leave. Just let her go. And you forget about this fucked up weekend. There is too much at stake. Man up, O!"

But his libido won out, and he crept into her bed well past midnight.

Oliver made Sunrise feel like a fully-grown, sexual being. She felt bolder and more mature with him. Although they were the same age, and she'd obviously seen much more of the world than he had, he was more knowing; he was surer of himself. Oliver walked in and quietly closed the door behind him. He moved her crutches across the room, as she watched silently. He knelt at her bedside and pulled her thighs over his shoulders. She was wearing no panties and was already

368

dripping. Oliver flicked his eager tongue against her throbbing clitoris, and she exploded against his open mouth. He covered the quivering with his entire mouth and French kissed her there, until the jerking subsided. Sunrise shuddered and bit down hard on the pillow she was using to stifle her lusty moans. Oliver lined the inside of her thick thighs with wet kisses and then moved to her taut belly, he climbed onto the bed and entered her with great familiarity.

The moon shone brightly over the bottle green rolling hilltops as Oliver stood over Sunrise admiring her complexity.

"Damn, this is hard. Harder than I expected, for real," he breathed. He shook his head, running his hands over his wild twists and down his neck. "A reset on this whole weekend would be nice."

"Yes, it would," Sunrise smiled shyly.

Oliver leaned over and kissed her passionately, and whispered goodbye against her ear, before dressing and leaving the room.

Monday morning Oliver woke up to the smell of coffee and bacon and the laughter of his nieces and their father. He showered and joined the Robinsons in the kitchen.

"Hey, Man! You want coffee?" Ali asked.

"Of course," Oliver said, looking around.

"They're gone. Sunrise got a call or something and had to head back East. Cami insisted on driving her to the airport. She should be back in about half an hour."

Ali slid the cup of coffee along the counter to Oliver.

"I hate that I didn't get to say goodbye to Sunrise," Oliver lamented.

"She's your neighbor now. You all live in College Park. So you'll be seeing her around."

Discussion Guide

❖··Why does the author introduce us to Sunrise in her childhood bedroom?

❖··Camilla is brutally frank and honest. Why doesn't she tell Sunrise the truth about their relationship?

❖··Do you think Sunrise's ideas about race change after her failed marriage with Xander? Does it affect her relationship with Gabe?

❖··Why is Sunrise willing to be angry and hold a grudge against Evangeline, but not with Camisha for shunning her?

❖··What impression do you have of Taliesan based on her actions and reactions, both verbally and non-verbally?

❖··What does the interaction between Beaux and James reveal about Beaux's character?

❖··Evangeline says that Camille has been around for her entire marriage (p. 301). Why did she stay married to James? Why does she accept Camisha, but refuses to accept Sunrise?

❖··"You look so much like her," Oliver whispers to a sleeping Sunrise. He rattles off differences between the mother and daughter and kisses her (pg. 353). Why do you think he kissed Sunrise in that moment?

❖··There are a lot of romantic attachments in *Sunrise Blues.* Many of them can be described as murky, at best. Where do the love lines lie?

- Lacey, Oliver, Isaac, Caspian

- Oliver, Farai, Sunrise, Lacey

- James, Evangeline, Camille

- Sunrise, Gabe, Oliver

Made in the USA
Middletown, DE
07 April 2017